GLADYS MITCHELL

Murder in the Snow

VINTAGE

1 3 5 7 9 10 8 6 4 2

Vintage
20 Vauxhall Bridge Road,
London SW1V 2SA

Vintage is part of the Penguin Random House group of companies
whose addresses can be found at global.penguinrandomhouse.com

Penguin
Random House
UK

This edition published in Vintage in 2017
First published in Vintage in 2014 with the title *Groaning Spinney*
First published in hardback by Michael Joseph Ltd in 1950 with the
title *Groaning Spinney*

penguin.co.uk/vintage

A CIP catalogue record for this book is available from the British Library

ISBN 9781784708320

Printed and bound by Clays Ltd, St Ives plc

Penguin Random House is committed to a sustainable future
for our business, our readers and our planet. This book is made
from Forest Stewardship Council® certified paper.

CHAPTER 1

Mrs Bradley Takes a Christmas Vacation

'Go, stop the swift-winged moments in their flight
To their yet unknown coast, go hinder night
From its approach on day.'

William Habington

Mrs Beatrice Adela Lestrange Bradley tapped with the corner of a stiff envelope on the edge of her writing desk. It was very seldom that she found difficulty in coming to a decision, but on this occasion she was conscious of doubt and hesitation.

She put the envelope down, took up a foolscap envelope instead, re-opened it, and re-read the letter it contained – an invitation to a conference of educational psychiatrists in Stockholm. The letter was warmly expressed, Mrs Bradley had spent an autumn and early winter in special and most fascinating research, and she badly wanted to attend the conference, whose views, generally speaking, would not accord with her own, but whose members would be interested in, if argumentative on, what she would have to say.

On the other hand, there was the invitation from the Cotswolds. Mrs Bradley's three marriages had provided her with a vast and varied tribe of spirited and gifted in-laws, some of whom she liked. The stiff envelope contained a letter from her favourite nephew who had obliged her by marrying the young woman of her choice. Mrs Bradley had greatly desired to find place in the family circle for the lovely Deborah Cloud, and her nephew Jonathan had been the vehicle for this inclusion. That he had chosen Deborah for his own and not for his aunt's reasons delighted that powerful but scrupulous mediator almost more than the actual fulfilment of her wishes.

'Now we've somewhere to live, won't you please come and spend Christmas? We are combining a Christmas party with a general house-warming, and are particularly anxious to have you,' Jonathan had written. 'Good company, Deb looking her best, and, what's more, I've achieved a bottle of Scotch, and if you stay until New Year's Day I swear you shall have a haggis.

'P.S. We don't care how many of your pet cases are going to collect *delirium tremens* at the festive season, or how many conferences you want to attend in January. Blood is thicker than water, and you always said you would visit us as soon as we were settled. You also promised to stay a good long time. So what about it? If coming, don't bother to reply.'

Mrs Bradley rarely acted on impulse and was averse to solving her difficulties by indulging in superstitious practices, but on this occasion her mind was so divided that she suddenly picked up two long spills from a jar near the fireplace and tossed them into the air. One landed on the rug and the other fluttered on to the writing desk. The tiny kitten on the hearth immediately pounced, and began to play with the spill on the rug.

'If you've got the longer one I'll go to Sweden, if the shorter, I'll go to the Cotswolds,' pronounced Mrs Bradley, solemnly. She picked up the kitten and took away the spill. She measured it against the one which had landed on the writing desk. The spill which the kitten had captured was the shorter by almost an inch. Mrs Bradley took up a telegraph form, scribbled rapidly on it, and rang the bell. She handed the form to her secretary with instructions to send the telegram at once. Then she seated herself, picked up the kitten and the two spills, looked thoughtful for a moment, and then, putting down the tiny animal, she looked closely at the two spills, which were home-made from strips of newspaper. Then she untwisted the ends.

'Oh, dear!' she said aloud. 'Now what have I done?'

The end of the shorter spill had been doubled over. As she straightened it out she discovered that the actual length came to several inches more than the length of that which she had decided at first was the longer spill.

'It ought to have been Sweden, after all!' she thought, with some amusement, crumpling the spills and throwing them into the basket.

'Well, the telegram's gone,' said her secretary, when Mrs Bradley told her what had happened. 'And I'm very glad. You need a holiday. You can go to Sweden *next* year!'

Jonathan Bradley and his wife Deborah had been lucky. A great estate in the Cotswolds had been offered for sale in two lots. Two-thirds of the property and the huge modern house had been sold to the Ministry of Education, but the remaining third of the land and the original manor house had been purchased by Mrs Bradley's nephew. It lay in typical Cotswold country, hilly yet gloriously open. It was partly wooded, had a dashing stream, and offered some shooting and the chance of going out with the local Hunt.

Jonathan and his wife had bought their share of the estate in January, had moved in in April, and had purposely refrained from inviting guests until they felt that they were settled and at home.

The month was now December, and Mrs Bradley arrived two days before Christmas Eve. She travelled by train, for her chauffeur had been given Christmas leave, and she had deliberately made no mention to her nephew of the time of her train, for his house was miles from Cheltenham, (her terminus), and she disliked to cause inconvenience.

Jonathan Bradley, however, was at the station to meet her.

'Deb wanted to come,' he observed, 'but I didn't know whether

I'd picked the right train. You didn't say, and I thought it was a bit too cold for her to hang about draughty stations. I wish I'd brought her now.'

He took Mrs Bradley out to his car, and saw her luggage put on. A few minutes later the car was slipping like a homing cat across the Oxford–Gloucester turning, past a fifteenth-century barn, past a country bus-shelter, and so along the Cirencester Road.

Great slopes brooded dreamily upon their lost summer treasure of wheat, clover and barley; little by-roads sloped quietly up or down to Coberley, Elkstone, Brimpsfield and Compton Abdale. After half an hour's driving, some deep woods, a lodge with its drive, a full stream at the bottom of steep banks, a straggle of black pine trees, a desolate farm, a narrower road, a sandy turning, and the entrance to a long and uphill lane, brought the car on to Jonathan's land.

The car crept onward up the steep, uneven lane. Mrs Bradley, seated beside her tall and black-haired nephew, looked out of the window with interest. To her left ran another small wood. On the right the treeless ground curved almost voluptuously downward to another noisy little stream.

'That turns the mill,' said Jonathan, jerking his head towards the sound. 'We've got a mill, a smithy, the pub and the post-office. Quite a model village, all told.'

As the rise mounted and the wood was left behind, the wet green slopes of the country filled the landscape. At the top of the rise was a grey and snow-filled sky, and, as the car climbed and the hills changed their contours, Mrs Bradley saw two small houses, one on either side of the way.

'What do you think of it?' asked Jonathan, touching his horn as the car approached the houses, and then changing gear as the slope became more gentle and a drive took the place of the lane.

'Desolate, enchanted, apt and supernormal,' replied his relative, gazing raptly at the charged and lowering sky.

'Apt for what?'

4

'For treason, magic, stratagems and snow. Who lives at the lodges now?'

'Will North, the gamekeeper, lives in the left-hand one. He's a grand chap. I've been out with him several times already and always had good sport. The other one belongs to the Woottons, Abel and Harry. They garden for us and for the College. Deb likes gardening, fortunately, so for us they don't do very much. They chop stuff down and burn it, and they tackle most of the digging. They work at the College mostly, but I was asked to let them stay on here at their cottage. They're most steady, respectable chaps. Abel is a widower with one kid, a boy of twelve. Harry is a bachelor. They've a sister who keeps the lodge at the College gates, and they go up there for their dinner more times than not. The sister's a dragon, but she has a keen sense of duty, sees that her brothers toe the line and don't spend their money at the pub, and she mends the kid's clothes and makes him go to church and get to school early and that sort of thing, you know. I really hardly see what they'd do without her.'

'Who looks after Will North?' Mrs Bradley enquired.

'Oh, Will? He's self-sufficient. Cooks and cleans, and is all kinds of a handyman. He gets food from our cook when he wants it, but he's remarkably independent, and a wonder with a gun or with snares. The last owner used to rear pheasants, but I don't know what happens now. Will finds me one or two to pop at, but the woods are no longer preserved. You can't get the food for the birds.'

'I think I shall like Will North.'

'I'm sure you will. He's a bachelor, sensible bloke! – and cares for nothing much except his dog and his ferrets. He's got what he calls his Dogs' Cemetery behind those bushes you saw by the drive. Properly dug, deep graves, headboards, last messages and all. If he takes a fancy to you you'll be shown it, I shouldn't be surprised.'

The drive curved in almost a semi-circle, and Mrs Bradley had her first sight of the house which her nephew had purchased.

It was of stone, and had the high gables and beautiful greyness of all early Cotswold manors. It had been built in 1560, but was simply designed and had the bareness and austerity of even earlier days.

Its tiles were of stone, too, and had weathered to a mellowness which was absent from the stark walls and the Tudor drip-stones above the windows. A broad archway led to the stables, and there was a large dovecot, almost the size of a cottage, at the side of the house. There was a row of plain stone shields cut just above the square-headed Tudor doorway, and beneath them was the lovely Deborah Bradley, waiting to welcome home the travellers.

'This is grand!' said Deborah, greeting Mrs Bradley. 'I betted Jon you wouldn't come! I said you'd be off on a toot to some conference or other. Do tell me what worked the charm!'

Mrs Bradley told the tale of the kitten and the two spills.

'Good for the kitten!' said Jonathan. 'Look here, Deb, it's barely three o'clock, and Aunt Adela says she had lunch on the train. We've time to go out and see a bit of the park.'

'Indeed you have not!' protested his wife at once. 'Aunt Adela is going up to her room, and then, when she's ready for it, I'm going to ring for tea, and by the time we've had tea it will be dark, and in any case you've got to go into Cirencester for those parcels. You had better go now and we'll have tea as soon as you get back. It won't take you long. I *thought* you were in a desperate hurry to put the car away!'

'Don't nag,' said Jonathan, kissing her.

'Do you like the house?' asked Deborah, when tea was over and Mrs Bradley had been taken upon a conducted tour of the oak-beamed, gloomy, friendly, surprising old place.

'Immensely,' Mrs Bradley replied with the utmost sincerity.

'Yes, so do I. I'm glad I'm going to have the baby here. He's twins and I'm going to call him Mary Crispin.'

'Indeed?' said Mrs Bradley, studying her niece-by-marriage with interest. 'This is glad news.'

'You'll be godmother, won't you? I do so much want you to be.'

'I shall be delighted. When do we first greet your heirs?'

'Not until May, I'm afraid. Can you bear to wait until then? I don't honestly think *I* can.'

'I shall count the days, and mark them off on my calendar.'

'You're nice,' said Deborah contentedly. 'I'm very, *very* glad you could come. Please will you come at the time? I shall feel safe with you in the house.'

Mrs Bradley lay that night in an oak-beamed, mullion-windowed room with a view to the west and an ash-tree outside the window. She thought of Provost M. R. James' story, but slept none the worse for that, and after breakfast she, her nephew and his wife went out for the promised expedition.

The weather was cold but not bitter, and the sky was still lowering and grey. They took a short cut from the house by way of a door in a wall, a path between centuries-old yew hedges, black, close-leaved and cleanly silent, and an iron fence over which Jonathan climbed and then lifted Deborah, and over which Mrs Bradley hopped like a robin.

This fence divided what might be called the garden proper from a paddock which climbed rapidly and (said Deborah, hanging on to Jonathan's arm) unnecessarily uphill to the woods.

Here a broad walk among beeches dropped downwards to the two lodges. Skirting these, the party continued through the woods, came out for a bit on to rough pasture from which a magnificent view across the valley showed the huge, rather ugly modern house (which was now a college) backed by a grove of trees, and then, keeping the little church and some of the stone-built houses of the village to his left, Jonathan led the way towards a narrow spinney, a mere straggle of trees where the woods petered out on top of the windy rise.

At the end of the spinney was a gate. Jonathan stood still and pointed.

'That's where our ghost hangs out,' he said. 'I think it must be genuine. Anyhow, everybody round here believes in it. It's supposed to be the local parson of about eighteen-fifty. He's to be seen hanging over the gate, a most realistic-looking corpse, on moonlight nights at between twelve and one, although some people claim to have seen him during the afternoon.'

'What is the story?' Mrs Bradley enquired, going forward to inspect the gate, which was of the ordinary country pattern, and which opened on to some rough ground pitted with rabbit holes.

'Nobody seems to know exactly. One story is that he was set on by robbers when he was coming back from visiting a dying parishioner, and another is that he had been celebrating rather too enthusiastically and just collapsed and died on the way home. He was found hanging over the gate and has haunted the place ever since. One can understand it if he was set upon, robbed and murdered, but if the other story is correct it's not very easy to see why he can't leave us alone. Dash it, he can't want the village to know that their parson was tight!'

'I expect he wanted to tell somebody something,' suggested Deborah. 'Which way are we going from here?'

'Oh, across old Daventry's fields, out on to the road, and as far as Tiny's and Bill's place. I rather want to see Tiny, and Aunt Adela may as well make his acquaintance, and Bill's, too. They'll be with us on Boxing Day, so she may as well meet them straight away.'

'Tiny's the agent,' explained Deborah. 'He agents for us and for the College. He's a most useful person, because he knows all the people round here and has introduced us to most of them. But Bill, his cousin, is nicer.'

'Yes, Bill's a good chap,' said Jonathan, 'but I think you'll like them both. Tiny's right up your street, as a matter of fact. He used to be in the Indian police. You ought to have plenty to talk about. He's got some amazing yarns.'

Tiny's and Bill's house proved to be a modern bungalow with a wonderful outlook over a deep valley. Tiny and Bill both were out when the party arrived, but the housekeeper was certain that they would soon return. She put out whisky and sherry, turned a red setter, two Manx cats and a bull-terrier out of the armchairs, repeated that Mr Fullalove and his cousin would be back at any moment, added that old Mrs Yates' roof did not really leak and never had, but that the Irish were like that, and left the company to themselves.

'Yes, Tiny and Bill are bachelors, lucky chaps,' said Jonathan, smiling at Deborah who was looking adorably beautiful that day. 'They've got a treasure in Mrs Dalby Whittier, their house-keeper. Oh, yes, she has to be given her full name. It's her only idiosyncrasy. She's a real find, though. Tiny says he doesn't know what they did before she came. She popped up out of nowhere and asked for the job. Just came up to the door two years ago and said she'd heard in the village that they had a vacancy for a cook-housekeeper. They've kept her ever since. It's a lonely spot up here, but she never minds being by herself. Bill is a bit of a natur-alist, so he says, and is often out at night badger-watching and all that sort of thing, and Tiny sometimes goes up to Town, but she never turns a hair. Queer, in a way, because she'd lived all her life in London until she came here, or so she told them.'

'What made her leave London, I wonder?' Mrs Bradley remarked. Her nephew had no time to answer, for at that moment both dogs began to bark, one cat jumped on to the window sill and the other on to the table. Jonathan went to the window and opened it, and an alert man of about fifty with a face almost as dark as an Indian's and small light-green eyes, climbed over the sill, shut the window, glanced down at his leggings, and then, with a cat on each shoulder and a dog's muzzle glued firmly to each knee, advanced to greet the guests.

'Get off, Mick. Get off, Deemster,' said he to the cats. 'Chuck it, Lassie. Go away, Cripes,' he added to the dogs. 'Hullo, Bradley. Good morning, Mrs Bradley.'

'This is Tiny Fullalove, Aunt Adela,' said Deborah. 'Tiny, this is Jon's aunt, Mrs Lestrange Bradley.'

'I am always taken aback when it is recalled that Deborah is also Mrs Bradley,' observed the reptilian, favouring Mr Fullalove with a leer. He responded with a gallantly meaningless remark, and began to dispense sherry.

Mrs Bradley, to her discomfort, was aware that she had conceived an instinctive dislike of her host. It was a feeling with which she was seldom troubled. Her dislikes were comparatively few, for she had a well-trained mind and a philosophical temperament, and a long succession of loathsomely egocentric patients had encouraged in her, in self-defence, a good-humoured tolerance of most of her fellow-creatures. But, in the present case, some female corpuscles, as it were, rose in revolt against something which they recognized in Tiny Fullalove. She had experienced the feeling once or twice before, and, in such cases, instinct had invariably proved reliable. There was a wife-poisoner, she remembered . . . a charming man in the opinion of everybody but Mrs Bradley. Even his unfortunate wife had adored him. He had poisoned her for her money . . .

'What do you think of Tiny?' Deborah demanded on the way back. She and Mrs Bradley had gone on ahead, leaving Jonathan to wait for Bill whom they had seen crossing the fields.

'What do you?' enquired Mrs Bradley.

'Oh, that's not fair! I asked you first.'

'It isn't fair to ask me what I think of a person I've met for the first time, is it?'

'I'm so glad,' said Deborah inconsequently.

'What about?'

'I know now that you don't like him a bit. And I don't, either.'

'Any reason?'

'Yes,' said Deborah, setting her jaw. 'I have a very good reason. But it's a reason I daren't tell Jon. Anyhow, it only happened once, and it certainly won't happen again. I've settled that. I detest men who can't behave themselves at *his* age.'

'Ah,' said Mrs Bradley, nodding. 'I'm glad you haven't told Jon.'

'Why do you say that?' enquired Deborah, struck by something in Mrs Bradley's tone.

'I shouldn't like my favourite nephew to be had up for causing grievous bodily harm. Jonathan is a quick-tempered man and very strong.'

'It's very odd that men can like men, and women can like women, whom the other sex can't stand,' pursued Deborah. Mrs Bradley agreed. She pointed out, however, that men could like women and women men whom their own sex could see through at the very first meeting, and that that was an odd thing, too.

'What about the cousin Bill?' she enquired. Deborah was again prepared to champion Bill.

'Like all Bills, he's nice,' she stated. 'I told him I didn't care much about his cousin's ways, and he said he'd take care that he behaved himself in future. I told him he need not trouble because I thought I had settled Tiny's hash, but I *think* there were words. Bill is an ex-Naval officer, and speaks his mind. Besides, Tiny had a black eye when Jon met him next day. He said he fell over one of the dogs, but I have my own views about that. Here comes Jon. Let's wait for him to catch us up.'

Mrs Bradley interpreted this last remark as a hint to drop the subject of Tiny Fullalove. Jonathan, who had sprinted after them, dropped into a walk beside his wife, and the conversation turned on the Fullalove cousins again, but upon a different aspect of them.

'I've had to ask both the Fullaloves for Christmas Day as well as Boxing Day, Deb,' said Jonathan. 'Sorry. I know you don't like Tiny, but I couldn't leave him out.'

'Who said I didn't like Tiny?' demanded Deborah. 'I've never mentioned such a thing!'

'Your face will never be your fortune, sweetheart. It gives too much away!' retorted her husband. 'Anyway, they've both accepted for both days, so you'll have to put up with them for lunch and probably for supper on Christmas Day, and tea and dinner on Boxing Day. And another sickening thing. They want us to put up a couple of pals of theirs. I'm awfully sorry. But they've very little room in that bungalow. Hullo! What's the matter with Worry?'

'I think he's seen your ghost,' said Mrs Bradley, closely scrutinizing a small lively dog which had come into view. 'That's the same gate again, isn't it? Who, by the way, is Worry's owner?'

'He's Will North's dog. The gamekeeper, you know,' said Deborah. 'Will must be somewhere about. Something *has* upset Worry! I wonder whether he's run a thorn in?'

She hurried down the slope. The terrier was standing about ten yards from the gate, yelping hideously, and all Deborah's cajolings could not persuade him to go any nearer. At this moment, Will North, the gamekeeper, came up and spoke to the dog. It nuzzled him, and, in a whining tone, began to explain its fears.

'Hallo, Will,' said Jonathan. 'Meet my aunt, Mrs Lestrange Bradley. She's a dead shot and a straight rider.'

'I've heard of you, ma'am,' said the tall man. 'You wrote a book I've got. *Psychoneurosis in the history of the Sixteenth Century*. I'm sorry about Worry. He isn't a silly chap really.'

'He's seen the ghost,' said Jonathan.

'Oh, yes, he *certainly* seems to have seen the ghost,' said Mrs Bradley. The gamekeeper capped them politely and walked on up the hill. The dog followed quietly at his heels, no longer afraid of the gate, and passed through it with him.

'The ghost has gone,' said Jonathan. 'I wonder why?'

Mrs Bradley watched the man and his dog until they were silhouetted against the sky at the top of the rise. Then she followed Jonathan and Deborah, who, by that time, were some way ahead.

When she looked back she had a sudden although transitory shock. A man was leaning over the haunted gate, and that man was certainly not the gamekeeper. Whoever he was, he straightened himself immediately he saw her looking back, and, turning, strode in the direction of the bungalow.

CHAPTER 2

The Shape of Things to Come

'. . . and if the night
Have gathered aught of evil, or concealed,
Disperse it, as new light dispels the dark.'

John Milton

The weather turned colder, and Deborah preferred the fire, so Mrs Bradley and Jonathan spent the daylight hours of Christmas Eve in tramping over the hills. She was astonished to discover the distances which could be covered without going outside the estate.

'Of course, a good bit of this is not mine,' Jonathan explained. 'It belongs to the College now. But the two parts have only been separated since this last sale, and I've permission to tramp where I like. Pretty good, all of it, isn't it? A chap named Daventry farms that bit down there. I've met him. He seems all right. His wife breeds Boxers.'

'Breeds what? – Oh, a type of bulldog.'

'Yes. I'm giving Deb a puppy for Christmas. She doesn't know yet. I hope she'll like it. They're a sensible, clean-looking breed, very companionable, I believe, and good guards, too. I've bought the puppy very young because I want him to grow up on good terms with Rhu, my Irish wolf-hound, but he's still to be weaned. Sally's looking after Rhu at present, but I'm fetching him in the car after tea. It's only fifteen miles. We're hoping to have her over for a weekend in the New Year. She's greatly looking forward to seeing you again.'

'What shall you call the puppy?' Mrs Bradley enquired, without making any promises which involved the New Year.

'Oh, Deb will name him. I shall suggest Bob Fitzsimmons, but I don't suppose it will pass! 'Morning, Ed!'

A carter was driving a heavy wagon along the rutted track. A jay alighted, with a noisy yell, about three yards in front of the wagon. It walked comically sideways, screeched hideously at the carter, and then flew up and almost tumbled on to the man's knee. There, balancing, it clapped its wings at him.

'Oh, there you are, then, you old boy, you,' said the carter. The bird scolded him roundly.

'Queer,' said Jonathan. 'Birds just come to that bloke. His name's Ed Brown. He carts for Daventry. The old women in the village swear he's a changeling, and, by the look of him, he could be, couldn't he? He reminds me of a satyr, or perhaps Puck, except that he behaves himself. There's only one person he doesn't take to, if rumour can be believed – and as it's pub rumour it probably can! – and that's our agent, Tiny Fullalove. It seems that Ed met Tiny out in India during the war and didn't like his ways with Army mules.'

'Odd that they should have met in India if, as I suppose, Ed Brown merely went there during the war,' Mrs Bradley remarked, 'especially if Mr Fullalove was in the police, and Brown a soldier.'

'Quite right; it was a bit of a coincidence. Their meeting must have been just one of those things. The Fullaloves aren't local people. It's a Yorkshire name, I believe. Tiny knew the former owner of this place and when he heard there was a job going here he asked to have it. He got it, packed up India (where, presumably, he knew there was no future for him) and came along. He had only been agent here for a couple of years when the place was sold. Fellow's gone to live in the South of France or somewhere. Made it a condition of sale that the College and I kept Tiny on. Fair enough. He's pretty good at his job. Miss Hughes, the College principal, doesn't like him, though. Moreover, she ain't tactful like Ed. She says it loud and clear, with Celtic oaths. Welsh as Llanfihangel. I love her.'

'Oh, it's a women's college, is it? I hadn't gathered that.'

'Yes. You must get Miss Hughes to tell you about it. She's coming over to Christmas dinner. Bit of a nuisance the Fullaloves have to come, too, but it can't be helped. One has to be matey in the country, and the College holiday only lasts a week, so Miss Hughes doesn't go down at all; just stays up getting ready for next term. It's one of these Emergency places, you know. They reckon to train their people in thirteen months. It must be the hell of a life for the Staff, I should think. Let's push in here and collect the pup for Deb.'

The guests bequeathed by the Fullaloves turned up on the afternoon of Christmas Eve. They were men of Jonathan's age, and, according to themselves, were respectively an archaeologist and a naturalist. The Bronze Age in Scandinavia and Denmark was Gregory Mansell's object of worship; Miles Obury studied British mammals, particularly badgers. During the previous summer he and Bill Fullalove had been out at night in the woods to try to photograph these animals and had built a watcher's platform in a tree. They took Mrs Bradley to see it, and Obury informed her that, owing to the legend of the ghost, the wood was called Groaning Spinney.

Obury and Mansell were agreeable and sociable persons, and the evening at the manor passed pleasantly. At just after half-past ten Deborah and Mrs Bradley went to bed, and Obury announced his intention of going up to the wood again to see how his badgers were getting on. Mansell, laughing, said that he would go with him and see whether it was the ghost's night to haunt at the top of the spinney. They took a nip of Jonathan's Christmas bottle of Scotch and set off in high fettle for the small wood which mounted the hill in the direction of the Fullaloves' bungalow. Mansell was particularly jovial. He was a complete sceptic with regard to ghosts and was not in the least afraid that he might see this one.

Jonathan did not accompany them because, in accordance with a humane custom introduced by Deborah, the maids had been granted Christmas leave from tea-time on Christmas Eve until ten o'clock in the morning of the day following Boxing Day, and he did not propose to leave his wife alone in a very lonely house. He did not realize that Deborah felt perfectly safe with Mrs Bradley there.

He lit a cigarette, stoked up the fire, went out to the kitchen to impound sausage rolls and mince pies in case his guests came in hungry, and then he sat down, picked up a book, and took no more notice of time. But at a quarter past eleven there came a quiet tap at the window. Jonathan was not at all startled. He had been accustomed for years (before his marriage) to admitting eccentric or delinquent friends by all manner of entrances to all manner of enclosures – school dormitories, College rooms, lodgings, fortified places of various types in various parts of the world, and once, against Admiralty regulations, to a submarine. So now he stepped over to the window and asked quietly who was there.

The reassuring and well-known voice of Bill Fullalove answered him.

'Thought I wouldn't knock at the door, in case I disturbed your missus.'

'All right,' said Jonathan. 'I'll go to the door and let you in. Come round to the front, will you? . . . Well, now, what can we do for you?'

'Oh, nothing, really. Tiny and I had a sudden flap lest we'd got the time of the invitation all wrong. You can't want us for mid-day dinner *and* supper tomorrow as well as to tea and dinner on Boxing Day, can you?'

'Yes, of course we can, you old ass! Why ever not?'

'Well—' Bill looked embarrassed. 'Fact is, it's all over the village that you've sent your cook and the maids home for Christmas Day and Boxing Day, and so we rather wondered – especially as we've saddled you with Obury and Mansell—'

'Whether you'll be asked to do the washing up? Well, you will! So if *that* puts you off, say so now.'

'Oh, Lord, no! Only—' he eyed the three empty glasses.

'Yes, Mansell and Obury have gone out ghost-hunting in Groaning Spinney,' said Jonathan, grinning.

'But tonight it's as black as a parson's hat,' said Bill, 'even out in the open! I know my way blindfold, but I've brought my torch, all the same. Anyway, I believe it's going to snow. Oh, well, I'll push off.' He eyed the decanter wistfully. Jonathan, who was a strong-minded, non-suggestible man, put the decanter into the sideboard cupboard and took out a bottle of gin. He grinned again as he put it opposite his guest. Bill laughed, and helped himself.

'You'll get one peg, and one only, tomorrow evening, and the same on Boxing Day,' stated Jonathan. 'That's the only bottle of Scotch I've been able to scrounge from anywhere, and I've had to open it already.'

Bill swallowed his drink, and had been gone half an hour when Mansell and Obury returned. They had signs and wonders to report. Between mouthfuls of sausage roll they reported them.

'Well,' said Jonathan, gathering what he could from the tale, 'everybody round here has seen him, so why not you?'

'But we *couldn't* have seen him!' said Mansell. 'Had it been moonlight, I'd have thought my eyesight was playing me tricks, but it was as black as pitch except for this queer light shining on a dead-white face. I'm convinced it was merely somebody playing the fool.'

'Then it must have been Bill Fullalove,' said Jonathan. 'He dropped in while you were gone. You'd better have it out with him tomorrow. He's coming to dinner.'

'When did he come?' asked Mansell.

'Oh, elevenish, I believe.'

'And when did he leave?'

'The same. I mean, he wasn't here more than ten minutes, I should say.'

'Must have been Bill,' said Mansell.

'Rot!' said Obury, flatly. 'It was the ghost. I won't be done out of my spook!'

Mrs Bradley, whose French chef, Henri, would never allow her to cook at home, begged permission to help with the Christmas dinner, and she and her nephew had the kitchen to themselves. Deborah, who was inclined at first to be obstinate and to demand the position of housewife, was turned out gently and firmly by her husband, and threatened with punitive measures if she returned.

So she went to church, leaving the new puppy and his mother at the farm, which was on her way, to be cared for there until the puppy was weaned. Obury and Mansell stoked up the drawing-room fire and settled down to enjoy a thoroughly lazy Christmas morning. They had offered to accompany Deborah to church, but were greatly relieved when she merely laughed. They watched from the window until they saw her join Will North, the tall gamekeeper, at the junction of the drive and the lane, and hand him over the puppy, and then they sighed luxuriously and settled themselves in deep chairs on either side of the fire.

'Shall you recognize the ghost if he turns out to be Bill Fulla-love?' Jonathan enquired, coming in to find out whether they wanted anything. Mansell and Obury were not at all certain that they would.

'Of course, we've both known Bill for some time,' said Mansell, 'but that rather sickening face we saw last night looked simply like nothing on earth. What did *you* think, Obury?'

'Oh, I agree. Bill or not, I shouldn't recognize it. But I'm still convinced it was the ghost. Anyhow, if it *was* Bill, well, although we went badger-watching together here during the summer, I couldn't swear to him at that distance and with that ghastly light on his face.'

They discussed the phenomenon of the ghost until Jonathan was needed in the kitchen and Mansell became bored and went to sleep. Obury then played with the cat, smoked, ate chocolates, read a novel and contrived to amuse himself until the busy Jonathan, his dark locks disordered and his middle girt about with a large white apron, rushed in again, this time to give his guests some drinks.

Obury woke Mansell, and as they were helping themselves the Fullaloves appeared at the front door, and almost immediately afterwards Deborah arrived from church, bringing with her the principal of the Emergency Training College, Miss Hughes, who had been invited for Christmas dinner and for as long as she cared to stay.

Miss Hughes proved to be a red-haired, hazel-eyed woman of forty-five. She had been for twenty years an outstanding success as a schoolmistress, although her first few years at her school-marming had been hell. She was highly intelligent and very strong-willed. Her intelligence saved her from pig-headedness. Her few friends she had made for life and their fondness and loyalty never faltered. She had, rather strangely, no enemies. She had been the third child of a family of twelve, and life in such a very large household had made her a competent improvisor, and her Welsh blood had supplied her with imagination and warm sympathy. She was hard-headed, too, as so many Welsh-women have always had to be, and to run a college, with its problems of discipline and catering, its servants, its workmen, its outside contacts with Education Committee and Ministry, and its own internal problems too numerous and, individually, too unimportant to name, came to her as second nature.

One great stroke of luck she had had, and that was in the situation of the College. The Cotswolds were not the hills of Wales, but they warmed her heart and reconciled her emotionally to what she knew she had sacrificed in leaving her own Welsh valley.

She had made it one of her first duties to call upon the tenants of the ancient manor house, and had taken to Jonathan immediately. Deborah she loved as she would have loved a daughter, and when she heard that Jonathan's lovely wife had lectured in English for a short time at the famous training college of Cartaret, their friendship was complete, and it followed naturally that Miss Hughes would spend Christmas with the Bradleys instead of remaining in solitary grandeur in the house on the opposite hill.

'Ghost?' said Miss Hughes, having listened with great interest to a conversation between Mansell and Bill Fullalove, in which Mansell challenged Bill to deny that he had been the ghost. 'I didn't know you had a ghost so near at hand.'

'Oh, but we have,' said Jonathan. 'A very well-authenticated ghost, too, and extremely well-behaved. He never comes nearer the house than that gate over which Mansell and Obury saw him leaning. I've been digging him up since we've been here. He's the Reverend Horatius Pile, who skippered this parish from 1801 until 1857, but nobody seems to know for certain how he came to be found dead, leaning over the gate. Yes, of course I'll take you along to see the gate. Have some more sherry. Aunt Adela brought it with her, so I know it's all right.'

'Well, I don't know what Obury saw, or Mansell, either,' said Bill. 'But, whatever they saw, it wasn't me. I went back through the stable-courtyard and up the village street. It was a darned sight easier way to take on such a pitch-black night. The last lap, up to our place from the village, was quite bad enough. I certainly didn't propose to walk back through Groaning Spinney. I didn't want to bash my brains out against an immemorial elm.'

'They're mostly beeches,' said Obury.

'Anyhow, I thought the ghost only appeared by moonlight,' put in Deborah.

'Ah, you'd probably only *see* it by moonlight,' said Miss Hughes. 'But that wouldn't necessarily prove that it wasn't there at other times. You've heard about ghosts which are only footsteps, but nothing seen? Well, in my opinion, such a ghost *can* be seen by

animals, particularly by dogs, who are well-known to be suscep-
tible to supernormal presences.'

'Talking of dogs,' said Mrs Bradley, 'it did seem as though the
gamekeeper's dog, Worry, disliked that gate the other day.'

The story of Worry was received respectfully by everybody
except Mansell, who continued to suggest that as there were no
such things as ghosts, even a dog would not be able to see them,
and Bill Fullalove who, rather surprisingly, said that dogs were
fools and cowards. Tiny Fullalove challenged this, and stated that
a good dog was better than a good man any day. The argument
was not entirely good-natured, although both cousins conducted
it smilingly. Mrs Bradley turned the conversation with great
adroitness on to the subject of the Roman antiquities found in the
neighbourhood, and the subject of ghosts was shelved in favour of
a discussion of the finds at Chedworth.

Ghosts cropped up again, however, on Boxing Day morning.
Snow fell on Christmas night, and in the morning the sun shone
brilliantly on pine branches laden with soft crystals, and upon
hills of purple-shadowed silver. Obury proposed to take a walk,
and invited others to join him. Jonathan intended to remain at
home in order to prepare the vegetables for Boxing Day lunch;
Deborah was not anxious to walk over snow, which she disliked;
Mrs Bradley was to help with the cooking again – her one chance
in the year, she explained, to practise the fascinating art, so
Obury, Mansell and Miss Hughes took a long cast upwards into
the hills, proposing to bear left at the top of the rise and to return
across the snow-covered fields which bordered the manor house
wood.

They returned to find that two more guests had arrived; these
were the village choirmaster, a delicate-looking young man with
effeminate hands and a cruel mouth, and a certain Mr Baird, a
retired stockbroker, a widower, who lived with his man-servant
next door to the doctor in a modern and delightful little house
just past the mill.

The introductions and greetings concluded, the stalwarts back from their walk had news to impart.

'The ghost leaves footmarks,' said Obury.

'Not boots or shoes, either,' added Miss Hughes.

'More like stockinged feet,' said Mansell, laughing. 'Anybody here guilty?'

'Let's all go and look,' suggested Jonathan. How this suggestion might have been received remained obscure, for at that moment a knock at the front door, followed by the clanging sound of its ancient bell, announced the arrival of the Fullalove cousins, who had returned home on Christmas night and now had come to spend Boxing Day. Cocktails having been handed round by the attentive host, and strange but palatable snacks having been supplied as the result of Mrs Bradley's experiments in the kitchen, the conversation became split like the effects of light in a prism, and the ghost's footmarks were left for the time in limbo, that magic fourth-dimension of the psychologists.

Mrs Bradley, returning from the kitchen with reinforcements of the dishes she had concocted, decided that her strong feelings about Tiny Fullalove had not altered at this second meeting, and she also found that she distrusted the bluff Bill as much as she disliked his brown-faced, jovial cousin. Bill was good company; there was no doubt about that. He was a man of wide experience and knowledge. He was good-humoured, good-looking and attractively jolly. No one would share her feeling about him except Miss Hughes, she thought.

She tried to rationalize her emotional reactions, but about both cousins there was something which repelled her; something which, to her analytical mind, did not ring true. She could not account for the feeling, for Jonathan most obviously liked Bill, and Deborah's little revelation that it was within Tiny's scope to play the wolf with a lovely girl affected Mrs Bradley not at all. Deborah, like most lovely girls, was very well able to lob back undesirable passes, particularly since her most happy and satisfying marriage, and a layman who never deviated from the path of monastic virtue was a phenomenon which, so far, Mrs Bradley had not encountered. It was not, therefore, Tiny as a potential home-and-heart-breaker to whom Mrs Bradley objected, nor to Bill as a lively good fellow. No; there was something else; but what it was she could not, so far, hit upon. She put the subject out of her mind and joined in the animated noise of a roomful of people, most of whom were obviously and heartily enjoying themselves.

Boxing Day lunch, tea and dinner passed pleasantly enough, and immediately dinner was over the Fullaloves and their two friends went off. Mrs Bradley was interested to observe the reactions of the others at their going, for it seemed early to break up the party.

The first thing she became aware of was that their going did not break up the party at all. The village choirmaster, deep in a discussion with Miss Hughes of the associations between heraldry and mass psychology, seemed not to notice their going. Deborah was obviously glad to see the last of them, and Baird, a semi-bald, shrewd Scotsman, looked up at them, nodded, and continued to talk to Deborah about the Edinburgh festival. Mansell and Obury were to return at about eleven, which accounted, perhaps, for the off-hand nature of the farewells.

'That's that,' said Jonathan, coming back from seeing the four men off. 'Now, then, people! Let's have some more port.'

'I thought you liked them,' Deborah remarked, passing on the bottle without filling her own glass.

'I did, more or less, Bill especially, until this Christmas,' replied her husband. 'But there's been something a bit wet-blanket about them today – or am I liverish? Anyway, to be frank and inhospitable, I'm sorry I asked them – all four of them – especially Tiny and Bill – and I'm glad to see the back of them, and yet I don't really know why.'

'I hope it's not my fault,' said the young choirmaster suddenly.

'I had a bit of a row with Tiny. He caught some of my choirboys on Christmas Eve pinching holly. He clouted them on the ear, and pretty hard. I'm not going to stand for that, and I told him so. In any case, the holly wasn't even on his ground. It was on yours, Mr Bradley. I've threatened him with a summons if he touches my kids again. He can keep his Indian ideas for Indians, and I hope they cut his throat for him, at that!'

'How long have you been choirmaster here?' Mrs Bradley tactfully enquired; for the young man spoke hoarsely and with what Mrs Bradley privately thought to be exaggerated and dramatic anger.

'Two years and a bit,' he replied, as though glad of the change of subject. 'I'm really a pianist, you know. I used to accompany professional singers in London, but I collected a bit of a packet during the war, and lost the use of one wrist. It's not much better now, but I can manage to play the organ in church. Anyway, the doctor told me I was crazy to stay in Town when what I needed were country air and a quiet atmosphere. Out here a room was going, and so I took it, and, although I don't earn much, I manage to get along.' He looked challengingly at the company.

'And have you benefited from the change of environment?' Mrs Bradley discreetly enquired.

'Well, I *might*,' said the young man, flushing, 'if I didn't straightway find . . . Oh, I'm sorry! You've had it once. Anyway, I can't stick Anglo-Indians. My father was one, and he and I . . .'

'I'll have a word with Tiny myself,' said Jonathan. 'If the boys were on my land I suppose he thought he had a right to interfere. Boys are destructive little beasts, and it's part of their lives to be so. Still, of course—'

'Yes, he *is* your agent,' put in Miss Hughes, without waiting for the sentence to be concluded, 'and boys can be cheeky and provocative. We should need to know the whole tale before we could judge. In my opinion—'

The young choirmaster seemed prepared to make an angry

reply to her eminently reasonable remarks, but he thought better of it when he met Miss Hughes' amused but challenging stare, and merely replied that he thought he could trust his choirboys to tell the truth even if they were not successful in the impossible task of shaming the devil.

'"Truth, they say, lives in a well,"' quoted Mrs Bradley solemnly. '"Why I vow I ne'er could see; let the water-drinkers tell; there she'll always stay for me."' In support of this statement she helped herself to port, a hybrid beverage which she had always detested. At this point Mansell and Obury came back.

'We didn't go all the way with them,' they said.

When young Emming had gone to his lodging, Jonathan remarked, 'First time I knew his father was an Anglo-Indian. I heard he was a London man, and that young Emming was – Oh, well! Not our business. What shall we all do tomorrow?'

'That young man reminds me of somebody,' said Mrs Bradley, refusing to be side-tracked. 'Tell me more about him, please.'

'I don't think we know any more about him, do we, Deb?' asked Jonathan.

Deborah hesitated. Then she shook her head.

CHAPTER 3

The Expected Begins to Happen

'Tis custom, Lord, this day to send
A gift to every vulgar friend.'
Nathaniel Eaton

However happy the Christmas, there is usually a deep-seated human instinct which feels tremendous relief when it is over. This emotion attacked all three Bradleys on the day which followed Boxing Day. Miss Hughes, Mansell and Obury all departed and the household sighed and settled down.

Deborah and Mrs Bradley remained indoors and took stock of the scraps. The servants, toiling loyally and stoically through the snow, which was now very deep, returned at approximately the appointed time. Jonathan went out for a scrambling walk through the drifts, and followed a track which led him a wild dance up to his thighs in the soft white morass on the hillside.

'What about the ghost's footprints?' asked Deborah, when he returned.

'Didn't go that way,' replied Jonathan. 'What about a bath? Is the plumbing, as such, in tune?'

'Yes. There's plenty of hot water. Go on up.'

Whilst he bathed, Deborah and Mrs Bradley looked again at their Christmas gifts.

'Book tokens; that means Cheltenham or Gloucester,' pronounced

Deborah, shuffling a dozen bright cards. 'When shall we go? – Tomorrow?'

'I don't know. I think I shall wait until I get to London,' Mrs Bradley replied.

'Oh, no. I want to go and choose my books with you. We can't go while the snow's so deep, that's one thing. I wonder what cook will manage for lunch? I do hope nothing weird and wonderful.'

To the surprise of everybody, the postman contrived to make his way to the house in the early afternoon. No one had expected him, for the snow began again at just after one o'clock, and fell silently and steadily until four.

However, at just after a quarter past two, when Mrs Bradley had gone up to her room to write letters which might or might not get posted that day, Sidney Blott, son of the postmistress and a postman in his own right, ploughed his way up the hill and delivered his cargo of letters, belated Christmas cards and presents.

He apologized for not having come in the morning, but the post, it appeared, was late because the road was almost impassable for the Post Office van. By the time the van had completed its journey, Sidney's mother had suggested that he wait until the morning, and the argument between Mrs Blott and her son had lasted until after the mid-day meal. Sidney had won by remaining silent until his mother had galloped herself tired, as he explained.

'Well, I rather agree with your mother, Sidney,' said Deborah, dragging him inside the hall door. 'Still, as you've been good enough to come, you'd better have something to warm you.'

'Beer, then, your ladyship,' said Sidney, 'if so be as his lordship has got any.'

The original owner of the estate had been a peer of the realm, and it had proved impossible to persuade Sidney and his mother to address Jonathan and Deborah by any other titles than the ones now loyally bestowed.

'But our letters and parcels come addressed to Mr or Mrs Bradley,' Deborah had observed. The postmistress had agreed.

'But,' said she, 'the old house always had a lord and a lady in it, and I've always voted Conservative and always shall.'

'Then, by rights, you ought to call Miss Hughes, up at the College, My Lady,' Deborah had pointed out.

'Oh, no, certainly not,' said Mrs Blott decisively. 'She's only a kind of housekeeper, when all's said and done. She has to work for her living, same as I do.'

'But so does my husband, and so did I until I married him.'

The postmistress was not to be persuaded, and re-opened the subject one day before Christmas when Jonathan was in her shop.

'And all of them racketeering young school teachers!' she said firmly. Even Jonathan felt bound to protest at this description.

'That's sheer libel, Mrs Blott,' he told her, counting out the money for his tobacco. 'Even if you mean racketing – and a woman of your education should know the difference! – it still isn't true. Those embryo schoolmarms are painfully, morbidly earnest. A good many of them have given up other and lesser jobs in pursuit of what they consider to be an ideal, and their zeal is positively nunlike – until, of course, they discover what the job really entails!'

'Not much ideal in learning how to learn young Bob Wootton and Tommy Mayhew,' retorted Mrs Blott with a sniff. As there was no possible answer to this except a direct contradiction which would have amounted to an equally direct lie, Jonathan pocketed his tobacco and his change, laughed, and wished her good-bye.

On the afternoon of Sidney's arrival in the snow, therefore, Jonathan and Deborah, having accepted their unwished-for titles without further question, went into the morning-room to examine the post.

'Oh, Lord!' said Jonathan. 'I do hope *this* isn't going to begin. Have *you* got one?'

'One what?' asked Deborah, opening some retarded Christmas cards.

'An anonymous contribution to your knowledge of my morals and conceits. I've got a beauty about *you!*'

'Show me.' She took the letter from her husband, and, to his dismay, flushed scarlet. 'Oh, dear!' she cried. 'Now who on earth could have known that!'

'Known what?' said Jonathan. 'Good Lord, it isn't true?'

'No, of course not. But I did have a bit of bother with him. It was very soon after we came. It's all right now.'

'But why the devil didn't you tell me? I'd have broken his neck!'

'Yes, I know, you idiot! That's precisely why I didn't tell you. But he got no change out of it, one way and another. But I wonder – what's the postmark on the envelope?'

'What you'd expect – Cheltenham. Anybody in the village has only to get on a bus.' He got up. 'I'm going into Cheltenham and I'm – dash! I suppose whoever it was just bunged it in the nearest pillar-box. Probably didn't even need to go into a post-office for a stamp. I know what I *will* do, though. I'll find out who in the village went to Cheltenham on the day before Christmas Eve and on what errand. That might give us a clue.'

'Oh, darling, I wouldn't bother. Some nasty person thinks she's got hold of a bit of scandal and wants to make mischief. That's all there's to it. Far better take no notice.'

'Well, I don't know about that,' said Jonathan, influenced already (although against his will) by his wife's calm reasonableness. 'You see, if this is just one nasty person's reaction to one particular incident, and that's the end of it, all well and good; but if it's the beginning of a poison-pen campaign, we ought to take strong action and try to nip it in the bud. This letter constitutes grounds for an action for slander, I should say, and, if it does, we'd be well advised, in my opinion, to push it as far as it will go. I suppose we're strangers here, and therefore, to that extent, resented, and, in somebody's opinion, vulnerable.'

'Well, look,' said Deborah, 'why not take the thing to the vicar? He's a sensible old darling, and will probably be able to put his finger on this anonymous Peeping Thomasina without much trouble.'

'Fine idea,' said Jonathan, looking grimly happy. 'I'll go over there right away.'

'Oh, wait until tomorrow, at any rate,' said Deborah. 'Aunt Adela will want her tea in another hour, and, anyhow, the weather's so frightful. Apart from anything else, it's snowing again.'

'Good heavens!' exclaimed the remorseful host. 'I'd forgotten Aunt Adela was here. Where's she got to?'

Mrs Bradley was discovered in the kitchen. She had finished her correspondence, and was now helping in the preparations for dinner and discoursing to an enthralled audience consisting of cook, Jane and Carrie, upon the subject of George Joseph Smith and his brides in the bath. They were preparing the vegetables, washing up her various utensils, and breathlessly hanging upon her words. Mrs Bradley, meanwhile, was engaged with savoury messes which carried their own recommendation.

'Cooking (vide Captain MacHeath's views upon women) unbends the mind,' pronounced Mrs Bradley, upon the advent of her nephew and his wife. 'And murder makes the whole world kin. There cannot be any doubt about that.'

'I remember,' said Mrs Fairleaf, the cook, 'a funny kind of case when I lived in Gloucester. It was somebody that murdered a grand-nephew because he believed in ghosts. And nobody could ever make out whether the ghosts committed the murder or whether the murder settled the ghosts, for they never had no ghosts after that.'

'Interesting,' Mrs Bradley remarked. 'I shall add it to my memoirs, Mrs Fairleaf.'

'I say, Aunt Adela,' said Jonathan, when Mrs Bradley was ready to leave the kitchen, 'what do you think about this?' He produced the anonymous letter. Mrs Bradley shook her head over it.

'I should keep it,' she said briefly. 'I suppose you do not recognize the handwriting?'

'No, I can't say that I do. But except for one or two communications from the original owners of this place, a letter or so from Miss Hughes, and several notes from Tiny Fullalove, all about the house and the estate, I don't think I know the handwriting of anybody in the village.'

'If you get any more anonymous letters I should submit them, together with the writings at your disposal, to an expert. You will, at that rate, clear your acquaintances of suspicion, even if you accomplish nothing more.'

'So far as I am concerned, they are cleared already,' declared Jonathan. 'Tiny Fullalove would hardly put me wise to his own dirty little games, and the others would have no interest in giving me this sort of information, even if they possessed it.'

'Are you sure of that?' asked Mrs Bradley instantly.

'What about Bill Fullalove?' asked Deborah.

'Bill? Well, he could have told me by word of mouth if he was going to tell me at all. That is, if he knew. *Did* he know, Deb?'

'Yes,' said Deborah, 'he did. I told him myself. I think he blacked Tiny's eye. He would hardly have done that if he intended to write you anonymous letters, would he?'

'I shouldn't think so. But I wish you'd told me, Deb.'

'She did well not to tell you,' said Mrs Bradley. 'It would be different if she had really needed protection. Was that the only letter?'

'No. But there was nothing for you,' said Deborah. 'There are one or two parcels, though, Jon. Let's go and open them, shall we? Come along, Aunt Adela. You can be the one to shake each parcel and guess what's in it. I haven't heard from Cecilia Randome yet, so one of the parcels is almost certainly from her.'

The rest of the day, the evening and the night passed without incident, but snow continued to fall, and, by the morning, although the house was not absolutely snowed up, Jonathan gave way to Deborah by putting off his visit to the vicar in favour of a day indoors by the fire. Mrs Fairleaf set to and baked some bread, and this was as well, for the tradespeople apparently considered that the toilsome, snowbound, uphill lane to the house was impassable and rang up to ask for instructions; this was as long as the telephone wires held.

'We can manage for a day or two,' said Deborah. 'There's stuff left over, and we've got some tins and plenty of vegetables. We shan't starve. I hope it doesn't get much worse, though.' She looked rather anxiously out of the window at the misty and whirling snowflakes as they dropped softly upon ledges and steps and drifted ever more thickly in the lane and against the banks in the garden and park, and upon the side of the house. 'There's something horribly eerie about snow in the country. I'd never realized it before. It's so silent. I'd rather have rain, and hear the sound of it.'

'I miss the newspapers,' said Jonathan. 'The wireless is all right in its way, but—'

'What did it say about the weather?'

'Snow on high ground, spreading eastwards and south.'

'Oh, dear! We may be cut off for days!'

'Yes. I think I'd better dig us out tomorrow. It will be something to do. I need exercise.'

'Yes, but not if it's still snowing, and it sounds from that weather report as though it will be. I wonder how Miss Hughes is getting on? I'm glad she's not alone up there. It's such an awful great barrack of a place.'

'I wish to goodness she'd stayed here. Still, one of her staff was coming back to keep her company for the day or two before the students arrived, wasn't she? I'm glad of that. All the same, if I *can* get out tomorrow, I'll go up there and see how she's getting along. I wonder—' He did not finish his sentence. His lips closed and his mouth tightened. That wretched anonymous letter, thought Deborah, had thoroughly upset him. For the hundredth time she wondered who could have sent it. That, and the snow and the lonely situation of the house, were enough to make people brood, and when people brooded trouble started. She put her hand on her husband's arm.

'That awful Amy Curtis has sent me an awful handbag,' she announced. 'Do you think I could send her that book token for a guinea which Myra Standish sent me and didn't sign, and buy myself some stockings with the money? I've had dozens of book tokens this Christmas and no stockings at all.' Jonathan laughed, forgot his cold anger against the oafish Mr Fullalove, and pulled Deborah on to his knee.

'You're an immoral little tyke,' he said, holding her. 'Do what you like, but it won't be for a day or two yet. I wonder' – he laughed again – 'I wonder how our ghost likes the snow?'

'Don't!' said Deborah. 'Snow scares me, I tell you. I didn't know it did, but it does. It's horrid and soft-footed and it acts like a great, thick blanket, stifling everything. I loathe it.'

'Here, here,' said Jonathan, protesting. 'Don't get fanciful! If you live in the country you've got to put up with the weather. Whatever next?'

It stopped snowing during the night, so on the following day he took a spade, a shovel and a hard broom and, dressed in breeches and leggings and a thick pullover, began to clear a path at each of the doors of the house. The snow was light and soft and the work was easy. By eleven in the morning he had got as far as the kitchen dump at the back of the house, and beyond the end of the lawn at the front. He went indoors for his elevenses, and then announced his intention of going up to the College to find out how Miss Hughes was getting on and whether her friend had arrived.

The snow had ceased at about five o'clock that morning. All the footmarks of the previous day were covered up. A wintry sun was trying to break through, but there was still plenty of snow in the sky, and Jonathan, glancing up at the heavens as he left the house for his long and difficult walk, began to wonder whether he had wasted time in clearing paths from the house.

He reached the College thoroughly tired. Some of the time he had been up to the thighs in snow, and the going everywhere was bad. He called at the lodge before going on to the main building, and was firmly jerked inside by the formidable Miss Emma Woot-ton, the sister of Abel Wootton and Harry Wootton, and Bob Wootton's painstaking aunt.

'Well, sir,' she said discouragingly, 'you *must* want something to do!'

'I came to find out how Miss Hughes was getting on,' explained Jonathan, feeling rather like a small boy with jam on his face. 'Did Miss Diana Bagthorpe turn up, do you know?'

'Being Physical, she did.'

'Oh, the PT lady, is she? I'm glad she made it.'

'The bus got stuck outside Stroud. She came that way. She walked it from there.'

'Good heavens! She *must* be an Amazon!'

'No. Little and good is what she is. One of the wiry, tough ones. She was about finished, though, when she got here, and wet to the skin, like you. She felt she *had* to get here, because of Miss Hughes. A grand little creetur, she is!'

'I should just about think so. I'd like to meet her.'

'Well, you will. Now, sir, you'll just get out of them there soak-ing trousers, and I'll have 'em all dried out by the time you get back here. It's not too bad from here to the College. Abel and Harry swept a path, so as long as you're back before the snow comes down again, you'll at least get up there dry.'

'But I can't—'

'Now just you do as I say, sir. I've got Brother Abel's velveteens as will fit you nicely. I always keep spare clothes here for my brothers. You needn't mind changing your trousers in front of me. I don't take no notice. I'm too used to men being wet through and dirty for that.'

So Jonathan changed obediently into Abel Wootton's cordu-roys, and very much more comfortable they were than his own snow-soaked garments. The swept path to the College, although only a couple of feet wide, was heaven after the ploughing uphill walk he had had after leaving the stable courtyard at the foot of his own hill. He was grateful to Miss Wootton, and regretted that he had ever referred to her in private as a bossy old cat.

All was well at the College. He found Miss Hughes and the lecturer for Physical Training taking their ease in front of a great open fire. One was nursing the College cat, the other was doing some embroidery. He stayed long enough to be assured that there was plenty of food in the house, including tinned milk, that bread could be baked in the College oven, and that neither of the ladies was in the least dismayed at the prospect of being snowed up. The students were due back in three days' time, but Miss Hughes was hoping that the snow would be melted by then.

She followed Jonathan's glance out of the window at the leaden sky, and shrugged and laughed.

'We must do what we can,' she said, comfortably. 'What is not to be won't be. There is no sense in worrying. If I know the students, they will get here somehow, luggage or no luggage. I shall do what I can with my car, but it won't be much, in this.'

She gave Jonathan some rum and lemon, for which he was grateful, and then she began to talk about the ghost. Miss Bagthorpe, who turned out to be a jolly, bouncing sort of person, rather like a solid rubber ball in human dress, expressed the opinion that to see a ghost meant death. Jonathan and Miss Hughes debated this point with her, and the argument went merrily until it was time for Jonathan to go.

Miss Wootton had dried his clothes but nothing was scorched. He did not know how she had managed to dry them in the time, and said as much. On impulse, he suddenly added:

'I say, Miss Wootton, I know you can keep your mouth shut. Who, in the village, is cranky enough to write me an immoral sort of letter?'

'That Mrs La-di-dah that does for Mr Fullalove,' Miss Wootton promptly replied. 'Nobody of these parts would do it.'

Jonathan thought this an unreasonable and prejudiced statement, so he nodded non-committally and started on his way home. Just as he began to mount the lane which led to the house he met the Fullaloves' gardener, a fellow named Anstey.

'The governor's bust his leg, sir,' said Anstey, 'and wondered whether you could go on up and see to him. I had a message. I wasn't to go up there myself. I was to come straight along here. Note pushed under my door.'

'All right,' said Jonathan. 'What's the other Mr Fullalove doing? – Mr Bill?'

'Called away to Gloucester, sir, or so the governor said yesterday. Don't see how he's going to get through. Here's the key, sir. The governor can't get to the door, so 'e says in the note. His leg must be pretty bad, I reckon. Anyway, I'm forbid to do aught except fetch you along.'

'Where's Mrs Dalby Whittier? Can't she let me in?'

'Gone to London for Christmas, sir, and the governor told me he'd wrote and told her particular she wasn't to try and come back in all this snow.'

'Right. Well, go on up to my house and tell them I'll get back as soon as I can. Then you'd better come up to Fullaloves' and help me.'

He opened the note and frowned at it. It was typewritten and ended in a couple of typewritten initials. Now had Jonathan not known that Tiny Fullalove did not possess a typewriter, and had he not received the scurrilous anonymous note about Deborah, and had Tiny Fullalove not been mentioned in it, he might have acted very differently from the way in which he did act. He turned left up the hill at first to go to the Fullaloves' bungalow, but, on a second thought, he climbed the fence which bordered Groaning Spinney and made his way back among the trees to his own house. He thought that he could at least test the information he had received. He did not propose to be hoaxed into taking the long, uphill walk through the deep snow to the bungalow if this should not be necessary. In other words he decided to telephone Tiny before he took any further steps.

There was not as much snow on the ground within the wood

as he had expected, but there were sudden swift falls from the overloaded branches. Jonathan hurried as much as he could. As he passed the bank where the badgers were known to have their holes, he noticed that the wooden platform, built by Obury and Bill Fullalove in the summer as a station from which to photograph the animals by flashlight, was now so deep in snow that he wondered whether it would collapse before the thaw came. It was built in the fork of a tree, about eight feet up, and the ground beneath was pitted with tiny holes, as though the thaw had already set in. He paid little attention, however, for he was soon struggling up to the thighs in the drift at the foot of the bank.

'You've been quick,' said Deborah, when Jonathan walked in. 'Anstey said you were going to see Tiny.'

Jonathan went to the telephone. To his annoyance, he could not get through to the Fullaloves' bungalow.

'Damn!' he said, giving it up. 'I'll have to go up there, after all. I still think the whole thing's a hoax, and I suspect our anonymous friend. Still, it won't do to chance things if the fellow *has* broken his leg.'

'Well, have something to eat first,' said Deborah. 'It won't be dark for another hour and a half. You can stay the night at the bungalow. Please don't try to come back.'

'We'll see,' said Jonathan. 'I'd better not stop now, though. See you later, I hope.' He picked up his stick and set off.

It was a brute of a walk. The snow had blotted out most of the landmarks. He climbed up through the wood without much difficulty, but, once he had to cross the open fields, there was nothing to go by but the general contour of the land. As he ploughed onwards, the countryside, lacking the colours and true shapes of the trees and hedges, made him feel like a man trying to pick an unknown track across a desert.

He climbed over the snow-laden ghost-gate, and when at last he reached the bungalow he produced the key and went in. The first thing he noticed was that the telephone was off its hook.

There was no sign of anyone in the place. Jonathan had been highly suspicious about the typed and initialled letter which had purported to come from Fullalove, and now he felt perfectly certain that it was a hoax. It was manifestly absurd to suppose that a man with a damaged (possibly a broken) leg, should have been able to sit down at a typewriter and then go out again. He was certain by this time that the anonymous letter-writer had heard that the Fullaloves were going to be away from home, and, for some reason unknown, had brought him out on a fool's errand. This looked as though the village pest, whoever it was, had decided to make a dead set at him. He wondered who, in the village, possessed a typewriter, and who, in the village, hated him. There was, too, the question of the doorkey. That had come from Anstey, it was true, but it had been enclosed in the envelope with the note. He wondered whether the writer had obtained possession of it by theft or by accident, or whether Tiny Fullalove had really sent it. It was all very puzzling and unsatisfactory.

Meanwhile, where was Tiny? And, equally, where was Bill? And, equally, where were the dogs and cats? Why could not Tiny's messenger – supposing that the note was genuine – have telephoned the manor house instead of pushing the note under Anstey's door? Nothing, so far, made any sense at all. Not knowing what else to do, Jonathan hung about for another half-hour. Then he locked up the bungalow and set out for home.

Hardly had he started, however, when he changed his mind. He would go first to Anstey's cottage and find out what he could about the typewritten note.

CHAPTER 4

The Ghost Faces East

'Get up! get up! thou leaden man!'
Thomas Campion

Thin, anxious-looking Mrs Anstey opened the door. Her information was very meagre. The note had been put under the door, and with it was a covering letter, also in typescript – she produced it – ordering Anstey to go to Jonathan's house, and on no account to go to the bungalow.

'That's all I know, sir,' she said. Jonathan believed her. It was obviously all that she knew. He looked at the whirling snow, which was falling fast again, and accepted the woman's offer of a cup of boiling hot cocoa. While he was drinking it Anstey got back from the village. He could add nothing to his wife's information.

'All of a queer do; that's what it is, sir.'

Jonathan agreed. He put down his empty cup, pulled his cap down over his brows, and set out for home. From Anstey's cottage, as from the Fullaloves' bungalow, it was far shorter to go downhill through Groaning Spinney than to walk back to the village and take the lane from the stable courtyard. He spent little time weighing up the chances. He knew that the short route was the hard route, but the evening was already drawing in and he had faith enough in his own powers to decide upon chancing the snowdrifts.

He struck off across a flattish field and kept close to the snow-covered hedge. Soon he reached the rough and pitted ground which separated the arable from the meadow and the wood. Here the going was extremely difficult, and he floundered his way down banks, and once went into a deepish hole and had to scramble out again.

Suddenly he caught his breath. His heart hammered, and a pulse jumped just behind his eyes. He had never credited the story of the parson's ghost, but he had been in some strange parts of the world and had seen some strange things, particularly in the West Indies and in connection with African witch-doctors. What he saw before him now, in the magic dusk of the snowdrifts, was the ghost in person, slumped over the five-barred gate in the position which village tradition assigned to it.

The story of the Abominable Snowman was immediately in Jonathan's mind. There was plenty of evidence for the existence of some monstrosity on the higher slopes of the Himalayas, and it flashed across his thoughts that here, perhaps, was something brought out of nothingness by the snow itself; a thing of fearful import; a creature, and yet not such because it was an emanation and nothing created.

Then he pulled himself together and floundered forward to discover what it was. He knew before he reached it. It was no ghost or demon, but a man dusted over into ghostliness by this last fall of the snow; and he had not been there on Jonathan's outward journey.

Jonathan climbed the gate to get round to the front of the man. It was Bill Fullalove, and there was no doubt whatever that he was dead. Moreover, he was already so stiff that Jonathan could not do more than ascertain beyond doubt that there was no way to help him. He had to leave him there whilst he himself, regardless of traps such as half-buried branches, and holes in the ground now filled with the drifted snow, plunged into the wood, and, instead of taking the short track homewards, went to call on Will North and send him down for the village policeman whilst he himself went for the doctor.

Will was reading *Paradise Lost*. He showed no sign of surprise at Jonathan's news. He consented at once to go to the policeman's cottage, and went with Jonathan directly downhill to the village. The snowdrifts seemed not to trouble him, and, however difficult the road, he seemed to find instinctively the most passable track. It did not take him more than half an hour to get them both to the house where the village policeman lived. They found him finishing his tea.

'Mr Bill Fullalove? Dead? Hanging over that there gate at the top of Groaning Spinney?' The policeman took it all in and appeared to remain impassive. 'That'll mean an inquest, that will. I'd better get along up there. Do Doctor Fielding know?'

'Mr Bradley will go for him,' Will replied. 'He'll be up there as soon as we are, to help take that poor fellow home.'

'Be you coming along of me, then?'

'Of course I'm coming along. And pretty bad going that is, all along up there, and the snow coming down the way it is.'

'Well, I'm glad ee be coming, then,' said the policeman, putting the last piece of bread into his mouth, and taking his helmet off its nail. He swallowed his half-cup of tea, put the helmet on, pulled on his uniform overcoat and his thick gloves, and put his head into the scullery.

'Shan't be long, lass.'

'Mind how ee go, then. 'Tis snowin' again.'

'Ah, I'll mind. I got Will North along of me. Mr Bill Fullalove have died of the cold up to Groaning Spinney.'

'Dear love! A strong gentleman like him! Whoever would have thought it! Got thy thick scarf I knitted for ee?'

'No.'

'You just take and put it on, then.'

The policeman unfastened his overcoat and picked up the scarf. Will North pulled his cap further over his eyes, re-buttoned his coat, picked up his stick, and the two of them set out through the wettish, now lightly falling snow and made for the top of the spinney.

Meanwhile Jonathan had gone for the doctor, and, on second thoughts, he decided to borrow the doctor's telephone and call up the Cheltenham police. Then he tramped doggedly uphill again to where he had left the body. His elderly aunt, wearing a ski-ing suit she had borrowed from Deborah, enormous gauntlet gloves of her own, and Jonathan's motor-cycling helmet, met him in Groaning Spinney, shone her torch to make sure it was he, and insisted on going with him.

'Why?' he enquired, as they turned further into the wood to gain a little shelter among the trees. 'I mean, how did you know anything about it?'

'Well,' said Mrs Bradley, taking out a second torch and switching it on, (for the evening was rapidly darkening and she was averse to taking a toss over roots of trees), 'I was watching what I believe to have been a hare. I was standing at my bedroom window, and I saw you silhouetted against the light from Will North's back door, and then you went off with him. As I knew you had been called previously to the Fullaloves' bungalow I thought that you had gone to the doctor, and it occurred to me that in a surgical case I might be of some assistance.'

'I see,' said Jonathan, and, as they struggled upwards through the spinney, he told her all that he had done.

'Ah, yes,' said Mrs Bradley. 'I wonder why you felt bound to telephone the Cheltenham police as well as going for your own police-constable and to the doctor? Is there something more in all this than you've told me?'

'Yes, there are one or two things a bit out of joint in the affair. To begin with, not only was there no sign of Tiny up at the bungalow, although he's supposed to have hurt his leg, but also I can't think who took that typewritten message to Anstey's cottage, or even, in fact, who typed it! Then, (although I don't know for certain, of course), I should hardly have thought that a fellow like Bill, who's been in the Navy and done convoy duty in all weathers, and that sort of thing, would just have collapsed and died like that from the cold. But, of course, you never can tell. The toughest-seeming people can snuff out as easily as any of us, I suppose.'

'But there's something else, isn't there?' said Mrs Bradley, prompting him.

'Only a small point, perhaps. I expect it was Anstey's mistake. He told me that Bill had gone to Gloucester.'

'Extraordinary, in this weather, surely?'

'Yes, although – oh, Lord! I do wish you hadn't come,' said Jonathan, floundering up to his knees. 'It's pretty rough going up this hill.'

'Nonsense!' said Mrs Bradley. 'Let me give you a helping hand!'

Soon they came to the bank where the badgers' earths were, and Mrs Bradley, flashing her torches, disclosed some long foot-marks only lightly powdered with snow.

'Bill's, I suppose,' said Jonathan. 'He must have come out, been overcome by the cold, and managed to stagger as far as the gate before he collapsed. Let's follow them. Here are mine, look, going along to the right. I kept under cover all I could.'

The footmarks were soon lost, however, for the trees thinned out towards the edge of the wood, and the snow there had already covered up any footprints.

Will North and the policeman, whose name was Tom May-hew, converged on the haunted gate as Jonathan and Mrs Bradley came out at the top of the spinney. Jonathan called after them, and the four struggled upwards towards the sagging, white, sack-like object which was still hanging over the gate.

There was a hail from lower down the slope, and the doctor soon joined them. There was not, as Jonathan already knew, the very slightest doubt that Bill Fullalove was dead, and, the doctor and Mrs Bradley having made what inspection was possible, with great difficulty the men managed to get the body to the bungalow.

They had just contrived to get their burden indoors and on to a settee when there came an eerie sound of groaning from the next room. Jonathan guessed what it was.

'Tiny!' he said. The doctor, who was again bending over the dead man, straightened his back. The groans came again, a little louder, and the doctor, after one more glance at the corpse, went into the adjoining room. Jonathan followed him. Tiny was lying on the floor. The door from the garden was open and there were still the marks of a dragging body to be seen in the snow.

'Well!' said Jonathan, leaving it to the doctor to break the bad news about Bill. 'What the deuce have *you* been up to, Tiny? And where are your dogs and cats?'

'Curse you, Bradley!' said Tiny, his little green eyes venomous, and, to Mrs Bradley's trained gaze, very watchful in spite of the fact that he was obviously in very great pain. 'Don't stand there like an ape! Give me a hand, can't you? – Fielding, leave me alone! I know what's wrong! It's my knee.'

Jonathan shrugged his wide shoulders.

'What I can't make out,' he said, 'is how you got that door open.'

'I had to drag myself up on my sound leg,' said Tiny, 'and use the doorkey, of course.'

'Who told Anstey to come for me?'

'How should I know? – Did someone?'

'Yes. Anstey got a typed message.'

'A *typed* message? I don't understand. – Ouch! What's the damage, doctor?'

'Kneecap,' said the doctor laconically. 'Have to get you into hospital. And, look here, Fullalove—'

'Well? Don't tell me I'll never walk again, or rot of that kind!'

'No, no. Only – well, look here, old man, it's Bill . . . Yes, dead. I'm sorry, Tiny. He must have had a bad heart. The cold, you know.

Too much. It packed him up, I'm afraid . . . Here, Bradley, let's give him a hand. If we heave him up on to his sound leg, he can hop as far as his bedroom. Take it easy, Tiny. Take it easy, old man.'

'Bill?' said Tiny. 'But he couldn't! Old Bill's as strong as a horse! He – ouch! Sorry! *Damn* this knee! He – Bill – couldn't – Oh, Lord, how it hurts! Oh, hell!'

CHAPTER 5

Parson's Farewell

'Wyd was his parish, and houses far asonder,
But yet he lafté not for reyne or thonder,
In sicknesse and in mes-chief to visite
The ferthest in his parisshe, smal and great.'

Geoffrey Chaucer

Jonathan, who, by inclination, was but an intermittent church-goer, had become very friendly with the vicar. The vicar was a bachelor and enjoyed a visit to the manor house for chess, sherry and a companionable pipe of tobacco, and Jonathan, elevated by his purchase of the manor house to the position of local squire, had been gently bullied by Deborah into setting an example to the parish by regularly attending Sunday Matins unless there was any good reason why he should not.

There was nothing surprising, therefore, in the fact that the vicar should pay a call on the morning following the inquest on Bill Fulla-love. He had come to the manor on his usual visit to have a comfortable chat. At least, so Jonathan supposed, but after some preliminary gossip the vicar came to the object of his call.

'It's like this, Bradley,' he said. 'I've received an anonymous letter.'

'Good Lord! Not *you*?' said Jonathan. 'What on earth have you been up to, padre?'

The vicar shook his head.

'It's really nothing to do with me,' he said. 'It accuses one of my parishioners. As you will see when I show it you, it does not give the woman's name, but you will see of what it accuses her, and you will see that it names the child – only the child is a grown man now – young Emming, our choirmaster.'

'How do you know it's one of your parishioners, then, padre?' Jonathan enquired, as he took the letter which the vicar handed him, and added, 'I had one, too, by the way. I think we ought to hunt out this anonymous scribe and hand her over to the police.'

'You say "her", as though you knew who it was.'

'Not as though I knew who it was, no. But I thought that the majority of anonymous letter-writers were women.'

'So they may be,' the vicar agreed. 'You think, then, that this letter consists of lies?'

'No,' said Jonathan thoughtfully. 'There's probably something in it. I say "something". I doubt whether that letter contains a grain of real truth, any more than mine did, but whoever wrote it probably has *something* to go on.'

'I don't understand you.'

'Well,' said Jonathan patiently (for he was particularly anxious to discover the identity of the anonymous letter-writer), 'it's like this.' He took his own letter out of a drawer and handed it to the vicar. 'I had that the other day. It's ridiculously untrue in the suggestion it makes, but the *fact* behind it is that Tiny Fullalove did make a pass at my wife, and she didn't tell me. I know why she didn't. I'm a short-tempered bloke and I should probably have gone straight to Fullalove and twisted his head off. It wouldn't have been necessary, of course, because Deb can look after herself, as she very rightly pointed out. But where she is concerned I have certain definite reactions which I shouldn't trouble to control. Well, that's that. It seems to me that this report' – he flicked at the vicar's letter – 'can't be *fact*, but there may be something about Emming's birth which he wouldn't care to have broadcast. Scurrilous comments are not facts, but once they become public property, which is what this anonymous pest is anxious for, they can be very damaging, and, of course, if you know what I mean, Emming is rather the village mystery man, isn't he? Anyway, there's nothing like a grain of truth for causing the water in the pot to boil over, so I expect the writer really has something to go on.'

'I see,' said the vicar, thoughtfully. 'But please do read it. I should like to have your advice.'

Jonathan read the letter.

'I'll tell you what,' he said. 'I wish you would let me show this to my aunt, who is staying with us. She's a psychiatrist, and she would advise us, I'm sure. By the way, what did you think of the inquest? Were you there?'

'Yes,' said the vicar. There was a pause. 'Yes, I was there.'

'Death by misadventure,' said Jonathan, beginning to fill a pipe. 'Could mean anything, when you come to think of it.'

'I don't like it,' said the vicar, taking out his own pipe and accepting the pouch which Jonathan pushed towards him. 'Mrs Blott keeps only one brand of tobacco, fortunately. No, I don't like it, Bradley. I don't mean the tobacco. I don't like what's happening here. There's something going on.'

'How do you mean?' asked Jonathan.

'The inquest, these letters, that injury to Tiny Fullalove. I don't know . . . In my work, Bradley, one gradually grows to believe in good and evil. *Really* to believe in them, I mean. The devil is about these parts.' He lit his pipe and the two men smoked in silence for some minutes. Jonathan waited. 'I wish you *would* let your aunt see this letter,' the vicar continued at last. Jonathan went to find Mrs Bradley and brought her back with him.

'This is leading to trouble,' she said, as soon as she had seen the vicar's letter. 'The next thing we'll be told is that Mr Bill Fullalove was murdered. What's more, the letter-writer will accuse the cousin, Tiny Fullalove, of being the murderer.'

'There you are, Bradley! That's what I meant,' said the vicar. 'Your aunt has the courage to put into words what I felt I could not say. If you and she, between you, would think the matter over—? Meanwhile, I shall pursue my own enquiries. Oh, dear! Oh, dear! And even a sensible fellow – a good fellow – like Will North, making the most fantastic observations. Of course I took it upon myself to question his statement, but what worries me very much is that he should have made it.'

'Will North?' said Jonathan. 'Like man, like dog, perhaps?'

In reply to the vicar's enquiring look, he told the story of the terrier Worry and the ghost gate.

'What did Will say?' asked Mrs Bradley, who had formed a good opinion of the gamekeeper.

'He said that he went up through Groaning Spinney with Tom Mayhew on the afternoon of poor Bill Fullalove's death, and that when they climbed a bank in which, apparently, there is a family of badgers, he noticed that on a wooden platform intended for a naturalist friend of the Fullalove cousins there was a greater depth of snow than there ought to have been. When Bill Fullalove's body had been carried up to the bungalow, Will returned by the same route, and noticed that the pile of snow on the platform was appreciably greater, although there had been no more than another light snowfall.'

'Odd,' said Jonathan. 'As a matter of fact, padre, I noticed the platform myself. There certainly was a deal of snow on it when I went up through the spinney. In fact, I remember thinking that the platform might collapse with the weight of it.'

'Indeed? But who would have gone up there in such weather merely to pile up snow?'

'What did Will think?'

'He didn't say. When I asked him why he had reported the business, he said he did not know. It had just struck him as being unusual.'

'But he made no investigation?'

'I did not ask him.'

'You know,' said Jonathan to his aunt, when the vicar had gone, 'the first person to be suspected of writing anonymous letters ought to be our undoubtedly innocent and frighteningly honest incumbent.'

Mrs Bradley cackled.

'Nothing could be more unlikely,' she said, 'than that anybody would believe such a tale. The vicar knows – or *should* know – all the scandal of the parish. He would not need to invent any!'

'But this idea of yours that the anonymous letter-writer will suggest that Tiny Fullalove murdered Bill is fascinating,' said Jonathan. 'It's just the sort of thing to be meat and drink to one of these cowardly sadists, a man dying suddenly, for no apparent reason, like that. Still, it can be so easily disproved that it wouldn't make more than a nine-days' wonder, I imagine. The village is fairly stolid.'

'I suppose it *ought* to be disproved?' said Mrs Bradley. 'Oh, I've nothing to go on,' she added, laughing at her nephew's startled expression, 'but I should like to talk to Mr Emming, all the same. It would be very instructive to know how much truth there is in this second letter, and whether he has any idea of which woman is meant.'

'You don't really think there was anything fishy about Bill's death, do you?' demanded Jonathan, continuing the line of thought which interested him most.

'On the face of it, yes, I do, and there are points which require explanation, apart from the typewritten note, which, except for the death itself, is the most mysterious feature of the affair.'

'Tiny explained quite a bit in the statement that was read at the inquest. He says he slipped while he was walking and crashed on to his knee on a boulder hidden by snow. He managed to drag himself back to the bungalow, but knows nothing of the note that was sent to Anstey. He is positive that he wrote nothing; he is equally positive that he does not possess a typewriter; and he can't explain how anybody knew he was injured.'

'One feels reasonably certain that he must know more than he says.'

'But what on earth would induce a man to go to all the trouble of typing the two notes if he was as badly injured as we know that he is? That knee of his is no joke.'

'I absolutely agree. Yet self-inflicted injuries have been known before this. I wonder what made Will North mention the pile of snow on that platform? And I wonder whether the choirmaster, Emming, has received an anonymous letter? He certainly seems to be affected. He is named as an illegitimate child. That ought to give us a clue to the letter-writer, you know. After all, Emming came from London. There is only one person in the village who might know the secrets of his youth.'

'Oh, you mean Mrs Dalby Whittier! But they may not have come from the same part of London, surely! It's quite a big city!'

'True,' said Mrs Bradley thoughtfully. 'But if they did not know each other in London, why should the vicar have received the anonymous letter about one of his parishioners? You see, the letter did not concern itself so much with Emming's illegitimacy as with his mother's character and misfortunes.'

'I see what you mean,' said Jonathan. 'And I'll ask Will North about the snow.'

'I think I had better do that.'

'All right, then. And you want to talk to young Emming?'

'Above all things, and the sooner the better.'

Will was preparing his dinner. He had opened a tin of stewed steak and a tin of baked beans, and had tossed the lot into the broth made from the carcase of a fowl. He had peeled a small cauldron-full of potatoes, and this was supported on iron rods on half the kitchen fire whilst the stew was to occupy the other half when the potatoes were three-quarters done.

Will welcomed the visitor and got out another large plate. Mrs Bradley accepted an old and comfortable armchair beside the fire, and gazed round the neat but very full room with interest. Nets, snares, the plumage of a jay for making fishermen's flies, a large kitchen table, a heavy curtain on rings to keep draughts out when the wind was in the east, a sink and draining board, several more chairs and a small table, a broad, high settee-bed used as a dump for guns, the gamekeeper's bag, and some books and papers, formed some of the furniture of a fair-sized stone-flagged room.

A window looked out over green and steeply undulating meadows to the rise of a hill, and between the window and the fireplace wall was the armchair occupied by Mrs Bradley. Beyond the armchair a heap of firewood, (logs and kindling), had been neatly stacked underneath two shelves which held cooking utensils.

In the opposite wall was the opening into Will's larder, and next to that was his gun-cupboard in which five more guns reposed. A step led down to his sitting-room, used by him in the winter as a bedroom and furnished with family furniture, a bedstead and some photographs.

'What can you do for me, Will?' asked Mrs Bradley, when she had taken her fill of the ship-shape arrangements of the living room. 'You can tell me, if you please, about the heap of snow on the badger-watching platform in Groaning Spinney.'

The tall gamekeeper studied her and took his time about replying. When he did speak, he said slowly:

'There was more snow on that platform than there ought to have been, ma'am. That's all I know about it.'

'Did you try to find out why it was there?'

'No. But of course I know now.'

'Oh?'

'Yes. I know now. That snow was covering up something that wasn't intended to be seen.'

'What something, Will?'

'Well, maybe I shouldn't say, ma'am. Least said the better, that's my meaning.'

'And you didn't make any investigation at all?'

'No, I didn't. I knew some of the boys from Mr Emming's choir had been up there, and I thought at first it was some of their games. If I'd guessed then what it was, I'd have had it all down at once, but there it is.'

'Did you see any footprints in the spinney?'

'I saw the same long marks as Mr Bradley told on – nothing more.'

'Did *you* think they were footprints?'

'Ah, that I did, ma'am, but they appeared to be double ones, if you understand my meaning.'

'Two people treading in the same tracks, Will?'

'Yes, that's it.'

'Well, you should know. You've had a good many years' practice in studying tracks of one kind and another. You want to stir those baked beans, or you'll have them stick.'

'Our vicar was here awhile, ma'am. Very worried he is, about these letters that keep coming. He think he knows who writes them.'

'You're a Norfolk man, Will!'

'Yes. Born and bred there as a boy; but haven't lived there for years. Thought I'd lost the talk, but I suppose one never lose that.'

'I hope not. What did the vicar have to say?'

'That say he can't understand Mr Tiny clouting the choirboys. That never happen before. Mr Tiny got a bad name from Ed Brown but nobody ever know him to hurt dogs, cats or children.'

'That might be important, Will. Did he say anything else?'

'Nothing much. Our vicar think Mr Tiny have something on his mind. He think Mr Tiny knows who writes the letters and don't care to give her away.'

'Her?'

'That's what our vicar think, ma'am.'

'Thank you, Will. The letters have been a nuisance. It will be a good thing when the writer has been discovered. It's of no use to ask you, I suppose . . . ?'

'I might guess wrong, and then that wouldn't do.'

'Do guess, Will. The person *must* be found. There's a great deal of mischief going on.'

'I know that. Well, from what I've heard, round and about, I'd be inclined to lay my finger on Mrs Dalby Whittier. If not she, then I'd say that the choirmaster, Mr Emming, know more than he say.'

'That coincides with my own ideas, but I suppose there isn't any proof of it?'

'No proof at all, so far as I'm aware, ma'am, but that young chap have no means of livelihood and yet pay his rent and eat and dress pretty fairly. But this is all village gossip, you know, and perhaps I shouldn't have taken notice of it. Leave gossiping to the old maws, I say. But sometimes, over a glass of beer, you know, ma'am—'

'I understand perfectly. Yes, Mr Emming somehow doesn't quite fit in with village life, but blackmail is an ugly word, Will, and I don't think we'd better use it.'

'Folks will talk, especially in a small place like this, but I wasn't thinking of going so far as that.'

'I'm sure you weren't, and I ought not to have done. Our task is difficult, though. Suspicion by the cartload, and not a spoonful of proof. And, talking of cartloads, what sort of fellow is Ed Brown?'

'Oh, pretty fair,' said Will; and did not enlarge upon this. He served his stew in great dollops on to the two large plates, and he and his black-eyed visitor ate in companionable silence.

CHAPTER 6

Saturday's Child

'Shepherds in humble fearfulness
Walk safely, though their light be less.'
Sidney Godolphin

Mrs Bradley did not need to wait long before she had her talk with young Robert Emming, for he came to the manor house on the Tuesday following New Year's Day to see Jonathan. He was a quietly angry young man, and when Jonathan had heard his story he suggested that Mrs Bradley should be invited to hear it, too.

The thaw had set in suddenly one afternoon at the end of Christmas week, and the snow had all disappeared by New Year's Night. Everywhere was either incredibly green or incredibly muddy, and the little mill stream was twice its usual size.

Emming had found the going slushy, to say the least, and was embarrassed at having to present himself to an elderly, leering, black-eyed lady at a time when he was bemired over the ankles, but he soon forgot the condition of his boots and trouser turn-ups in telling her his tale, for her attitude was friendly and sympathetic, and her questions were pertinent. The anonymous letter-writer, it appeared, had been at it again, and Emming had received two vituperative notes. The first had been delivered at his lodgings. He lived in two rooms at the carpenter's house and was looked after by the carpenter's wife, and the letter, which had come by post from Cheltenham, had been delivered by Sidney Blott on Christmas Eve. The second letter had been addressed to the village school, (apparently in error), and Sidney Blott had been far too intelligent to deliver it there; so he had handed it in to the carpenter's wife with the remark that he supposed Mr Emming would like to have it before Old Mother Acres (the school cleaner) went and trod on it or lit the fire with it or something.

The carpenter's wife had propped it up against the tea-caddy on the kitchen mantelpiece, but Vera, her eldest, had got the tea that day, and had left the envelope lying flat on the high shelf when she reached the caddy down, with the result that when she returned the caddy to the mantelpiece she stood it on the letter without noticing, and her mother had forgotten all about the letter until the next day, when she was dusting and it fell into the hearth.

Emming, having read it, and then compared it with the first one, had decided to come to Jonathan, (who was a Justice of the Peace in addition to being now the local squire), with both epistles. They were, as the vicar's had been, in typescript, and the first one, in content, was worded in much the same terms as was the one received by the vicar. It commented on Emming's birth, contained some coarse remarks, and then added something which had not been in the vicar's letter.

'And we know what you done about it, too, so don't think we don't. You can't keep *everything* dark for thirty years, you—' Followed a rude description.

'And the second letter?' said Mrs Bradley, when she had been told the tale up to this point and had read the first letter. 'To what extent does it embroider the theme?'

'To a very considerable extent. It states that Bill Fullalove was murdered, and accuses me of murdering him to shut his mouth,' said Emming. 'Absurd, as well as nasty, because if this—' he hesitated – 'this person knows something about me it wouldn't be much good my murdering Fullalove. The whole thing's ridiculous, but it stinks, and I want to know what I ought to do about it. Of course, even if Fullalove *did* know anything about me, I really

can't see that he would be particularly interested. After all—'
he gave a short laugh – 'I'm not the only bastard in the country!'

'So the actual fact is true?' said Mrs Bradley. She had been
wondering how to put this question (although she had guessed
the truth from a remark made previously by her nephew) but now
the way was clear. The young man's expression became good-
humoured. It was obvious that he was relieved.

'Well, yes,' he answered frankly. 'It is perfectly true in a way.
But I was registered in my present surname owing to the kindness
and decency of my father's brother. He married my mother at
once, saying that it was no fault of hers that my father had been
killed before he could fulfil his obligations, and then he himself,
poor, decent chap, went into the trenches and was killed within a
month. That's my family history, and I don't see why I should be
ashamed of it. But the thing is – well, you know what it's like in a
village. I was conceived out of wedlock, although I was born in it,
so to say. If people in a small place like this intend to make a
mountain out of a mole-hill they'll do it, and it's a bit awkward for
the person who's then got to climb the mountain.'

Jonathan nodded. Mrs Bradley cackled and poked her nephew
in the ribs. Emming showed neither embarrassment nor resentment at her reactions.

'Let's all have a drink,' said Jonathan, 'and, Emming, while I'm
getting it, you can tell my aunt what your alibi is for the time of
Fullalove's death. No, I'm perfectly serious! I'm beginning to get
a line on this anonymous letter-writer. He or she knows that
something was wrong about that death! There's some grain of
truth in every one of the letters, underneath all the nastiness. A
chap like Bill Fullalove doesn't snuff out like that, a mile and
a half from his home. Of course, I don't necessarily mean the poor
old chap was *murdered*, but, once mud begins to fly, you never
quite know who'll be plastered. Tell her about your choirboys'
pig-club, Emming, and what a stink *that* made in the village.'

'I sometimes think my nephew has an odd fashion in words,'

said Mrs Bradley, joining in Emming's laughter as Jonathan went out. 'Please tell me about the pig-club. Did you cheat the government out of their half of the pig-meat, or did you undercut the village butcher's prices?'

'We haven't a village butcher. Of course, if somebody kills a pig— but really, though,' said Emming, firmly refusing to be side-tracked, 'what am I to do about this business?'

'We must all set to work to find out who writes the letters,' said Mrs Bradley. 'You know the people in this village pretty well by now. Have you no suspicions on which we could set to work?'

'Never a one,' replied the young man promptly. 'Except for Tiny Fullalove, I haven't made an enemy in the place, so far as I know. Besides, I can't think of more than one person besides myself who could possibly have known . . .'

'Jon,' said Mrs Bradley, when the guest had gone, 'be careful what you say. My secretary sometimes talks about sticking one's neck out, and if I understand her metaphor—'

'You mean that supposing there *did* happen to be something queer about Bill's death, and it could be shown that Emming had a motive for causing it—'

'I am not so much concerned about Mr Emming,' said Mrs Bradley. 'It's you I'm thinking of.'

'Me? Oh, Lord, that business about Deb, you mean! But that was Tiny, not Bill.'

'I know. But you know what gossip can do. And if, as this anonymous correspondent suggests, that whole episode was Deborah's fault, how are you going to prove that it might not have been Bill as much as Tiny who tried his luck? – No, don't fume. It suits your saturnine cast of countenance, but it doesn't assist a reasoned argument.'

Jonathan laughed. Then his face lengthened again into its usual melancholy furrows.

'You're taking a very serious view of these letters, aren't you?' he said. Mrs Bradley nodded slowly and rhythmically.

'A *very* serious view,' she agreed. 'I begin to see the pattern behind them. We must certainly watch our words and not appear to know more than we do. There is a great deal more in this business than the desire to give pain and anxiety. Another thing: Mr Emming has just told us that the only enemy he has made (to his knowledge) is Tiny Fullalove. I suppose Tiny isn't our anonymous friend? We *did* wonder whether he sent the notes himself to you and Anstey. Couldn't he—'

'Oh, he isn't the type. These people are always thwarted spinsters and so forth. Fullalove is a hairy-heeled brute, but he's definitely not thwarted—'

'Except by Deborah,' Mrs Bradley pointed out.

'And he's definitely male,' concluded Jonathan, scowling again, however, at the reference to his wife. The rest of the conversation was interrupted by a call on the telephone.

'I can't talk over the 'phone, Bradley,' said Doctor Fielding's voice, 'but if I could come along when I've finished my round, I'd be glad.'

'Another anonymous letter?' said Jonathan, putting down the receiver. 'Will you bet on it?'

'No,' replied his aunt. 'I regard it as a certainty, and it is my practice only to bet on certainties when I myself have proposed the wager. At what time do you expect him?'

'Oh, at about half-past twelve. He's got nobody but Baird's man Evans, down with flu, and young Bob Datchett, with broken chilblains on his feet, and old Mrs Dear with her arthritis.'

'I wonder whether he'll expect to stay to lunch?' asked Deborah anxiously, when she was told of the visitor. 'There are exactly three chops.'

'Then he can't,' said Jonathan decisively. 'I'm not giving up my chop to anybody, and you're not to, and Aunt Adela is our guest and therefore can hardly be mulcted of hers, because that would bring shame on the household. He'll have to trot back to his bit of corned beef, or *gaucho* horse, or whatever it is. I can give him a drink, and that's all.'

'I don't suppose he'll accept one,' said Deborah, 'if he's got another round this afternoon.'

'He can't possibly have another round this afternoon. There's nobody to go round to, unless he goes and looks up Tiny Fullalove in that nursing home. Anyhow, you'd better put lunch off until two. He's got something important to say, and it may take some time.'

'All right. Was your parcel this morning what you wanted?'

'No, it wasn't. It was simply a lot of tripe about the geology of the Pitcairn Islands, and as I can't work if I can't get the materials I want, I'm going to smoke a pipe and read the new Nicholas Blake.'

'You can't. I've got it.'

'Then,' said Jonathan, 'you can jolly well hand it over.'

Doctor Fielding came at ten minutes past twelve, accepted gin and tonic, and came at once to the point.

'It's your aunt I want, not you. At least, I may want you later as a witness. I'm getting anonymous letters.'

'Been accused of poisoning the patients?'

'Much worse. I could disprove that easily. This would mean an exhumation job if the writer's serious and chooses to follow up the matter.'

'Oho! Don't tell me. I can guess. Bill Fullalove.'

'Who told you? Have *you* had one too?'

'Yes. So has young Emming, the choir bloke. So has the vicar. But they're not all about the same thing.'

'I say, we don't want a public pest in the village! That sort of round-robin stuff can have serious consequences. How many letters have you had?'

'One. Emming's had two, and the vicar's had one about Emming.'

'So have I, dash it! Two letters, I mean. The first one suggested that Bill Fullalove had been murdered, and the second one accused me of being aware of the fact and of conspiring to hush it up.'

'Good Lord! The idiot must be crazy!'

'That's just the trouble,' said Doctor Fielding. 'She probably is, but there's just the chance she might not be. That's why I want to talk to your aunt. She's better qualified than I am and she's seen plenty of corpses, murdered, suicided and just plain. I'd like her professional observations on Fullalove's death. She saw the body when I did.'

'I'll fetch her. Help yourself to another drink.'

'A short one, then, if I may. Don't be long. Lunch is at one, and I've promised faithfully to be back because Millie wants to go into Cheltenham this afternoon, and the shops shut at five or thereabouts.'

'He doesn't propose to stay to lunch, and he wants Aunt Adela,' announced Jonathan. His aunt accompanied him to the study and Doctor Fielding was brief and lucid.

'Not to beat about the bush, Mrs Bradley,' he said, 'I've been informed by an anonymous correspondent that Bill Fullalove was murdered.'

'Yes, that's my opinion, too,' said Mrs Bradley.

'Your opinion? Do you mean—?'

'It is impossible for me to make any clear or even rational state-ment in support of my opinion,' said Mrs Bradley, 'but I had some opportunity of observing Mr Bill Fullalove during Christmas, and there seemed no reason to suppose that he would collapse and die of cold during a walk in the snow. But, of course, I did not test his heart, and, in any case, it is not my business to challenge the verdict given at the inquest.'

'Quite so. Well, if he *was* murdered, I'm in the cart, and in it with me is the police surgeon. We both examined the body and there was no sign of foul play, and no possible symptoms of poisoning.'

'Did you look particularly? – I mean, had you poison in mind?'

'I did not think of *murder* by poison. Such an idea would never have entered my head. But one does think of suicide and accident, naturally, and had there been the very smallest grounds for suspicion, I'd have seen about an autopsy. But I can assure you solemnly that there was not the slightest suggestion of anything of the kind. You're an authority on forensic medicine, and you know all the signs of death by poisoning as well as I do.'

Mrs Bradley nodded.

'It couldn't have been poison,' she said, 'in the accepted sense of that term. Now, would you be prepared for an exhumation? – I mean, if there were anything else to go on besides these anonymous letters?'

'I don't know. It's rather sticking my neck out, isn't it?'

'The days of the martyrs are over, of course,' said Mrs Bradley, with an amused glance at her nephew.

'No, but look here,' said Doctor Fielding, 'if anything seems likely to blow up, I'm prepared to repeat, very loud and clear, what I thought at the time – that I was astonished that Fullalove died like that. Not that he'd ever been my patient, mind you.'

'Good,' said Mrs Bradley. 'I, too, saw the body, as you say, although I did not examine it closely owing to the difficulties out there in the snow and the degree of *rigor*. But let us risk a stern rebuff, and see what the police surgeon has to say.'

The police surgeon, as was only to be expected, was rather terse.

'Plenty of people die of cold and exposure in weather like that,' he said. 'And hadn't the man lived in India?'

'No. He was ex-RN,' said Jonathan (having put down the receiver) when Mrs Bradley appealed to him. 'It was Tiny who'd lived in India. I'll go and see Tiny in that nursing home. He should be able to tell us more about Bill's health than anyone else can except Bill's doctor, and we don't know yet whether Bill ever went to a doctor.'

'We might also try to find out where Mrs Dalby Whittier is staying,' suggested Deborah, who had come in. 'She might know something, too.'

'I suppose she'll come back when Tiny is out of the nursing home,' said Jonathan.

'I suppose so – but Bill Fullalove – it's incredible!'

'Well, if it *should* turn out to be murder, and if I had to bet, I think I would bet on Tiny,' said Jonathan thoughtfully. 'For one thing, I can't see who else would have known Bill well enough to have murdered him, or even to have *wanted* to murder him.'

'These are deep waters,' said Mrs Bradley solemnly. 'But I've been promised a chop for lunch. Give me, please, a glass of your excellent dry sherry, and let us forget these incalculable and meretricious problems, and concentrate upon food.' She thought of the long spill and the short spill, and said no more.

Doctor Fielding rang up Jonathan next day with the tidings that he had received a visit that morning during surgery hours from the police surgeon and an inspector from Cheltenham. There had been some discussion, but of an abortive type, the doctor thought.

'Still, they're obviously interested in our anonymous correspondent,' he added. The next visitor was for Deborah. Doctor Fielding had a very charming daughter of twenty. She was a level-headed and intelligent girl, and she came to give Deborah some news which Deborah was to pass on or not, at her discretion.

'Proposed to you?' said Deborah. 'When was that?'

'Last October. I turned him down. He seemed quite philosophical about it, that's one thing.'

'What did he say?'

'Oh, he just said, "Righto. I didn't think I had an earthly, and you're quite right – I'm much too old for you. Still, if you *should* change your mind, remember I'm still in the market. I suppose you wouldn't like to kiss and still be friends?" I said that I shouldn't. He tried to grab me, but I smacked up at him pretty hard and turned nasty, so he chucked it. He went pretty soon after that, and when he was going I laughed – because he looked rather pipped and deflated – and told him that if I ever changed my mind,

I'd let him know. I was sorry as soon as I'd said it, because he perked up quite a bit and looked hopeful again, so I added that I didn't suppose I *would* change my mind because, as far as I knew, I didn't particularly care whether I got married or not. He took that quite well, and went off more jauntily than I had expected. There must be something in me which appeals to the Fullalove family. Tiny proposed to me too – that was last August. It's very embarrassing for a poor girl who only wants a bit of peace and quiet to get on with her work.'

Deborah recounted this conversation to Mrs Bradley.

'Although I can't imagine,' she added, wrinkling her brow, 'that Bill Fullalove would have been the type to commit suicide because of a girl. Besides, if there was no injury and no symptoms of poisoning, how did he manage to do it? Would he just have lain down in the snow? He was leaning on that gate when he was found.'

'What is Miss Fielding's work?' Mrs Bradley enquired.

'She's going to be a research chemist. She's on holiday at present. Most of her time she is in London, at college, of course. I believe she's exceptionally brilliant. Doctor Fielding doesn't say much, but he's frightfully proud of her.'

'Ah,' said Mrs Bradley vaguely. Deborah glanced quickly at her, but the sharp black eyes and beaky little mouth betrayed nothing. Deborah knew better than to ask questions. She turned the conversation on to her bulbs, which seemed, she thought, in need of care and protection. Mrs Bradley accepted the change of subject gracefully, and no more was said about poisons, chemistry, and violent death until the telephone rang and a voice asked for Jonathan.

Jonathan, not too pleased at being disturbed, went to the telephone and listened. His brow creased perplexedly.

'What was it?' asked Deborah, when he put the receiver down.

'The nursing home rang up. It seems that Tiny Fullalove – whose knee is still very painful – it looks like being a long job – has had an anonymous letter telling him his cousin's body is to be exhumed. He's in the devil of a state, naturally, and the matron is so worried about him that she got my telephone number from him and rang to see whether I could throw any light on the matter. I couldn't, of course! Told her (not too truthfully) that I hadn't the ghost of a notion of such a thing, and added that it must be quite ridiculous.'

'What else did you tell her?'

'The verdict at the inquest – misadventure – heart-failure due to cold and exposure. Told her as well that there were no queries from the jury, and that the medical evidence was perfectly straightforward.'

'You reassured her, then?'

'Good heavens, yes! Told her that, as a matter of fact, there had been one or two of these anonymous letters going round, and that we were going to get the police on to it.'

'Yes, I see.'

'She sounded a sensible sort of woman,' Jonathan continued, 'so I hope she can calm Tiny's mind. Rotten thing really to be tied down like that with all this dynamite whizzing round the village . . . Do you *honestly* think Bill was murdered? If so, how?'

'My present theory is quite unsupported by facts. Did I hear you say that Sally was coming over?'

'Yes. She's bringing Rhu, and she's longing to see you again.' He accepted the change of subject with a grin. He knew that his aunt's brain was never more busy than when she went off on a conversational sidetrack.

CHAPTER 7

No Names, No Packdrill

'Why art thou for delay?
Thou cam'st not here to stay.'
Richard Baxter

The arrival of Sally, niece to Mrs Bradley's first husband and cousin by courtesy to Jonathan, (she was on the Lestrange family tree and had no blood relationship with the Bradleys), coincided with that of the police.

She came in a Hillman and the police in a Morris, and the two cars ground up Jonathan's wet and muddy drive with Sally in the lead and the police about thirty yards behind.

'Good Lord!' said Jonathan, who knew Sally very well and had once thought of asking her to marry him. 'Don't say you're going to be pinched on my very doorstep! Don't you know that I'm a Justice of the Peace?'

'I do know,' said Sally. 'I've been terrified. They began to follow me just as I turned out of Cirencester, and they've been tagging along ever since. I thought at first it must be accidental, but when they came into the village behind me and then turned up this drive . . .'

'I beg pardon, sir,' said a very smart sergeant of the Gloucester-shire constabulary, 'but might I have a word?'

'Certainly. Come in here. Deb, look after Sally. You do know one another slightly and you both know me a lot, so . . .'

'I'm sorry to intrude, sir, on top of visitors,' said the sergeant. 'Well, yes, I will, sir, if it's all the same. Many thanks.'

Jonathan poured out a couple of beers, asked the maid to find Mrs Bradley, and produced a pipe for himself and cigarettes for the Law.

'Stop me if I'm wrong,' he said, when Mrs Bradley had been found, and the sergeant had taken a long, refreshing draught and had lighted a cigarette, 'but I take it that you've come about those wretched anonymous letters that some of us have been receiving.'

'In a sort of a way, yes, sir. A Mr Baird, down in the village, has complained, and, previous to that, we heard from a Mrs Dalby Whittier, who was housekeeper to the two Mr Fullaloves.'

'Oh? What did Mrs Whittier have to say?'

'Something which got us rather . . . shall I say interested, sir? The fact is – you'll please to keep this to yourself, sir – she gave us a piece of news which made us look twice at Mr Bill Fullalove's death. Of course, the inquest went straightforward enough, and the doctors both gave the only evidence they *could* give, medically speaking, which, as you remember, was heart failure due to cold and exposure. Anyway, sir, when this letter from Mrs Dalby Whittier turned up, we naturally took steps to verify her information.'

'I thought you always proceeded,' said Jonathan.

'Beg pardon, sir?'

'Oh, nothing. Sorry. Have some more beer.'

'Well, thank you, I don't mind if I do. Well, sir – lovely drop of stuff, this. I always say you can't beat the West Country for beers – it turns out that Mrs Dalby Whittier's yarn is true. No longer ago than last September, Mr Bill Fullalove got himself medically examined for a life insurance policy. It seems he thought to get married at some time or other. Now comes the interesting part, sir. Mr Tiny, according to the doctor what has been attending him in that nursing home he's gone to, is no great shakes as a life. Not terrible bad, you know, but long years in India haven't done his constitution much good. Mr Bill, on the other hand, was a remarkably good life. The insurance company's doctor – we've been in personal touch with him – states he has never seen a healthier man or tested a heart in better condition than when he examined Mr William Fullalove, address as we all know it.'

'Oho!' said Jonathan, obviously and greatly interested.

'In view of which,' pursued the sergeant, 'although against the grain in a local matter, we are applying to the Chief Constable to see what he thinks about asking for an exhumation order. It's really our own surgeon's wish, sir, him not liking the idea that he made a wrong diagnosis. He says he's sure there was nothing over-looked at the post-mortem, and he's got his professional pride.'

'Well, that should settle matters, one way or another. By the way, now that Bill has gone, how does his will work out?'

'That's the curious part, sir. Got the lawyers tied up properly. There's no question of the insurance people not paying up. The verdict was clear, and they can't go again' it and don't intend to. The amount is five thousand pounds. Now, that's not a big insur-ance, as such things go, but it might tempt *some* people. Well, the funny thing is that we don't know who it might have tempted . . . that is, if the death *wasn't* quite all it appeared to be. The will is made out in favour of—' he took a notebook out and passed a formidable young thumb over its pages – 'my dear wife Amabel Lucinda.'

'No other clue to the lady's identity?'

'None at all, sir. And Mr Tiny swears he wasn't married. It all adds up a bit odd, sir.'

'So that, unless the lady comes forward and stakes her claim, Tiny, I suppose, gets the lot – the money Bill left and all the insur-ance, too.'

'That's the size of it, sir. Been very short with the lawyers, Mr Tiny has, and you can't hardly blame him, really. Challenged them to produce a marriage certificate and said that whoever Mr

Bill might have *intended* to make his wife, he was absolutely certain he'd never actually married.'

'Unless, for some reason, he kept the marriage secret. Still, no doubt that if she exists the lady will come forward, marriage lines and all, as soon as she hears of the death.'

'Yes, very likely, sir. Perhaps I should give the name of the beneficiary we've got in our mind, sir . . .'

'Yes?'

'Mrs Dalby Whittier, sir.'

'But, good Lord, she was just the housekeeper and not a young woman, at that!'

'Hot stuff, sir, I wouldn't be surprised,' said the sergeant. 'Little and good, you know. Good for what, says you? Perhaps good for nothing, says I! Thank you very much, sir. I really don't mind if I do. Yes, sir, there it is. He might have married her secretly, as you say. It don't take long, with a registrar and a special licence. Although why he should want it secret, an independent gentleman like him—!'

'So you rather want to see Mrs Dalby Whittier, I take it?'

'Well, there's the five thousand pounds, sir. It's a lot of money to anyone in Mrs Dalby Whittier's position. The only thing is—'

'Yes, what?' But Jonathan had an inkling of what was coming.

'We can't trace her, sir. After she left the bungalow she was supposed to go to her relations in London. She never turned up. Not that they seem to have troubled themselves about that. Just said they thought she'd changed her mind and have been waiting for a letter to that effect. Seems it was years since they'd seen her, and we gathered they wouldn't lose sleep if they never saw her again. Hinted as how she had been a little bit of a bad 'un. Blotted the family copy book, we were given to understand, and had been more or less kicked out when she eventually got married. What do you think about that, sir?'

'You'd better ask my aunt,' said Jonathan.

'So that, if she *did* marry Mr Bill Fullalove, it would have been her second marriage?' Mrs Bradley enquired.

'That's the size of it, ma'am.'

'Did she have any children by her first husband?'

'Yes, one child. A boy. The choirmaster here – Mr Emming. That doesn't surprise you, ma'am?'

'Not in the least. I had guessed it. I wonder whether *she* left a will?'

'If she's really disappeared we'll have to trace her, particular as there's going to be an enquiry into these here anonymous letters.'

'*And* if there is going to be another enquiry into Bill Fullalove's death,' said Jonathan. 'By the way, what was the post-mark on this letter she sent you?'

'London, W.1, sir. And her relations live in Lewisham.'

'Still, it means she did go to London.'

'Yes, sir.'

'Was her letter written by hand?' Mrs Bradley enquired.

'No. In a sort of careful print done in pencil, ma'am, and just signed D. D. Whittier.'

'So it may not have come from her, you mean?'

'Well, I must say we took it that it did, ma'am. No reason to doubt it, I should say.'

'So there it is,' said the Chief Constable. 'We can find Mrs Whittier, of course, but, short of exhuming the body, there's nothing more we can do, and in spite of what the inspector and his police surgeon say, I'm dead against it.'

'You can track down this anonymous letter-writer, anyway, can't you?' demanded Jonathan.

'It isn't easy, you know.'

'But, hang it all, the person, whoever it is, and my bet is that it's a woman, is somebody living in this village! What's more, it's somebody who has access to a typewriter. All the letters I've seen have been typewritten, except the one which came first to me.

Yes, and that reminds me! There was the very odd business of that typed note pushed under Anstey's door. We've never found out who did that.'

'There's nobody in the village with a typewriter. That brings us up all standing. Two of the blue-stocking ma'ams at the College have got one, but I can't get at even the smell of a typewriter here, and when we tested the College ones they proved to be out of the question. The doctor writes everything by hand, and so does the vicar. There isn't even one at the post-office. You haven't got one, have you?'

'Yes, of course I have, but the type is quite different from that used for the letters. You're welcome to test it for yourself. In fact, I wish you would. The point is, not that there *isn't* a typewriter, but that you haven't found it. Moreover, whoever types or writes the letters goes into Cheltenham to post them. All have a Cheltenham post-mark. Isn't that anything to go on?'

'Half the village goes into Cheltenham at least once a week. Some go oftener. You can't get anything from that. They go there for shopping and the pictures,' said the Chief Constable, shaking his head.

'In other words, you're hedging. You don't want to ask for an exhumation, but you're afraid you'll have to. That's about the size of it, isn't it? I can't see what you're waiting for! If the poor bloke was murdered you've got to investigate, and if he wasn't an exhumation will stop this scandalmonger's tongue. There's nothing to lose! For goodness' sake get on with your job and stop stalling!'

'It's no good your turning nasty, my boy,' said the Chief Constable, kindly. 'I know what's the matter with you. You've got your own reasons for wanting this poison pen tracked down and exposed, and I quite understand your point of view. But this person is just some lunatic trying for a bit of notoriety, that's all. My reaction is to leave the whole thing to die down. What this letter-writer wants is a bit of excitement. If we fail to provide it, he or she will give up trying. It's not as though the letters were of really virulent type. I mean, nobody's going to commit suicide because of these letters. No, what this condemned scribe wants is to have us do just exactly what I for one am not prepared to do – exhume Bill Fullalove's body and have newspaper headlines about it, and, in the end, make ourselves a laughing stock. That would be meat and drink to this sort of reptile.'

'You're prepared, then, to disregard the opinions of your own policemen?'

'Look here,' said the Chief Constable patiently, 'your own Dr Fielding and the local police surgeon gave perfectly clear evidence at the inquest. Plenty of people die of cold and exposure. If those two doctors are going to turn cranky enough to deny their own sworn statements, they're asking for trouble, that's all. As for the insurance bloke, he must have made a mistake. I suppose even doctors can be deceived. He may have *thought* that Bill was a good life, but the fact remains that the poor chap wasn't, that's all.'

'Doctors can be deceived, eh? There you are, you see! And your own police bloke is ready to admit that *he* might have been deceived, and yet you refuse to act! Well, whether Fullalove died naturally or not is no actual business of mine, but this poison pen is everybody's business, and I give you my word that if any more anonymous letters are written, I'll track down the writer myself, and I shall make no bones about what I say to the police if I do. As for the exhumation, I don't care whether you have that or not, because if there *was* anything wrong about the death it'll be your affair, not mine, as I say. But I *know* there was something wrong!'

'Hang it, man, what have we got to go on? I can't just back up an unsubstantiated opinion.'

'There's Mrs Dalby Whittier's disappearance.'

'We can tackle that, of course, but as for the other matter – this exhumation – well, if Mrs Bradley, whose opinion, needless to say, I respect, can give me a definite pointer . . .'

'Suppose another letter – Oh, well, never mind.'

'Suppose another letter named names and made another

definite accusation against somebody? I don't know, at the moment, what I should do about that. There would have to be some sort of evidence. The letters, so far, contain no real facts at all.'

'But they *do*, you know! All of them! Every one! Oh, well, let's forget it,' said Jonathan, 'but remember that you'll be responsible as soon as something blows up!'

But no one was permitted to forget it. The next complaint that an anonymous letter had been received came again from the nursing home where Tiny Fullalove was mending his damaged knee.

'It's quite absurd,' he pointed out, 'but some damn' feller has written accusing me of doing in poor old Bill. What do I do about it?'

'Nothing, apparently,' said Jonathan. 'That's the Chief Constable's view, at any rate. You grin and bear it, that's all.'

'But can't *you* do anything? Damn it, you're a Justice of the Peace.'

'Yes. *That* has its humorous aspect,' replied Jonathan, still angry with Fullalove over Deborah. 'You'd better ring up the police and leave it to them.'

The Chief Constable visited Jonathan again the next day.

'Here's our next definite accusation all right,' he said triumphantly, 'and it only bears out what I said. This individual is so anxious to get herself into the papers that she hasn't even taken the trouble to find out that, even supposing the death wasn't natural, Tiny Fullalove is the one person who couldn't have had anything to do with it.'

'His busted kneecap?'

'Exactly.'

'We've no clue to when he did it, have we?'

'Yes, near enough, I think. Anstey met you at about a quarter past four. Bill was not dead when you went up through Groaning Spinney. You found his body propped against the gate on your return journey.'

'So what?'

'So Tiny had got his injury before Bill died.'

'Tiny could have delivered the note himself, and then gone off and killed Bill. We don't know when that note was pushed under Anstey's door.'

'But how could he know he was going to be injured like that? The injury is his alibi.'

'Some blokes in the Army . . .'

'Yes, I know. But – do you think Tiny's that type? – And a smashed kneecap is so damnably painful that it's not the kind of injury to be deliberately self-inflicted.

'I don't know what I think about that, but it was all a bit odd about that note. There's something that doesn't make sense. And I suppose you haven't found Mrs Whittier yet?'

'Look here,' said the Chief Constable, 'I'll tell you what. You set to work quietly and track down this village pest and we'll force her into the open with her proofs. You don't want a lot of policemen nosey-parkering their way round the place. Our bird would soon smell a rat, and might go to earth.'

Mrs Bradley, who was privileged to overhear this startling metaphor, cackled with deep appreciation.

'Ah, yes,' said the Chief Constable. 'The very person! What has morbid psychology to say about this anonymous scandalmonger, Mrs B.?'

'Plenty,' Mrs Bradley replied. 'It is a pity that you can't issue a general search-warrant so that you could find that typewriter. There are several significant features which, put together, could only belong to one individual machine, and that machine, I may add, is *not* the one in this house.'

'Yes, but we've no power to issue such a warrant. Besides, I don't want those kind of practical suggestions from *you*. I want to know what's behind these letters. What makes people sit down and write 'em? . . . apart from the general human desire to see what happens when you start a bit of muck-raking, I mean, or touch off a bomb.'

'Often the letter-writer is airing a grievance against society. Sometimes he is externalizing a personal hatred or jealousy. Often he is a person with too much time on his hands. Sometimes . . .'

'But in this case?'

'In this case I have the definite impression that a crime lies behind all this. We may be looking for a murderer, and therefore the anonymous letter-writer . . .'

'You really believe that? . . . That Fullalove was murdered? Well, look here, then! If I get a shred of real evidence that any-thing fishy (apart from the letters, of course) is going on, I'll apply for an exhumation order.'

'Is that a promise?' demanded Jonathan.

'Yes, it is,' said the Chief Constable, after a moment's thought. Mrs Bradley cackled.

'You won't need to keep it, child,' she said.

'Why not?' asked the Chief Constable, studying her expression and changing his own to one of anxiety.

'Because there is no question of shreds of evidence. You'll find that your hand will be forced. You will *have* to get that body exhumed and examined.'

'And why?'

'Because I am quite sure that whether anybody knows any-thing definite about the manner of Mr Bill Fullalove's death, there is something criminal connected with Mrs Dalby Whittier's disappearance.'

'Well, Scotland Yard have taken that over. Her letter to us, as you know, was posted in London. The point is – is Tiny Fullalove involved?'

'I'm almost certain of it . . . Oh, I don't mean that Tiny murdered Bill. He may have done, of course. But I firmly believe that there is something very strange about that five thousand pounds' insurance money. Consider the facts. A man with an excellent constitution gets his life insured for what is, to one in his position, a considerable sum of money. The same man dies of cold and exposure. His will leaves his property to a so-far unidentifiable wife. His cousin, with whom he lives and who might be expected to have knowledge of his affairs, declares that there is no wife. If this can be proved, the money all comes to the said cousin, as next of kin.'

'I can't make any sense out of it, except that I can't see Tiny Fullalove as a murderer.'

'I know. It is very mysterious in itself, this whole business, and I feel that somewhere behind it there is another mystery. If we could solve this second mystery I believe the first would solve itself.'

'The first job is to trace the wife,' said Jonathan, 'but I imagine that that's being done. Trouble is that, being a sailor, Bill may have married abroad.'

'If you will allow me to offer one piece of advice,' said Mrs Bradley to the Chief Constable, 'it is that you have the body of Mr Bill Fullalove exhumed as soon as may be.'

'But – oh, hang it! Why? The thing is, I don't want to!'

'Because from the wood beyond the world the world should be visible.'

'You talk in riddles,' said the Chief Constable, uneasily.

'So does the Sphinx, yet it preserves its reputation for wisdom,' said Jonathan, grinning. 'Be a man! Ask for the exhumation order and let's get cracking. It's a shame to tease him,' he added, when the Chief Constable had gone. 'Do you really know anything? If so, I wish you'd tell me.'

'What I surmise isn't knowledge. I wonder how Tiny Fullalove's knee is getting on?' said Mrs Bradley. Her nephew, regarding this as a change of subject, nodded.

'I really must go and see him,' he said. 'Of course, a nice smack on the kneecap with a hammer . . . but why should I part with my theories any more than you do with yours?'

'I daresay we are both being quite unfair,' said Mrs Bradley. 'Yes, go and see him, by all means. You ought to have gone before, as you suggest. You've been most unneighbourly!'

'You're perfectly right,' said Jonathan. 'I *ought* to have gone before, but I do hate going into nursing homes and hospitals. Besides, I've conceived a dislike of the swine since Christmas.'

He went that same afternoon. Tiny was pleased to see him, but looked at him with shrunken little eyes. He said that his knee was going on as well as could be expected, but that he supposed it would be a long job. He asked about the inquest and the funeral, and then mentioned Mrs Dalby Whittier.

'I feel worried about her,' he said. 'She hasn't written. Anstey has a key to the bungalow and sends on letters. It seems queer that she should just pass up on us. On me, I mean. She was going to stay with relatives in London, but she didn't leave any address, so I don't know how to contact her. I owe her a month's pay, too. She wouldn't take December's money before she went. Said that for one thing it wasn't due, and for another that she'd only spend it in London. I hope she hasn't gone down with flu or pneumonia, or something. The weather must have been even worse than it seemed, to finish poor Bill like that.'

'I rather wanted to ask you about Bill,' said Jonathan, 'if you didn't mind. How long was he out that day? – and where had he been?'

'As I wrote in my report to the coroner, I'm most uncertain, actually. The poor old chap was mad on natural history, as you know, and he'd been out to the badgers' earth in Groaning Spinney. At least, that's where he intended to go, because he said so.'

'Anstey seemed to think he'd gone to Gloucester,' said Jonathan. 'How did he get hold of that idea?'

'It's a queer business,' said Tiny, passing a hand across his eyes. 'Damned queer. He was a far better life than I was, don't you know. I should never have thought . . .'

'No,' agreed Jonathan. 'I don't think anybody would. By the way – this woman to whom he left his money? Have you any idea? . . . Or am I being too curious? I mean, I'd no idea old Bill was married.'

'As I've told those damned lawyers,' said Tiny, 'I don't believe he was.'

They talked on other subjects for about half an hour, and then Jonathan, rising to go, cleared his throat and spoke his mind.

'By the way, Fullalove, I have perhaps strange views on the subject, but when you are up and about again I shall be very much obliged if you'll bear in mind that the very slightest attempt on your part to embarrass or annoy people will result in your being back in this nursing home immediately and probably permanently.'

'I apologize most humbly,' said Tiny at once. He kept his eyes on Jonathan's face. 'It was . . . well, dash it, you *must* know how these things happen. It certainly won't occur again. Just a moment's sheer idiocy . . . I'm really most terribly sorry. I wouldn't for the world have been offensive.'

'All right,' said Jonathan. 'So long as that's completely understood. And I shall also be obliged if you'll refrain from clouting kids you find on my land.'

'They were doing damage, you know, and I am your agent,' said Tiny, with considerably more assurance.

'Take their names, then, next time, and keep your hands to yourself.'

'Damn it, Bradley . . .'

'All right. But don't forget.' Jonathan, feeling relief at ridding himself of his temper, suddenly grinned. 'Look after that knee, now, and let's soon see you hopping around. Oh, and Mrs Dalby Whittier's being looked for. She seems to have done a disappearing trick. As far as is known, she never turned up in London – at least, the police don't think she went anywhere near her relatives.'

'Good Lord!' cried Fullalove. 'I hope nothing serious has

happened! She *would* take the short cut through the woods and over the estate! I *told* her to go round by the road!'

'Well, there it is!' said Jonathan. 'And, of course, it wasn't snowing then!'

Fullalove looked at him closely, but Jonathan gave nothing else away.

CHAPTER 8

Reappearance of a Housekeeper

'My tale was heard, and yet it was not told;
My fruit is fallen, and yet my leaves are green.'
Chidiock Tichborne

Chiefly because her niece Sally proposed to extend her visit into February, Mrs Bradley was persuaded to stay on at the manor house much longer than she had intended. There was already, even at the end of January, the faintest feeling of spring, and what with that, the fact of Sally's visit and the even more important fact that Deborah wanted her to stay as long as she felt she could spare the time from her work, Mrs Bradley became almost one of the family and was soon as well known in the village as Jonathan himself.

There were no more anonymous letters, and there was no more news about a possible exhumation. The whole subject of the death and of the poison pen might have been allowed to drop, in fact, but for Sally, who said one day, when she and her aunt were walking briskly back to the house after their morning constitutional:

'Talking of anonymous letters, did you know we had a maid once who wrote them?'

'No, I didn't know.'

'I thought not. Mother would hate the family to think that she'd engaged an unsatisfactory servant.'

'How did you discover what was happening?'

'Well, we didn't, for nearly four months. She used to write the letters on her afternoon out and post them in various pillar-boxes, so it wasn't at all easy to find her out. But one day she was a bit too clever. She wrote a letter to Mother and put in something which only a person living in our house could know.'

'What was that?'

'Where Mother kept the wine-cellar key. Even Higgs, our butler, didn't know. You see, Mother's got a "thing" about drink, and she said she would never put temptation in anybody's way. But this girl found out one day about the key because we were having some house repairs done and she came in just as Mother was taking out the key to hide it somewhere else from the workmen. She accused Mother in the letter of being a secret drinker, so, of course, we tumbled to her.'

'I see,' said Mrs Bradley, very thoughtfully. 'Too clever, but not quite clever enough to hide the fact. Go on. You've something else in your mind.'

'Well, it's only this – and, mind, I may be talking medical rubbish. But – well, when doctors fix the time of death, don't they go by the stiffness of the body?'

'Yes. What about it?'

'Take Mr Fullalove,' said Sally. 'He might have been dead longer than the doctors thought. If so, Mr Tiny would have had time to establish an alibi for the time of his cousin's death. He could have typed the notes to Anstey and Jonathan. He might have taken the risk of being seen pushing them under Anstey's door, for there was nobody to fear, I suppose, so long as Anstey or his wife or Jonathan didn't catch him at it, and he could then have damaged his knee.'

'You are referring to the fact that the weather was so cold,' said Mrs Bradley. 'But there is Jonathan's evidence to consider. The body was not hanging over the gate when he went up to the bungalow, but it *was* there when he returned. That fixed the time of the death almost more surely than the medical evidence, you know.'

'Oh, of course!' said Sally, crestfallen.

'I am more interested, really, in the anonymous letters,' Mrs Bradley continued. 'You see, the fact that they have suddenly ceased is rather curious.'

Sally looked at her sharply.

'You mean that the person who wrote them may be dead? And the police are still looking for that Mrs Dalby Whittier? Do you think *she* wrote the letters?'

'I don't know. In any case, how could she have typed them?'

'Yes, the typewriter *is* the snag. But Bill Fullalove made a will and nobody has turned up to claim the money. The lawyers have advertised. I should think they'd have to let Tiny have it in the end. And if he *did* kill Bill—'

'Killed Bill, watched for Jonathan to leave the bungalow, carted the body through deep snow and flung it over the gate before Jonathan got there, staged his own injury, crawled back, and waited to be found by the people who brought home his cousin's body . . . the snow having blurred, or, with luck, covered up all traces . . . yes, I know,' said Mrs Bradley. 'But there's no *proof* that Bill was killed, Sally. The death was by misadventure. He died of cold and exposure. No exhumation will prove otherwise.'

'I know. But just suppose! Nothing has gone wrong, so far, and once it is clear that there is never going to be any claimant for Bill's five thousand pounds, Tiny will be entitled to collect it, and there is the motive for murder. That's how it seems to me, anyway.'

'Your remark about your maid, the too-clever one, opens up a field for speculation,' said her aunt. 'You see, if Tiny has anything to hide, one would imagine that the last thing he would want is to have his cousin's body exhumed. Therefore, unless he also is trying to be too clever, he is not the author of the anonymous letters. Yet the letter sent to Anstey was typed on the same machine as all the anonymous letters which have been shown to the police. Now it seems more and more certain to me, as time goes on, that

Anstey's note *must* have been sent by Tiny, whether he did the actual typing or not. I wish we could see the letter which he himself is supposed to have received at the nursing home. According to the matron there, it really did come by post and it really did give him a bad shock.'

'There's no doubt that by getting Bill exhumed he thinks he can dispose once and for all of any doubts about Bill having died a natural death,' said Sally, 'but—'

'Why should he suppose that people would suspect anything else, though?' Mrs Bradley enquired. 'The verdict at the inquest was quite clear. I don't think for one moment that Tiny wants Bill's body exhumed.'

'Well, somebody evidently does. And, look here, Aunt Adela! This business that the anonymous letters have ceased! It means that Tiny *did* write them, only he now has no opportunity of getting them posted secretly. All his correspondence is sent out from the nursing home, and is posted by one of the staff, so he daren't send the anonymous ones out, or somebody might suspect! How's that for a reconstruction? And you're wrong about the cold and exposure! Tiny poisoned Bill and somebody found it out – Mrs Dalby Whittier, I expect.'

'Is there *really* a secret poison unknown to science? It is certainly true that there are poisons which are very difficult to detect after death. Unfortunately for the convenience of murderers, however, they leave very decided symptoms at the time the victim dies, even if the poison itself leaves no trace afterwards.'

'You're pulling my leg,' said Sally. 'All the same, I still think there was something fishy about Bill's death. He dies in the snow – and a perfectly healthy man, according to the insurance people, shouldn't really have done that! – Tiny gets injured – nobody knows quite how or exactly when! – and the housekeeper (who might know something awkward) disappears! Then there are all these letters, and now, as you say, they have ceased. I think you ought to start throwing your weight about. It's more than time these mysteries were all cleared up. If you sat down for a couple of hours and made your mind a blank, you'd get on to the truth in no time!'

Mrs Bradley received this involved tribute with an appreciative hoot of amusement.

'What you want is a nice brisk walk,' she said. Sally shuddered.

'What a horrible idea! I took Rhu out to Topstone before breakfast and nearly walked my legs off up those hills!' she protested. Hearing his name, the great dog got up from the hearthrug and poked his nose affectionately into Sally's hand. 'Nothing doing,' she told him. The dog lay down again. The Boxer puppy burrowed against his side.

'Well, I'd like a walk, but not with Rhu, nor even with *you*, Sigfried,' said Mrs Bradley. 'I think I'll adopt your valuable suggestion, Sally, and make my mind a blank. It will be just as useful as continuing to allow it to run round like a white mouse on a wheel. The fact remains that we have no evidence, and suspicions without evidence are merely tiresome.'

She clothed herself for her walk, and Sally watched her out of the window as she crossed the lawn towards the rhododendrons.

'Where's Aunt Adela? It's almost lunch time,' said Deborah, an hour and a half later.

'Hurrying uphill towards us at a pace that can't be good for her,' said Sally, again at the window.

'Goodness! She *must* be hungry!' said Deborah anxiously. 'She *certainly* ought not to hurry uphill like that! Or else – you don't think anything else has happened, do you?'

'She's positively sprinting,' said Jonathan, watching his elderly aunt with narrowed eyes.

It was not because she was hungry that Mrs Bradley was hastening towards the house, nor even because she might be keeping lunch waiting. She had news, and the news was of such a nature that all else, even lunch, had to wait whilst she told her tale.

'The body of a woman identified by Will North, myself and

Farmer Daventry (who had met us and was walking with us at the time) as that of Mrs Dalby Whittier, is lying in a deep dip in one of the farmer's fields. If Will North had not spotted a hawk, and if Mr Daventry had not decided that a sheep which he lost in the snow, and which has not been found yet, might be the reason for the hawk's appearance, we should not have known she was there.'

'Then you've actually seen the body?'

'Yes, I have. Both men plunged down the hillside and I followed. Will has gone for the village policeman, Mr Daventry has gone for Doctor Fielding, and I've come back to tell *you*.'

'I must ring up the inspector in Cheltenham again,' said Jonathan. 'We'd better have lunch at once, Deb. There may be plenty to do later on. Oh, Lord! First Bill and then . . .'

'Lunch!' said Deborah, horrified. 'You surely can't want *lunch*?'

'Of course, chump. Get a move on,' said Jonathan, with the brusqueness he felt was needed. 'Damn it, we're not going to starve! Whatever next? We may be kept busy for hours!'

CHAPTER 9

Bridge of Sighs

'Before I pilgrim it to Rome, I will
seek – Saint Truth.'
William Langland

The inquest on Mrs Dalby Whittier was held in the village school-room as the day was Saturday. The schoolchildren, to their annoyance, were, of course, strictly excluded, but everyone else in the village attended the interesting and melancholy ceremony.

The coroner, Mr Baird's lawyer from Cheltenham, was capable and precise. His jurymen, dressed in their Sunday clothes, comported themselves with the stiff dignity shown by all villagers on solemn occasions, and listened with rather anxious attention whilst the coroner gave them the usual little homily . . . 'formed any previous opinion . . . verdict based solely on the evidence . . . types of witnesses . . . enable this poor woman to be buried . . .'

Evidence of identification was given by Tiny Fullalove, who slightly exaggerated his limp as he walked from his seat to the witness box.

'When did you last see the deceased alive?' he was asked. Tiny did not hesitate.

'On the afternoon of Christmas Eve, December the twenty-fourth.'

'When did you next see her?'

'When I was first called upon to identify the body.'

Farmer Daventry was next called. He described the finding of the body. Then the doctor gave evidence.

'I was called by John Daventry to the dip in what we call Swallow Field. There I saw the body of the deceased. She had been dead for several weeks, perhaps four and possibly for as much as six.'

'You can't put it nearer than that?'

'No.'

'Will you tell the jury what you found when you examined the body?'

'I found that the deceased had taken poison.'

'And that was the exact cause of death?'

'Yes. I discovered that the deceased had taken an overdose of belladonna.'

'It would not be in the public interest to ask you to specify the amount of the dose. You are satisfied that it was sufficient in itself to cause death?'

'Yes, I am quite certain of that.' This was the outline of the inquest which Jonathan gave to Deborah when he and Mrs Bradley (who, after all, had not been called as a witness) returned to the manor house. The verdict of death by poison but without sufficient evidence to show how or by whom the poison was administered had been anticipated. What also occasioned no surprise was the Coroner's Warrant which was issued to the police inspector who was present, and the intimation that the inquest would be adjourned to allow the police to make some further enquiries.

'The interesting thing is,' said Mrs Bradley, later, 'that if the two deaths are connected, and the persons were murdered, the murderer must either have had alternative plans, one of which depended on snowy weather, or else the murders were committed on the spur of the moment.'

'One would think,' said Jonathan, 'that it would be easy to detect both the murderer and the method if the murders were suddenly thought of and were executed at short notice. I would plump for careful, long-term planning and then a patient hope that the weather would at some time fit in. These deaths were planned for deep snow, without a doubt. The snow *must* have been the deciding factor. Don't you think so?'

'Yes, I'm sure it was. It hid the body, it covered vital tracks, and it brought with it the right temperature . . . or, rather, the right temperature brought the snow. I shall be thankful for all the help the students will be able to give.'

'Miss Hughes' young schoolmarms, do you mean? What on earth can *they* do to help?'

'I don't know yet, but it may be that a series of regional surveys would help our enquiry. The students could carry these out more quickly than we could. I must see Miss Hughes about it. The students perhaps could undertake to show that the geography, particularly the topography, of even very small areas may help to account for the mentality, prejudices, speech and reactions of the people who live there. They could apply their findings to Gloucestershire.'

'Old stuff,' said Jonathan rudely.

'I was hoping it might be new to the students,' said his aunt. 'They can begin with obvious analogies; the people of Scandinavia and the people of Spain, for example.'

'Lovely!' said Deborah derisively. Mrs Bradley cackled.

'Think of something else, then, between you,' she said benignly. 'You both know what we want to do. We've got to find out how Mrs Whittier got to that field, and for that the ground must be quartered.'

'We'll try your idea first,' said Jonathan.

'But what *is* all this about the students?' Deborah enquired. 'I mean, if you really want to study the local geography, what's the matter with the Ordnance Survey?'

'Nothing, but it doesn't give quite the kind of detail we're looking for.'

'What *are* we looking for? . . . I mean, what *shall* we be looking for? Clues of some sort, do you mean?'

'I'm going to ask to be allowed to keep that to myself for the moment. I already have one important clue which, needless to say, I have shared with the police. Well, now! Beaters make a very loud noise to frighten the quarry, do they not? Very good. We will have such a noise. By the time I have enlisted the geography class and any other student volunteers, we shall see what the College can do for us in the way of obtaining not clues so much as reactions.'

'What I can't understand,' said Deborah, 'is why the body wasn't discovered before. How could it have lain there unnoticed for so long?'

'If you saw the place I think you would understand,' Mrs Bradley replied. 'It was in that deep dip about three quarters of a mile beyond the field where they've cut down those elm trees. There are brambles at the bottom of the dip and nobody ever goes there in winter. I should imagine it is an old stone quarry.'

'But hasn't she been searched for by the police?'

'Yes, but their enquiries have been at railway stations and along bus routes. Nobody thought of her not even reaching the station.'

'No, of course not. Shall you go to the resumed inquest?'

'Yes, I would not miss it for the world.'

'To every principal of an Emergency Training College,' stated Miss Hughes, 'is granted a sum of money to be spent on outside lectures, therefore why should you come for nothing? If you come to us as an outside lecturer we shall be gratified. This would also account for your rambling with the students over the hills. Now what do you want to find out?'

'Primarily, why Mrs Dalby Whittier should have selected the most dangerous way to get to the main road from the Fullaloves' bungalow. Could the students be told that this is an experiment in local geography, or something of that kind? And could they make sketch-maps, do you think?'

'They'd love that. They are most earnest, and append sketch-maps automatically, likewise diagrams, explanatory drawings, underlinings in coloured inks, and all types of fancy paper-fasteners, to distinguish and to present everything they send us in.'

'Excellent,' said Mrs Bradley briskly. 'Then I'll come and lecture as soon as you like.'

'And we'll run a project, or a centre of interest, based on the lecture,' said Miss Hughes, grinning. 'Such things have been filmed before now for so-called educational purposes. So that's that. It will do the poor things all the good in the world to chase about over the hills and imbibe the fresh air and plot out the lie of the land. And they won't miss much, I can assure you. By the way, one of them, Miss Golightly, is an ex-policewoman. Would you consider telling her in confidence what you're after? I take it that you suspect murder?'

'I don't think we had better tell her that. It might be embarrassing for her to be compelled to keep silence, and I don't think it would help us much to have her know the real point of the project.'

'Right. I'll put everything in train. But you do think the poor woman was murdered?'

'That is not an admissible question, but, in your private ear, yes, I am pretty sure of it.'

'Bets have been made in the Common Room, I believe. We have remarked on your continued presence in the neighbour-hood, and have come to the closely reasoned conclusion that it is not for nothing. By the way, I take it that there is little likelihood of the students' finding anything gruesome?'

'Oh, I'm sure they won't.'

'Good. Then I'll put in a memo, and send you an official invitation to lecture.'

The next day Mrs Bradley received this formal invitation and she answered it by return of post, giving the written answer, in fact, to Sidney Blott in person when he delivered Miss Hughes' official letter.

The lecture itself was a great success. Mrs Bradley had been pulling her nephew's leg when she had announced her subject. What she did lecture on was the use of a theodolite in surveying, and what she demonstrated was the construction of a home-made one which could be guaranteed to function. The students ('poor brutes' as Deborah observed) were interested in anything which they thought they could pass to the children in their classes later on, and they fell for the home-made theodolite with a zest which warmed Mrs Bradley's heart although it burnt a hole in her conscience.

A second lecture saw the amateur surveyors well on the way to the completion of their instrument, and, the weather turning suddenly spring-like, Miss Hughes altered her time-table sufficiently to give the students a chance to wander off in groups and couples into the hills to test their new toy and tabulate the results.

Reports and observations, drawings and sketch-plans, maps and charts came in after that as fast as even the devoted Deborah could deal with them, and Mrs Bradley, besides enjoying her own share of the field-work, spent long evenings looking for clues among the students' handiwork – or so Deborah fondly and erroneously imagined. She had forgotten Mrs Bradley's abstruse references to beaters, noises and quarries.

Jonathan, who had been to Gloucester, came back one afternoon to find his aunt and Deborah in full session. As soon as he had had his tea, Mrs Bradley invited him to crouch or squat beside the one-inch map and check her findings.

'It begins to look as though Mrs Dalby Whittier did not choose her own route or lose her way,' she said. 'Tomorrow I wish you would come with me to the spot where we found the body, and then you can pick holes in my argument, and then if you can find a flaw in my reconstruction I shall be most relieved.'

She took her nephew by the hair and gently directed his attention to the Ordnance map by pulling his face almost on to it.

'Eh? Oh, yes, rather, of course! I say, Deb—'

'Good,' said Mrs Bradley, cutting him short. 'Well, now, look, Mrs Dalby Whittier set out from the bungalow, according to the evidence we have, at about a quarter to four. She was to get the bus at ten to five. She should have had ample time to do this if she went by the sensible and obvious route which leads straight across the footpath over Mr Daventry's field and joins the road through the village. At the end of that road is the bus route. Now the interesting thing is this: the snow did not begin falling until Christmas night, by which time Mrs Dalby Whittier should have been in London for more than twenty-four hours.'

'Well, but . . .'

'Quite so. She may have left the bungalow at the time that we suggest, but she may have had some reason to return to it later. On the evidence of her London relatives, she certainly never reached their house. Therefore—'

'If she did come back the idea would be, of course, that she had something she particularly wished to do. Perhaps she had left behind her a Christmas present for one of the relatives she was to visit. At any rate, it would have been something for which the telephone, or even a letter, would not have been adequate, I suppose,' said Jonathan.

'It is impossible to say. But we shall know a good deal more when the inquest is resumed. The police are now in a strong position to assume that she was murdered. One of the symptoms of poisoning by belladonna, which, as you know, is the product of the deadly nightshade, is intense vomiting.'

'No sign of that?'

'None.'

'So she *was* carried to where she was found!'

'That is the logical inference, and that is the clue to which I referred the other day. Under cover of the students' activities I have verified that Mrs Whittier was not sick anywhere near that dip or on any direct or indirect line to it from the bungalow.

Moreover, you will be interested to hear that even the Chief Constable seems impressed. There is something more to be discovered, or so he informs me, about these mysterious deaths. (Please note the plural.) I am afraid he sometimes jumps to conclusions.'

'Do you think *he* suspects murder this time?'

'Yes, but, of course, he is far too obstinate to say so.'

'Has he got anyone in mind, I wonder?'

'At present, no, child. Whom could he have in mind?'

'Well, Tiny,' said Jonathan baldly. 'It's a bit too much of a co-incidence for two people in one small place to die under such peculiar circumstances. I mean, why should they?'

'A reasonable question, child. But, of course, the after-Christmas weather was very severe. However, there seems little doubt that we've had two murders and that both were planned. I think they were quite well planned. The anonymous letters, as it happens, may have been rather a mistake, but one can't foresee everything, and murderers are curiously fallible. On the other hand, we cannot rule out the possibility that there may be no real connection between the deaths and the letters, and there may be no connection, either, between the deaths. We may be looking for two criminals, not one; and there may be no murderer at all. We must, above all things, be open-minded. The furthest that the Chief Constable will go is to suggest suicide in both cases.'

'I suppose Mrs Whittier knew something which Tiny was afraid she'd give away,' said Jonathan, adhering to his own point of view.

'I am not certain that we ought to bring Tiny Fullalove's name into this, you know. There is no *proof* of anything wrong, so far as he was concerned, except the curious affair of those notes to Anstey.'

'What do you call proof? Isn't it enough that those two people have died for no obvious reason, and that both of them were directly connected with him?'

'Perhaps, circumstantially, it is. But the Law is always amoral, and circumstances are often misleading.'

'I thought that justice and morality were supposed to be the same thing.'

'Then why bring in mercy to temper justice?'

'Do you feel merciful?'

'No,' said Mrs Bradley decisively. 'I do not. But neither do I feel myself to be the instrument of justice or the law. Revenge is my aim, in this instance.'

Her nephew looked as much taken aback as he felt.

'Revenge for what?' he enquired. Mrs Bradley eyed him solemnly.

> 'I do not like thee, Doctor Fell;
> The reason why I cannot tell,'

she answered briefly.

'Meaning Tiny Fullalove, Aunt Adela?'

'Meaning unnatural death. And there is no doubt in my mind that these deaths should not have occurred. Anyhow, the Chief Constable is now fully armed with his exhumation order, and intends to go ahead with the business.'

'Will it help him?'

'No. It will help nobody but the murderers, and perhaps not even those. By the way, I was in Groaning Spinney with two of the students and young Robert Emming this morning, and he made – Hullo! Here's Sally!'

'Jon, dear,' said Sally, 'can you mount me? I can't display my prowess to the Cotswold. That's flying much too high. But a boy I know told me that your local pack can do pretty well behind a local fox, and there's a meet over at Tivingbridge next Wednesday. What about it?'

'You can have Three Legs,' said Jonathan decisively. 'I'm not having you ruin my best hunters over stone walls.'

'I promise not to put Truelove to a single wall.'

'Your promise is void, dear girl. You don't get Truelove for love, truth or money.'

'Oh, but—'

'Three Legs, or nothing. I'm going out on Truelove myself.'

'Well, Deb won't want to go, with Mary Crispin on the way. What about lending me Moonlighter?'

'Oh, *no!*' said Deborah, horrified into inhospitality. 'And, Sally, don't go hunting next week. The snowdrops are out, and—'

'All right. I'll take Three Legs, and if I'm brought home on a stretcher I suppose you won't let it lie on your conscience,' said Sally, ignoring the snowdrops. Her cousin grinned, and winked at his wife.

'As Three Legs has never been known to risk even a two-foot furze-bush, there's no danger that you'll need a stretcher,' he said. 'You just give him his head. He's old, but he's useful because he knows all the gaps and gates. Talk to him nicely, and you'll be in at the death all right. Will North was telling me that he's made a very good false earth on Wyeman Hanger, and has had a vixen in it all winter. Besides, Three Legs won't catch his feet in rabbit holes if they find over at Groaning Spinney, and that's always something to be grateful for.'

'There are five foxes at least in Coverdale Woods,' said Mrs Bradley.

'Who said so?'

'Will North, of course. Is there anything Will doesn't know?'

'Yes. He doesn't know who committed the murders,' said Sally. 'And what were you all talking about so busily when I came in?'

'Young Emming and two students,' said Jonathan.

'Good heavens! What on earth can they see in *him*?'

'Oh, it wasn't like that,' said Deborah. 'It was something he made.'

'Well, it couldn't have been a daisy chain at this time of year. What was it?'

'It was a great discovery,' Mrs Bradley replied. 'He was poking into the badgers' sett and he unearthed two leather leads and two chains. I want Jon to see them.'

She went up to her room and came down with the evidence. Jonathan said:

'No fingerprints?'

'Nothing at all. I have tested them very carefully, and Mr Emming, the students and I were all wearing gloves.'

'Those belong to Tiny Fullalove,' said Jonathan. 'He chains up those tykes of his at night, and those are their leads, too. Anstey says Tiny told him he was sending the dogs to boarding kennels and the cats to a home, but Anstey can't believe it, and neither do I.'

CHAPTER 10

Peculiar Persons

'Did his foe slay him? He shall slay his foe.'
Giles Fletcher, Junior

Deborah had been right about the snowdrops. They were spread almost as thickly as the snow itself on a great slope where the lawn rolled downwards towards the beech trees.

'What do you hope to gain from our little stroll today?' Jonathan asked his aunt when he had gathered a bunch of the snowdrops for his wife to wear, and the three of them with Sally were out for a short walk in the woods.

'I am going to trace history backwards,' Mrs Bradley replied. 'We will walk to the Fullaloves' bungalow from the spot where we found Mrs Dalby Whittier's body, and when we get there we will call on Mr Tiny and put some leading questions.'

'Trap him, do you mean?' asked Deborah, with distaste.

'Certainly not. He won't allow us to do that if he is guilty, and if he is innocent he cannot harm himself, whatever answer he gives.'

'I like your moral sense,' said Jonathan. 'Anyway, it will be nothing more than neighbourly to call on him and ask how the knee is getting on and whether he's had any more anonymous letters. Shall you say anything about the dog-chains and leads?'

'No. At any rate, not yet. And I beg that you will allow me to order the conversation.'

'Only too glad. It's got too hot for me to handle!'

'I *am* silly!' said Deborah suddenly. 'I knew there was something nagging at me. Was Mrs Dalby Whittier's identity card in her handbag?'

'Certain to have been; and her ration book, too, if she really intended to go to London. Why?'

'Well, her signature would be on her identity card, and her ration book would be more useful still, because she'd have written her address as well on that.'

'I still don't see . . .'

'Oh, but *I* do,' said Mrs Bradley. 'If we could see her book and card we could decide – or an expert could decide for us – whether *she* wrote that first anonymous letter. All the others were typed, but—'

'I'll turn up that letter the minute we get back,' said Jonathan. 'What a good thing I didn't give it up to the police.'

'I'm not so sure!' said Mrs Bradley drily.

The place where Mrs Dalby Whittier's body had been found was in a direct line with the bungalow, according to the students' careful maps and plottings. Mrs Bradley led the way back. The walk was uphill and hard going, and in snow would have been almost impossibly bad, but – as Jonathan remarked – it had to be borne in mind that the reverse direction would have given anyone who was walking the benefit of the downhill slopes.

'I wonder how much she weighed?' said Mrs Bradley, as though to herself. 'She looked quite a small woman, but most people would look small against all these shining slopes of snow.'

'She couldn't have weighed much above eight stone,' said Jonathan. 'She was one of the small, spare, energetic kind. You said before that she could have been carried to where you found her.'

'It would have been easily possible,' said Deborah. 'I wish we knew, though, irrespective of whether she walked or was carried, whether she was coming from the bungalow to the village or from the village to the bungalow. You see—' She broke off as they came in sight of the bungalow, although it was still some distance away. The map Mrs Bradley was following traced a route across the middle of a field. They had taken this route, and now, keeping the bungalow squarely in front of them, they were soon at its garden gate. 'You see, it's the one thing I cannot deduce, and it might make all the difference in the world, don't you think, between Robert Emming and Tiny (or, possibly Bill) as Mrs Whittier's murderer.'

'It could have been both the Fullaloves,' said Sally. 'I don't understand about Emming, though. After all, she was his mother.'

'I think I'll go back,' said Deborah, who had turned very pale. 'Would you mind very much?'

'I'll come with you,' said Sally, at once. 'I don't want to meet Tiny Fullalove. Those two can easily cope.'

A woman from the village was looking after Tiny Fullalove. She opened the door to the visitors and showed them into the lounge. Tiny was able to get about on two rubber-shod sticks. He seemed pleased to see the visitors, invited them to be seated, and asked Jonathan to forage for drinks.

'I'll get one for you, if you like,' said Jonathan, 'but I won't have one at this time of day, thanks.'

Tiny flushed.

'You needn't keep up this business of being sore with me,' he growled, in an undertone, as he and Jonathan stood together by the cocktail cabinet.

'That's all right,' said Jonathan lightly. 'As a matter of fact, we came on business. At least, I did. Can you tell me anything about the fencing at the foot of Deepdene Spur? I thought it was agreed with Daventry that it was his job to renew it. You know the place I mean. Mrs Dalby Whittier's body was found not far from the middle of it.'

'Yes, I know,' Tiny responded. 'As a matter of fact, Bradley, and strictly between ourselves, I'm not too well satisfied about Mrs Whittier's death. I've a moderate hunch that it was suicide.'

'Really?' said Mrs Bradley, turning with great interest to the speaker. 'And what gives you that idea, Mr Fullalove?'

'Well,' said Tiny, 'it's *only* an idea, of course, but I do know that she was being pestered by that anonymous letter-writer, because she showed me one of the letters and asked my advice. She seemed terribly worried, and when I heard that her body had been found right away from any possible road to the bus stop, don't you know, I couldn't help being puzzled. I mean, why *should* she wander off like that? It wasn't really dark when she set out, and she knew the way as well as I do myself.'

'What communication was received from the friends she was supposed to visit in London? Do you know?' Mrs Bradley enquired. But Tiny was not to be drawn into contradictions.

'I haven't the foggiest idea. Nothing's come here. Naturally, tied up in that nursing home as I was, I've had very little opportunity for knowing anything much about it,' he replied. 'Her death was a shock, of course, especially coming right on top of poor old Bill—'

'But not the same kind of death,' said Mrs Bradley.

'No. But the weather – I mean, it wasn't such a coincidence, I suppose.'

'Well, I thought it *was*, rather,' said Jonathan. Tiny turned his small, intelligent, green eyes on him.

'Well, I know what you mean, of course,' he said. 'You mean it wasn't snowing when the poor old girl set out. She must have decided to come back for something after Christmas, I suppose, and just couldn't make it in the snow. That's if she ever went to London.' He turned his head away, and there was silence until Jonathan said, not very kindly:

'Well, we just thought we'd look you up as we were out for a stroll. How long will it be before you can manage without – those?' He pointed to the rubber-shod sticks.

'Well, not just yet, of course. Still, I'm hoping. I've got to have exercises soon – to make sure the articulation is going to be all right, you know.'

'May I look at your knee?' asked Mrs Bradley.

'Sure. Help yourself. The surgeon's made a wonderful job of it – better than at first he thought he could.'

He lowered himself carefully into an armchair and pulled up his trouser leg.

'May I touch it?'

'Sure. I shall probably yell, but you mustn't mind that. It's very sensitive still.'

'It must be,' said Mrs Bradley drily; but her exploratory fingers were gentle beyond belief. 'Yes, that seems to be going on well,' she continued. 'Tricky things, knees. Limber, prayerful, romantic . . . There is no end to the part they can play in human destiny.' Tiny looked at her oddly. 'Who has been looking after your dogs and cats whilst you've been in the nursing home?' she went on. Tiny did not hesitate.

'Oh, luckily I sent them to homes over Christmas,' he replied. 'Knew we were going to be out a good deal, don't you know. I expect you noticed they weren't here the night I busted my leg. I'll have to send for them soon. I'm getting damned lonely without them.'

'And now,' said Mrs Bradley, when she and Jonathan had caught up the two women, who were loitering among the trees of Groaning Spinney, 'for Mrs Dalby Whittier and her handwriting. Jonathan, take your anonymous letter to the police as soon as you've had lunch, and get them to compare it with the writing on her identity card.'

'Do you think they've still got her identity card?'

'Yes, child, I know they have. Whatever the verdict of the coroner's jury may have been, the police are not lacking in intelligence, and, as we know, they are no more satisfied about Mrs Dalby Whittier's death than we are. Meanwhile, let us see what we can tabulate.'

'Right,' said Jonathan. 'Where do we begin?'

'We begin with the unexpected call which Mr Bill Fullalove

made here on the night of Christmas Eve. It *was* unexpected, I take it?'

'Oh, entirely, and his excuse for coming was a bit dim, actually. It was to check the invitations for Christmas Day and Boxing Day. Now, I had made those invitations perfectly clear, I'm sure. There was no need for Bill to come. He had some other object. I was pretty sure of that at the time. However, whatever it was, it wasn't actually stated. I half-wondered whether he came to look up Obury and Mansell, those pals of his who were here.'

'It didn't, of course, occur to you that the cousins might have quarrelled, and that he might have come out to give Tiny a chance to cool off or go to bed before he got home?' suggested Sally.

'No, it didn't. There was nothing in Bill's manner to suggest it, and when they both turned up on Christmas Day and again on Boxing Day, there was nothing wrong between them. Bill was no good at hiding his feelings, and Tiny is a complete and utter oaf. If they'd had a row, he'd have continued it, even in someone else's house.'

'I agree,' said Mrs Bradley. 'Next came the business of the ghost. Mr Obury and Mr Mansell said that they saw something leaning over that gate at the top of Groaning Spinney. The point is, what did they see? – that is, if they saw anything, and weren't making it all up.'

'You tell us,' said Jonathan. Mrs Bradley looked at him expectantly.

'No, no,' she said. 'Your turn.'

'Well, I still think they saw Bill.'

'Then why should he have lied about it?' asked Deborah. 'There was no reason why he should have denied being the figure with the white face, is there?'

'Every reason, if he was there for some bad purpose. Look here, let's suppose that Bill lied. He *was* at the top of Groaning Spinney, and we may ask ourselves what his reason could have been. If he did lie, he might have been Mrs Dalby Whittier's murderer. But, of course, he may have told the truth, and, in that case, who was the ghost? – because I quite refuse to believe that there was a real one!'

'And that's not the only question,' said Deborah. 'There's still the main point about Mrs Dalby Whittier to be solved. If she left the bungalow on Christmas Eve, as she is supposed to have done, where was she between about four o'clock on Christmas Eve and the time when she was first hidden away in the snow?'

'Where *she* was, or where her dead body was . . . Yes, that could be the hell of a gap,' said Jonathan. 'I don't see how we can possibly fill it up. The police can't, and they've far more chance than we have.'

'At any rate, we can begin to try,' said his aunt, 'and the first move now, as I see it, is to find out (through the official channels, of course) whether she wrote that first anonymous letter. If she wrote *one*, she may have written more, and therein may lie the motive for her death, particularly as her murderer can hardly have complained to the police.'

'Ah!' said Jonathan. 'Now you're talking! And, rather than that the anonymous letters should cease suddenly, the murderer typed a few more. He didn't dare write them because of the altered handwriting! I say! That opens a considerable field for research! We shouldn't need to worry all that much about the Fullaloves. The murderer could have been anybody! There isn't a clue!'

Official channels were far from slow, but, all the same, before the comparison of the first anonymous letter with Mrs Whittier's ration book had been made, Mrs Bradley's enquiry had taken a livelier turn.

'Mrs Dalby Whittier?' said Anstey. 'I don't know for sure, I'm sure, ma'am, what time she left the bungalow for to go away on Christmas Eve, except she was there at the mid-day. Anyways, I didn't know she was going right up to London. She never mentioned it to me or the missus. Cut her stick, so I always understood, and come to live out here a-purpose. The missus always reckoned her husband had left her, but I don't know, I'm sure. Least said, soonest mended, about them there sort o' matters.'

'Ah,' said Mrs Bradley. 'And now about this message which came from Mr Tiny Fullalove on the twenty-ninth of December. At what time was it slipped under your front door?'

'Oh, that would a-been a matter of – let me see, now. It were the old woman as found it. Oo – see here, now, lass!' He turned his head and called out through the half-open kitchen door. 'What time did you pick up that there note, like, from Mr Tiny?'

'Oo, that would a-been about three o'clock, I reckon. Who wants to know?'

'Friend o' the squire's.'

'What friend?'

'His aunt,' said Mrs Bradley, neatly inserting this reply. 'It is rather important. There is a question of Mr Bill's will.'

'Oo?'

'Yes. So if we could establish whether Mr Tiny was injured before or after Mr Bill's death, it might make a difference to the disposition of the property.'

'I see. Well, I knows the note weren't here at half-past two,' said Mrs Anstey, appearing in the doorway, 'but I reckon it were here by three.'

'Talking of Mr Bill's money, whatever it might be,' said Anstey suddenly to his wife, 'didn't Mrs Whittier once tell Mrs Blott, down at the Post Office when she was drawing out of her Bank book, as she might have expectations there?'

'By the way,' said Mrs Bradley, hoping that her nephew would betray neither surprise nor unseemly curiosity at these interesting tidings, 'do you mind telling me, Mr Anstey, how you knew that Mrs Dalby Whittier was at the bungalow at mid-day on Christmas Eve?'

'Sure I'll tell ee, mam. You remember, mother?'

'Yes, that nasty curry. Her sent little Bob Wootton over with it in a basin, but none of us can abide the stuff, so, without saying nawthen to young Bob, I just gives it to father and tells en to give it to Lassie and Cripes.'

'The dogs?'

'Ah.'

'Did they eat it?'

'Ah. Been brought up to it, you see, Mr Tiny living like that in India. He never had his curries hot, like some folks makes 'em, so the dogs, they was quite accustomed, as you might say, and the little cats, too.'

'Why did Mrs Dalby Whittier give the curry away?'

'Her said, according to young Bob, as Mr Bill 'ad refused it. Said it give 'im the – well, the—'

'Us calls it the backyard trot,' put in Anstey, helping her out. 'You understand, mam? And he didn't want that over Christmas. Young Bob, 'e said she were proper put out about it, and said she'd made it very special, and Mr Tiny 'adn't even tried it though she'd made it just the way 'e liked. Said 'e 'ad to go over to Fairford, so she eat what she could of it 'erself and saved 'is 'ot, and sent us over what Mr Bill wouldn't eat.'

'At what time, then, did he leave for Fairdyke?'

'W'y, at about a quarter to twelve, I reckon, but when Mrs Whittier left, well, to be exact to an hour or so, I couldn't say, I be sure. I never see 'er go.'

'You did think that Mrs Whittier might have claimed to be the wife?' said Jonathan, as he and his aunt walked homewards down the hill. 'If so—'

'It all keeps coming back to Tiny, doesn't it?' said Deborah, later. 'And yet I can't think of him as a murderer. He doesn't seem the type.'

'There isn't a type,' said Mrs Bradley. 'There is no common denominator. Neil Cream and Hawley Harvey Crippen are as far apart mentally as Charlotte Corday and Constance Kent; a murderer such as George Joseph Smith is not really akin to one like Patrick Mahon. A savage and a sadist such as Jack the Ripper is not really much like Seaman Thompson. The extraordinary tavern keeper George Chapman bears no traceable resemblance to the equally unusual chicken farmer, Norman Thorne, except that both had what is oddly known as a Christian upbringing. We could multiply instances—'

'I'd rather hear the stories,' said Jonathan. 'At least, I'd like to hear the ones I don't already know. And what about the murderer of Steinie Morrison?'

'He bears no resemblance to the murderer of Mrs Buck Ruxton, except that neither was an Englishman. But now to our own problems, for, although Mr Fullalove's knee was not so badly injured as he would like us to suppose, it was quite bad enough to have prevented him from propping his cousin's body up against that gate where Jonathan saw it, and I cannot believe that he would have had time to watch Jonathan go to the bungalow, move the body, damage his knee, and so on. He had an accomplice.'

'Do we *know* that?' enquired Sally.

'Yes, we do, and the snow must have been falling at the time they carried Mrs Whittier,' said Jonathan. 'He would have needed that to cover his tracks – the accomplice, I mean.'

'Yes, I can see that, of course. Besides, if it was snowing and you wore protective colouring, you might easily not be seen, either,' suggested Sally.

'Oh, as to that, the chances are that nobody would be about, anyway. These hills are lonely in bad weather,' said Deborah.

'The curry did the trick, of course,' said Jonathan, 'and that would account for the disappearance of the dogs. You couldn't have poisoned dogs *and* a poisoned woman. The inference would be obvious.'

'Well, he murders Mrs Whittier because she knows something about him which she may mention in an anonymous letter. Why does he murder Bill? – a row, or to get Bill's property, or to leave a clear field to propose again to Miss Fielding?' Sally enquired.

'The answer might come if a claimant now came forward for

that five thousand pounds' insurance. That is, if the money was the motive,' said Mrs Bradley.

'Who are Bill Fullalove's executors, by the way?' demanded Sally.

'Baird and Daventry,' said Jonathan. 'Bill once asked *me*, but I dodged the job. I'm jolly glad now that I did. I say, it *would* put the cat among the pigeons if some woman came forward and proved she had a claim to the money! That is, if Tiny is guilty, and the money *was* the motive.'

'I still don't think Tiny is a murderer,' said Deborah, 'whatever Aunt Adela may say about there being no particular type. But it's queer that the anonymous letters should have stopped after Tiny went into the nursing home. I do admit that rather goes against him. But it's probably only coincidence. As for the curry, you can't *prove* whether it was poisoned.'

The report from the handwriting expert to whom Jonathan's letter and Mrs Dalby Whittier's ration book had been sent, stated, without doubt or condition, that the address on the ration book and on Jonathan's anonymous letter had been written by the same hand.

'The thing to find out now is whether Mrs Dalby Whittier wrote out her own address on her ration book,' said Jonathan. His wife and Sally looked at him in great admiration.

'That certainly *is* a point. It can be cleared up by sending her identity card for comparison,' said the latter. But the police had been intelligent enough to anticipate Jonathan's thought. The first anonymous letter had undoubtedly been written by Mrs Dalby Whittier, but whether, as Jonathan pointed out, of her own free will or under duress had still to be proved.

'Of course, she may have been in love with Tiny. In that case she would have hated anybody in whom he seemed to take any sort of interest,' said Deborah. 'We always thought of her as practically middle-aged, but she was younger than Tiny or Bill.'

'It's not the first letter that matters so much, except to us personally,' said Jonathan. 'We've got to find out whether Mrs Dalby Whittier wrote any more of the things before we make sure of Tiny.'

'I wonder where that typewriter is?' said Deborah.

'At the bottom of the millpond, most likely,' said her husband. 'The police ought to drag every pond in the neighbourhood. Ten to one it's been thrown away somewhere.'

The next piece of news was brought by Farmer Daventry.

'I've been going through poor Mr Bill Fullalove's papers,' said he, 'and I find he used to have a typewriter, but there isn't any typewriter in the place now, and Mr Tiny, he declares there never *has* been one at the bungalow. I don't know what to make of it, I'm sure.'

'I suppose,' said Jonathan casually, 'you didn't happen to find any typewritten papers among Bill's effects?'

'Yes, I did; only one, though. It was in a kid's book on Mr Bill's bookshelf. There beant many books at the bungalow. Mr Tiny and Mr Bill each had a shelf of 'em in 'is bedroom.'

'What did you do with the paper?'

'Nothing. Left it where it was. But I did mention it to Mr Tiny. He agreed that Mr Bill must have used a typewriter at some time, but he went on and said that there never had been one brought to the bungalow, same as he told me before. Proper put out he was about it.'

'Ah!' said Jonathan. 'Look here, Daventry, are you going back that way?'

'Well, I wasn't, but I could do.'

'Good. Come along, then. I want to borrow a book. I suppose that will be all right?'

'Oh, no, I don't think so, sir. There's the question of probate. I think we ought to keep all the stuff together just now, do you see.'

'Oh, yes, I'd forgotten all about that. All right, then. But I'd like to see that bit of typing. Bill joined Tiny here at the bungalow as soon as he gave up the sea, and surely he wouldn't have had a typewriter on board ship with him? If he had, he'd have brought it along.'

'He may have had regular lodgings ashore, sir. Portsmouth, or Southsea, or somewhere.'

'Oh, yes, of course. Well, come on, and let me see this typewritten paper.'

The paper was a quarto sheet torn raggedly at the bottom, and bore, in careful typescript, the excerpt from Sir Thomas Browne's *Christian Morals*:

'Lastly, if length of Days be thy Portion, make it not thy Expectation. Reckon not upon long Life: think every day the last, and live always beyond thy account. He that so often surviveth his Expectation lives many Lives, and will scare complain of the shortness of his days. Time past is gone like a Shadow; make time to come present. Approximate thy latter times by present apprehensions of them: be like a neighbour unto the Grave, and think there is but little to come. And since there is something of us that will still live on, join both lives together, and live in one but for the other.'

Jonathan read it through twice. He had a quick hand and eye, and found no difficulty, while affecting to put the paper back inside the book, in secreting it from Farmer Daventry and, later, in transferring it to his pocket-book. He thought it might interest his aunt.

He was disappointed, therefore, when she declared, after closely comparing it with the typescript of one of the anonymous letters, that it had been done on another machine.

'Are you sure?' he demanded. Mrs Bradley handed him her magnifying glass.

'But, all the same, this is a clue of the first importance,' she assured him, as he handed back the glass and she picked up the piece of paper. 'If we could only discover who typed it and which of the inmates of the bungalow had taken the trouble to keep it, we should be able, I think, to eliminate one of our suspects. What was the title of the book in which it was found?'

'It was a kid's nature study book. What not to pick and eat on country walks. Not exactly, one would imagine, the particular cup of tea of either of the Fullaloves.'

'I don't know,' said Deborah. 'I knew a sailor once who used to take *Little Meg's Children* to sea with him every voyage, and read it at least twice before he came home again. He said it used to make him cry just as well as if he had gone to the pictures.'

'It's frightfully odd, that, about the pictures,' said Jonathan. 'Lots of fellows have confessed to me that they cry at them. I suppose there's a psychological explanation. Most of the chaps are quite tough, in the normal way, too.'

'It's the darkness, and the feeling that you can release emotion without anybody knowing,' said Deborah. 'Most people say they feel all the better for a good cry. Personally, if I *do* cry at the pictures, I come out feeling completely chewed up and with a frantic headache.'

Mrs Bradley, who had not cried since she was four, but who believed that crying at the pictures was a morbid symptom and reflected deep-seated neurosis built on self-pity, made no contribution to the discussion. Neither did she return the typescript to her nephew, although, in the privacy of her room, she studied it long and thoughtfully. She could think of nobody in the village who would be at all likely to type out and keep a longish and very apt quotation from Sir Thomas Browne. Then a possible explanation came to her, and she smiled.

CHAPTER 11

What's in a Name?

'I have and always had the manners of a hawk,
I am not lured with love; there must be
meat under the thumb.'

William Langland

Nothing out of the way occurred for about another fortnight, and then Jonathan received a telephone message from the farmer.

'Rather a facer for Mr Tiny, I'm afraid, sir. He was telling me he thought he would be entitled to claim Mr Bill's insurance money, as he was positively certain Mr Bill wasn't married, whatever he might have put in his will. But now, it seems, somebody has turned up, and reckons to be the lady Mr Bill had secretly made his wife. Myself, I've been expecting her. Stands to reason Mr Bill had something up his sleeve to make such a will as that.'

'Good Lord!' said Jonathan. 'That's torn it!' He hastened to communicate these tidings to his aunt. Mrs Bradley was delighted.

'In Shakespeare's words, "This falls out better than I could devise,"' she observed. Her nephew studied her, and then said:

'You know, you are pretty sure that you know the name of Tiny Fullalove's accomplice.'

'Am I?' enquired his aunt. 'I see no reason for your having come to that conclusion.'

'Go on,' said Jonathan.

'I need not. I had hoped you might have thought of something else.'

'And that is?'

'No. *You* tell *me*. I should like to check my findings.'

'Well, don't laugh, then. I have at times rather wondered whether Bill was killed in mistake for Tiny, that's all. There's the question of the curry, you know. Tiny loved it, apparently. Bill didn't like it at all. The murderer (if not Tiny) might not have known that.'

'What a different light would be shed upon the affair if your words were true!' said Mrs Bradley.

'Yes. For one thing, I might be very seriously involved, if the thing did turn out to have been murder.'

'You?'

'Well, perhaps not involved, exactly, but I might find that I had some awkward explaining to do. After all, I am known to have a grievance against Tiny Fullalove. Suppose that it was Tiny, and not Bill, who had been found dead? After all, I'm known to have been the one to find the body! Where should I stand?'

'Upon honour, scruple and your dignity, child, as you do now. And remember what I have already said upon the subject.'

Jonathan laughed, but Mrs Bradley, humming a few bars from the *Mikado*, regarded him dolorously.

'No, but, really,' he continued, watching her face, 'it could be deuced awkward, and it's of no use to blink the fact. Still, we're tilting at windmills, aren't we? All the same, somebody took a fair amount of trouble to make certain that it was I who found the body. I wonder, though . . .'

'Say on, child.'

'Well, the point about the whole thing that baffles me is the time-scheme. It goes back to what Sally once said. How *could* Tiny Fullalove (supposing him to have murdered Bill and Mrs Whittier) have known that Bill would pass out just when he did? I mean, he had to cook up this alibi about having damaged his knee, he had to time it right, he had to get me up to that gate at the top of Groaning Spinney to find Bill's body, and he had to fit in his own re-entrance to the bungalow. Suppose he did fake his accident, he had to time that crawl pretty carefully. He had to damage himself sufficiently for the injury to pass muster with the doctors, too, and yet not sufficiently to cause permanent inconvenience to himself. You know, the more you look at it . . . yes, I *do* see what you mean about the time of Bill's death – rigor mortis and the cold and all that . . . but *I* think it would have taken somebody with even more brains than Tiny possesses to work all that out, and put it over. By Jove . . . !'

'Ah, you think you know someone who would have the brains that you doubt whether Mr Tiny Fullalove possesses?'

'Well, if Bill was murdered, and if it wasn't old Tiny who did it, there *must* be somebody else, accomplice or not.'

'You do not suggest that Mr Bill was in some way hoist with his own petard? . . . You don't think . . . enlarging on your previous suggestion . . . that Mr Bill intended to kill Mr Tiny, and that something went wrong, and Nemesis very rightly took a hand?'

'No,' said Jonathan. 'No, I don't see Bill as a person trapped in the pit he had dug for another. Besides, he wasn't poisoned. We can't even prove that he was murdered, and it's my belief we never shall.'

'You forget the dogs' chains and leads, child, and the fact that they were found by Mr Emming in my presence and that of two other witnesses.'

'Emming, yes. He's quite the village mystery man, isn't he? But we can't prove anything against him. I mean, anybody grubbing about in Groaning Spinney might find almost anything. I daresay Anstey hid the chains and things when they found the dogs had died. That is, if the dogs *did* die.'

'We shall trace those dogs, alive or dead,' said Mrs Bradley. 'By the way, I wonder how much Mr Bill liked the Navy, and I wonder how much Mr Tiny liked giving up the Indian Police? – And, talking of the Indian Police, are you *quite* sure that you do justice to Mr Tiny's mentality?'

'So we've come back to Tiny, have we?'

'Not at all, child. We have never left him. However, we are still waiting for evidence (of which there is still almost none) for our theory that the first death was murder. As for Mr Tiny . . .'

'What about him?' asked Jonathan, watching her. 'And, by the way, that idea that Mrs Dalby Whittier might have been married to one of the Fullaloves seems to have sprung a leak, doesn't it? – But what was that again about Tiny?'

'I wonder what his Christian name is, child, that's all.'

'Oddly enough, it's William. Bill's real name was Clarence, so, of course, he had to be called Bill.'

'Yes. Clarence Fullalove does not, somehow, suggest a Naval officer. And Tiny, I suppose, rather liked his nickname?'

'Very pleased with it. Introduced himself to everybody as Tiny. It is only by the merest chance I know his name was William, and I'm sure he doesn't know I know. I borrowed a jacket from him when I arrived at the bungalow wet through one day, almost as soon as I came here, and I wore it home. I shoved my tobacco pouch into the pocket, and, when I went to pull it out, I pulled out his identity card with it. I'd never given it another thought until now. I say, though . . . !'

'Yes, yes, and indeed yes,' said Mrs Bradley. 'It certainly gives one a reason for deep thought and dark suspicions.'

'Still, it would be the insurance company's business, to begin with, I suppose?'

'Undoubtedly. Our Mr Tiny may or may not be a murderer, but there is some reason for thinking that he has had an opportunity for fraud.'

'But he's a murderer, too!' said Jonathan. 'On that motive alone he must be! Look here, how about this for a reconstruction? Bill decides to marry. He may even have got married. It certainly seems as though he did. He doesn't tell Tiny. The reason he doesn't we don't know. Bill thinks a married man ought to insure his life, but he knows he's not a good bet from the Company's point of view. Right, says Tiny, (not realizing, of course, that Bill is married), let me go and be vetted. I can give my own name, which is William, so there's no catching us out on *that*. Meanwhile, if I conk out, you can collect the boodle in the name of William Fullalove, and, as everybody knows you as Bill, there you are, as right as a trivet, same as me if *I'm* the lucky bloke.'

'Very nice,' said Mrs Bradley, 'Bill was the sound life and Tiny the uncertain one, and Bill it was that died.'

'All right. That doesn't affect my argument. Take it the other way round. Bill takes out the policy under the name of William, and the insurance doctor, perhaps a bit dubiously, passes him. Well, the other one is still sitting pretty. Either of 'em can be William Fullalove: Tiny because it's his name, and Bill because everyone not in the know thinks Bill is the shortened version.'

'I should like to be there when the lawyers interview this woman who claims to be the widow,' said Mrs Bradley with apparent inconsequence.

CHAPTER 12

Enter Two Gravediggers

'Benigne he was, and wondrous diligent,
And in adversitee ful pacient.'
Geoffrey Chaucer

The woman who had come to claim Bill Fullalove's property was named Carol Letchworth Fullalove, and was less than thirty years old. Local gossip suggested that she would have difficulty in proving her case, unless her marriage lines were quite above suspicion, but once she had come and gone – for she returned to her home in Portsmouth after spending a couple of nights in Cirencester – talk and speculation died down and Tiny merely shrugged when her name was mentioned.

His knee mended, and soon he was able to reduce his two sticks to one, and limped only very slightly as he went upon his lawful occasions. He was not asked to the manor house any more as a visitor. If he came, it was strictly on business connected with the estate, and he interviewed Jonathan alone and always in the library.

Towards the end of February Jonathan had received a letter from Miles Obury. Obury proposed to stay at a hotel in Cirencester, but asked to be made free of Groaning Spinney so that he could continue his badger-watching. It was time for the cubs, he pointed out, and although he had some excellent and quite remarkable pictures of adult badgers, he had none of the youngsters. He added that Mansell would be staying in the neighbourhood also, for he had permission to make a trial trench in the mound at Cissington to find out whether a summer dig there would be valuable.

Jonathan groaned, and tossed the letter to his wife.

'Oh, bother!' said she. 'I suppose we must ask them to stay here. I wouldn't mind if the food weren't such a business. They'll have to exist on Mrs Humper's chickens, that's all!'

'No, I'm not going to ask them to stay,' said Jonathan, with spirited inhospitality. 'I'm damned if I am. Could you manage a couple of lunches, and perhaps a dinner? And I'm damned if I'm going to ask Tiny. After all, they were more Bill's pals than his. Look here, don't let's ask them at all.'

'Oh, I expect we can manage,' said Deborah. 'It's really break-fast that's the worst. People always expect a cooked one in other people's houses! So long as they're not here for that!'

Miles Obury's first task on the day which followed his arrival at the inn, not in Cirencester, after all, and distant only three miles or so from the manor house, was to reconstruct, with the aid of the suspected changeling, Farmer Daventry's carter Ed Brown, the platform in the tree from which to take his flashlight photographs.

It was Jonathan who had recommended Ed.

'If there are any badger cubs, they'll probably amble out and climb all over Ed,' he had observed. 'And, if they don't, at least he won't frighten them away!'

He said nothing of Will North's theories about the extra snow, and Obury and Ed made the platform safe again for the spring and summer, and, greatly to Obury's joy, on the second day he was there he saw two cubs gambolling outside the sett in broad daylight. The early light of the year was not very good from a pho-tographer's point of view, but he got what he hoped would be a reasonably clear picture, and presented Ed with five shillings.

A robin, which, in the friendly manner common to his species, had followed the proceedings from a very short distance away, flew up to Ed and perched upon his shoulder. Jonathan, who was with the two men, laughed aloud, but the robin was not alarmed.

'Well, then, you old you, you,' said Ed. The robin cocked an eye sideways, and, apparently not caring much for Obury and Jonathan, flew into a bush from which he continued to watch the three men.

'Very tame, aren't they, robins?' said Obury, packing up his traps.

'Ah,' agreed Ed. 'This wood be full of they grey squirrels, too. Will North, he shoots 'em. Pests they be, he says. Queer how nature prey on nature. Parson talk about the brotherhood of man, but Nature know better, I reckon.'

'How do you mean?' enquired Obury. But Ed had shot his bolt, and made haste to change the subject. At least, Jonathan thought that the subject was changed, but his aunt, when she heard of it, thought otherwise.

'I see Mr Bill Fullalove, day he died,' Ed observed. 'Didn't he used to come out along of you to study these here old badgers?'

'Once or twice, yes, I believe he did come along,' Obury agreed.

'Ah,' said Ed, nodding. 'Many's the time I see you and him together, up along over here. Ah, many's and many's the time.'

'Not as many times as all that,' retorted Obury. 'I don't suppose I was out with Mr Bill Fullalove half a dozen times altogether.'

'Well, 'tweren't Mr Tiny you was out with,' countered Ed. Obury glanced at him sharply, but the carter's serene face gave no sign that he was arguing the point. Jonathan, deeply interested in what was, in effect, a dispute, took no obvious notice. Ed left them at the bottom of the wood, and Jonathan took Obury home to dinner. Mansell also was expected, and turned up in good time for the sherry.

Mansell had great things to report.

'I believe I've struck something really good,' he said. 'You know where that road goes up by the side of the village pub and becomes a narrow lane? Well, I don't know how much you know of the country beyond it? Can one get round that way?'

'It makes a pretty good walk,' said Jonathan. 'You've got to go the hell of a long way if you don't want to come back by the same path.'

'Oh, but there *is* a way round, is there? I wish you'd come with me tomorrow. I've spotted a most useful place for my trial dig into the hill just north of the long barrow up there. I'll show you. And then you can take me for the round tour. I'd like that immensely.'

'Good idea,' said Jonathan. 'It's wonderful weather for it, too. Rather different from the last time you were here.'

'Yes, rather. Anything more come up about that business?'

'Nothing of any significance,' said Mrs Bradley, before her nephew could reply. 'Some young woman – probably an imposter – is making an attempt to claim Bill Fullalove's money.'

'Oh, really? Well, if she's an imposter she won't get far without proof.'

'She's got a very sound-looking certificate of marriage, according to old Baird,' said Jonathan. 'I had a telephone conversation with him this morning. He seems frightfully interested. I don't believe country life suits him too well, and I suppose any bit of news makes a change.'

'Bachelors are always gossips,' said Deborah unreasonably. 'May I come with you on your walk? I'd love to see where you're going to begin your dig,' she added to Mansell.

'I should be delighted to have you come,' said Mansell politely, 'if it wouldn't be too long a walk.'

Mrs Bradley, Sally and Obury promptly added themselves to the party, and next day the company set out. They started immediately after breakfast, and the plan was to return to a late lunch. Mrs Fairleaf, Deborah's cook, was to make it a meal which could be delayed if necessary beyond the time which had been allowed for the walk, and, the weather being fine and the air sharp, the party stepped out along the drive and were soon on the road which led uphill through the village.

At the village public house they turned left and were soon on another and a steeper uphill road which degenerated into a narrow lane and then into nothing more than a track.

There were banks and hedges on either side, and, on the lower slopes, the track was muddy and slippery. As it mounted it grew drier, and at the end of half a mile of stiff walking the ground flattened out to a small plateau. The hedges disappeared, and ahead of the walkers was the hill on which was the long barrow where Mansell was to make his trial dig.

About a mile further on, the ground began to fall again, and the track followed a stream. Soon the party came to two small houses. They seemed incredibly remote from the village, although, as the crow flies, they were within a mile or two of a small church which the walkers could see in the distance.

The track forked beside the houses. Mansell unhesitatingly took the left-hand fork, and the party walked alongside the stream, which, here and there, crossed the path in a tiny cascade over grey, clean stones. It was nowhere sufficiently wide to cause the walkers inconvenience, and the party made very good progress until again the ground took an upward slope.

At the top of the rise was the long barrow, a whale-backed object higher at one end than at the other, and commanding a magnificent view over the valley of the Severn and away to the Forest of Dean and the Welsh mountains. The situation of the barrow was romantic, and, although lonely, not desolate.

Mansell spent some time in demonstrating exactly where he proposed to make his trial dig. This was not into the barrow itself; that had long since been excavated and its contours carefully restored. His idea was to determine whether, at a short distance from the barrow, there had existed a sacred site of the Neolithic Age. Mansell had an archaeologist's reasons for believing that such a site was there. He put forward these reasons concisely, and the company, whether they were edified or not by what he said, gave a civilized impression that they fully understood and appreciated his statements, and listened with apparent interest to what he had to say.

'What interests me,' said Obury, the only one of the party to appear a trifle restive during Mansell's lecture, 'is the fox's den which I see has been made into the lower bastion of the camp.'

'Not camp; not bastion; theatral area, if you like,' said Mansell, with a slight touch of condescension which was not lost upon his hearers.

'I think we ought to be getting along,' said Jonathan. 'We've still the longer part of the walk in front of us. How do you feel, Deb?'

'Fine,' said Deborah, who looked so.

Beyond the long barrow the track forked again, and, keeping to the left, the party climbed a knoll and saw in front of them a small wood. A lonely cottage seemed to be the only dwelling-place, and as they came up to it they saw a woman in a dark-blue dress slip in by the side door.

Beyond the wood there was a village. They by-passed this, led by Jonathan, until they reached the church which they had seen from some distance away. Once past the church, low walls of Cotswold stone enclosed the little road, and another steep climb brought the party to the turn which indicated the road home. Here they bore sharply to the right, along a lane which bordered upland pasture, and then took a downhill track between haw-thorn hedges to a farm.

'There's our village,' said Jonathan, pointing. 'We keep along this track until we come to the stream, and we follow that until we come to our own church.' He took out his watch. 'Two hours and a quarter. Good going.'

'I say,' said Deborah, dropping behind to walk beside Mrs Bradley, 'did you notice that woman in the blue dress who slipped inside that lonely cottage as though she didn't want us to see her?'

'Yes. It was the woman who claims to be Mr Bill Fullalove's widow,' said Mrs Bradley. 'At least, so Will North informed me yesterday.'

'That's who I thought it might be. But what is she doing there, I wonder? She's supposed to have gone back to Portsmouth.

Besides, the cottage belongs to Tiny Fullalove. He lived there before he had the bungalow built. He's said nothing about letting it to anybody.'

'I'd like to see that woman's marriage certificate,' said Mrs Bradley. 'If she is put down as the wife of Mr *William* Fullalove we've quite a lot to think about, and so have the police and the lawyers.'

'You mean . . . ?' asked Deborah.

'Mrs *William* Fullalove isn't Bill's wife but Tiny's,' said Mrs Bradley. 'I heard from Jon that Bill's real name was Clarence. I've a good mind to go to Farmer Daventry and find out whether he's seen the marriage certificate, and, if so, what is on it. You see, if we're right, it would be just as easy, when once her claim is substantiated, for Tiny Fullalove to share the five thousand pounds' insurance with his wife as to inherit it directly! In fact, from *his* point of view, if Bill's death was no accident, it would be much the safest way to get hold of the money.'

'Oh, dear!' said Deborah. 'It's all horrible and all interesting.'

'That's due to the devil,' said Sally, who had joined them whilst the men walked on ahead. 'The trouble about horrors is that they *are* interesting. Deb, Jon is looking round anxiously. I think he is afraid you're getting tired.'

'No, that Aunt Adela is,' retorted Deborah. Mrs Bradley cackled.

'Nonsense, child,' she said. 'He never thinks of anybody else when you are one of the party, and quite right, too. I *like* young husbands to be obsessed with their wives' charms. Far too many of them are not. It may be rather hard on the wife to be an object of worship, but to an observer it is undoubtedly fascinating. The exalted primitive theory that the primary deity is a woman . . .'

Deborah made a face at her, tripped over a tree-root and would have fallen but for Mrs Bradley's iron-fingered grip on her elbow.

After lunch Deborah had to go into Cheltenham and Sally went with her. Jonathan went out with the limping Tiny Fullalove to look at the pigs. Mrs Bradley went up to her room to write letters,

Mansell went out to co-opt labour for his dig, and Obury sought out Ed Brown. He observed to the others that he had taken a great fancy to Ed because of his knowledge of the countryside and the strange attraction he had for animals. He proposed to accompany Ed on his afternoon round.

Jonathan was not at all certain that this programme would appeal to Ed, or to Farmer Daventry who employed him, but he supposed that the day would end with beer for two at the village pub, and he trusted that this would compensate Ed for any boredom or embarrassment which he might suffer during the afternoon. As for Farmer Daventry, he probably had the wit to leave a good carter alone.

Left in the house, except for the servants, Mrs Bradley sat at her window for some time looking out over the hilly fields and pastures. Then she gave one glance at her unanswered letters and went downstairs and out to the front door.

There she paused whilst she surveyed the scene. She returned to her room, put on walking shoes and an indeterminate ulster, and strode out into Jonathan's drive. She followed the rough, downhill path as far as Will North's house, and then struck up into Groaning Spinney. She walked on the soft humus and the fallen pine needles until she reached the sturdy tree in which Obury and Ed had rebuilt the badger-watching platform.

She took off her ulster and tossed it over a shrub, and then climbed up to the platform. Here she squatted like a benevolent toad and appeared to lapse into meditation.

Around her the signs of spring, in the form of shining buds and a lively blackbird, gave colour, perhaps, to her thoughts, for she descended from her perch after a while, and, taking out a small lens, diligently surveyed the trunks of various trees. She then transferred her scrutiny to the badgers' sett and even poked experimentally into a hole with the end of a long rod which she fitted together from parts which she took from the pocket of her discarded ulster.

Obtaining no apparent results from these probings, she abandoned them, and, instead, began to scrape aside the layer of humus formed by the fallen leaves of the tree in which the platform had been built. She looked up to see Jonathan and Tiny approaching her. Tiny seemed to find the soft going difficult, and Jonathan had to give him a hand down the bank. Just as they descended, Mrs Bradley bent down, inserted a yellow claw into the hole she had previously probed, and popped into her skirt pocket an object which neither man, at that distance, should have been able to identify. She then looked up, grinned like a crocodile at them, and allowed Jonathan to help her on with her ulster.

'And what are you supposed to be doing?' he enquired. 'I thought you stayed in to write letters? Never mind. You can come with us now to see Will's ferrets.'

'Yes,' said Mrs Bradley, 'and then I must catch the bus.' She accompanied them as far as Will North's house and then hurried off down the lane for the village street and the bus stop. She grinned hideously at the recollection of Tiny's face.

When she glanced back the two men had gone. Mrs Bradley dived into her skirt pocket, took out the object which she had secreted there, and, upon arriving at the mill-stream, she threw it in. It was a cardboard container which had surrounded a bottle of aspirin tablets. She leaned on the miller's railing, and watched the small package float away downstream.

Then she walked briskly to the high road, took the bus into Cheltenham, and went to a cinema. She remained there until seven, dined alone at an hotel, and returned on the half-past eight bus.

'I say,' said Deborah, when she returned, 'Jon's had another anonymous letter.'

'What about this time?' But Mrs Bradley did not seem surprised.

Deborah giggled.

'About you. You are supposed to be corrupting the minds of the village children. What have you been a-doing of?'

'I suppose my immediate removal from the vicinity is demanded?'

'Oh, yes, of course. There's a postscript which says that all witches ought to be burnt. Who on earth *does* write the beastly, silly things?'

'Was it written or typed this time?'

'Oh, typed again, and on the same typewriter. At least, Jon thinks so.'

'I'd like to see it.'

'Oh, you shall. He's taken it to show the vicar and Mr Baird. He says you said they were to be called in to conference. He's gone in the car. He went directly after dinner. I don't expect him home until after midnight. He'll go to Mr Baird second, and they're certain to gossip.'

'I wonder what luck Mr Mansell has had in getting people to work on his trial dig?' Mrs Bradley enquired.

'I don't know. We shall hear from Jon when he comes home, because Mr Baird knows everything. I shall wait up, I think. What would you like to do?'

'Knit,' replied Mrs Bradley. She went up to her room and returned with a repulsive bundle of dead-looking natural-coloured wool. 'Do you think purple or puce would look better as a contrast with this?'

'Good heavens!' said Deborah, expressing simple horror. 'It's bad enough as it is!'

Mrs Bradley grinned amiably and set to work on huge wooden needles to fabricate what appeared to be some sort of shawl, a type of garment which, needless to say, she never wore.

Jonathan came back earlier than his wife had expected. He was in the house by half-past ten, and brought news that Mansell was experiencing some difficulty in recruiting men for the trial dig. He seemed rather annoyed about it.

'It's a lot of ballyhoo,' he said. 'They don't fancy the job for some reason, so they are saying they don't like to interfere with something which has been there for hundreds of years. Just imagine chaps like these Gloucestershire fellows talking such rot!

No, there's something the matter with them, and I don't know what it is.'

'Perhaps they haven't the time to spare,' Mrs Bradley suggested. Her nephew snorted.

'He's prepared to offer handsome pay for next Saturday afternoon,' he said. 'They'd jump at it if they really wanted the work. No, there's something up, and I'd like to know what it is.'

'What about this anonymous letter?' Mrs Bradley enquired. Jonathan grimaced.

'I'd almost forgotten it,' he said. 'I showed it to old Baird. He doesn't seem particularly impressed. Says it's not scurrilous, blasphemous, improper, or in any way actionable, so I've brought it back with me.' He produced it and handed it over. 'It was typed on the machine we've heard of before. It was not posted, but was found on the ground outside the post office by young Bob Wootton, and he handed it in. It was stamped, but the stamp had not been cancelled. Sidney Blott obligingly brought it along. That's all. Here it is.'

'Very interesting indeed,' said Mrs Bradley, examining it. 'Look at the spelling of "inditing". I remember the same word being used in another of the letters. The spelling – correct enough according to the Concise Oxford dictionary, is in the unusual form "enditing". Apart from the fact that it is not a word which an uneducated person would commonly use, the rather extraordinary spelling marks it, I think, as the product of an individual mind.'

'And you mean that it narrows the search?' said Jonathan. 'Yes, I can see that, all right, if we take it for granted that the writer is somebody living in the village; but—'

'Well,' said Mrs Bradley reasonably, 'who, living outside the village, would know that I am here?'

'Don't be modest,' said her nephew. Mrs Bradley contented herself by leering tenderly at him, and then she said:

'Except, of course, Mr Mansell and Mr Obury. And now, take Deborah to bed. "The iron tongue of midnight hath tolled twelve."'

'"Lovers, to bed; 'tis almost fairy time,"' said Jonathan, breathing the words into Deborah's hair. 'Yes, and that reminds me,' he added. 'That's the most exasperating thing about this digging business of Mansell's. Fairy time, indeed! Grown men of the twentieth century, and not Cornishmen or Irishmen mind you, but sober, and, one would have said, God-fearing West-Country fellows.'

'I say, though! This spelling bee of yours! You don't mean the vicar?' asked Deborah. 'Now that I come to think, that old-fashioned spelling comes in the English liturgy of Edward VI. Would anybody but a clergyman be likely to know that?'

'Think it out for yourself,' said Mrs Bradley. Jonathan smacked his knee.

'Oho!' he said. 'I've got it! But has he a typewriter?'

'At any rate, he must have access to one. I should say, on the whole, he must possess one.'

'Do tell me,' pleaded Deborah.

'You use your gump. It was you that recognized the Prayer Book of Edward Tudor!' retorted Jonathan.

'Psalm 45,' said Mrs Bradley.

CHAPTER 13

The Dragon's Teeth Are Sown

'On what wings dare he aspire?
What the hand dare seize the fire?'
William Blake

The empty packet of aspirin tablets which Mrs Bradley had found in the badgers' sett had certainly not been there when the snow was on the ground. It was dry, and in good condition. Whether it had been left there without malice, or whether (as she strongly suspected) to drop a broad hint of the manner in which Bill Fullalove had met his death, she could not decide. She had done the only possible thing under the circumstances: she had destroyed it. It was not evidence, and therefore it must not, she felt definitely, complicate a business which was already not very simple.

The insurance plot, she was almost sure, had been made by the cousins jointly. One policy between them, obtained on the strength of Bill's health, was a neat form of economy and the fraud was quite likely to have gone undetected. She wondered whether the cousins wrote an identical hand. At any rate, they had probably practised a signature.

One other point arose from all this. The fact that a claimant had turned up in the person of a wife no longer held the importance that Mrs Bradley had at first assigned to it. She was now prepared to believe that the woman, although doubtless legally married to one of the cousins, was no more than a business associate, or, baldly, a partner in crime. Her share in the plot was to turn up at the crucial moment to claim the money. It was a business deal all round, Mrs Bradley thought. Having received her share, she would disappear again into the limbo from which she had come, unless she decided to try blackmail on whichever cousin lived to claim the money.

However, if all this were true, there could be no doubt that Tiny might have been tempted to give his cousin an overdose of aspirin before he went out into the snow. Once Bill had fallen asleep, nothing could save him in such weather.

If Tiny, therefore, were the murderer, it could not be he who had dropped the aspirin packet. The people who had access to Groaning Spinney were many, if one counted the servants and all others who worked on the estate, but it should not be difficult to find out which of the many had been through the little wood during, say, the past week.

She decided to talk to Will North again and to the Wootton brothers, and also to take counsel with the carter. Among them, these four men should be able to supply the information she wanted.

Aspirin, of course, suggested the presence of a woman. She thought she would also go up to the College and question the students. They had free access to the whole of the estate, and if one of them had dropped the packet there would be no need of further enquiries.

Miss Hughes, although not immediately visible, was soon run to earth by the College secretary, who found her supervising a group of history students.

'Good to see you,' she said to Mrs Bradley, as soon as they met. 'The students are always asking when you are coming to talk to them again, and when you've another job that you want them to do.'

'I'll come when you like,' Mrs Bradley promised, 'provided it can be fairly soon. I really ought to go back and look at my clinic next month.'

'Well, these students go down in May. We only have them for thirteen months, as you know. What about one day next week?'

The arrangements were made there and then, but before Mrs Bradley was able to come to her real business Miss Hughes began to talk about the inquest on Mrs Dalby Whittier.

'I am interested that the jury brought in an open verdict,' she said. 'You know, it never seemed natural to me that that poor woman should have wandered so far from the track and died in the snow, and when I looked at the students' maps and plans of the hillsides it seemed more unreasonable still. And, by the way, talking of hand-written anonymous letters – well, I didn't intend to mention the fact because I put the thing straight on the fire and took no further notice – but I had one myself last term.'

'Last term? Before Christmas?' said Mrs Bradley, producing from a capacious skirt pocket the inevitable notebook.

'Yes. Last November. About the middle of the month. It accused me of knowing the students to have immoral relations with the brothers Wootton who do the gardening here and look after the boilers. It added that I did nothing to prevent this.'

'Indeed?' exclaimed Mrs Bradley. 'That is more than interesting!'

'If you knew the complete detestation and fear in which the younger Wootton, Harry, the unmarried one, holds all women, not even excepting his own sister,' said Miss Hughes, with a deep chuckle, 'you would also find it more than amusing. But no! Anonymous dirt is never that! I'm sorry now that I didn't keep the letter, but it was a real piece of nastiness and I didn't like the idea of leaving it about. My secretary is utterly discreet, of course, but naturally she has access to all my drawers and pigeonholes. I must confess I never faced the fact that there might be other letters. I thought it came from one of the villagers who disliked having the College take over the biggest house in the place . . . a sort of perverted local patriotism, you know.'

'I see.' Mrs Bradley nodded. 'Still, it establishes my theory that at least one other person must have received one of these hand-written letters besides yourself and my nephew, and that that person may have killed Mrs Dalby Whittier and dumped her body where we found it.'

'The easiest place to have killed her . . . and the safest . . . would have been at the bungalow, where she lived,' said Miss Hughes, 'but that would involve one of the Fullalove cousins, would it not?'

Mrs Bradley hesitated, and then decided against telling Miss Hughes the story of the curry and the disappearance of the dogs and cats. Miss Hughes glanced at her face and asked no questions.

'Of course, we know Mrs Whittier left the bungalow before Christmas: that is to say, before the snow fell,' she said, 'but I repeat that if she was killed at the bungalow it would be fantastic to suppose that someone other than one of the Fullaloves killed her, unless . . .'

'Unless what?' asked Mrs Bradley, who was anxious to have her own theories tested in every possible way.

'Unless some friend of one of the cousins had access . . . that is to say, a key . . . to the bungalow. And that opens up matter for speculation.'

'And adds up to the answer I first thought of,' said Mrs Bradley. 'But I came upon a different errand. I wonder whether you would be willing to help me?'

'I *think* the students are all litter-conscious,' said Miss Hughes, when she had heard about the empty aspirin packet, 'but one never knows. People are so very remiss over these things. Question them, by all means. Will you know whether they are being quite truthful?'

'What are psychological tests for?' Mrs Bradley enquired. Miss Hughes, who had often wondered, smiled amiably and went off to arrange for the following day a period during which every student should take Mrs Bradley's test.

The result was gratifying. It was clear, from the papers sent in, that none of the students had been in Groaning Spinney since they had made the survey of the neighbourhood for Mrs Bradley.

'And now, what are you going to talk to us about?' enquired Miss Hughes, when Mrs Bradley had been to the College again to announce the result of the test. A subject was soon agreed upon, and then Mrs Bradley walked through the lovely grounds to the village street, and, when she reached it, stopped at the house where young Emming, the choirmaster, lodged. He was at home and was mending a puncture in the back tyre of his bicycle.

Mrs Bradley came to the point at once.

'I am beginning to discover,' she said, 'that other people besides my nephew received hand-written letters of abuse. These were in addition to the typewritten ones of which we have all heard.'

Young Emming straightened his back, glanced rather wistfully at his upturned bicycle, and asked her to come inside the cottage, for they were in the front garden. Mrs Bradley complied.

'Now, then,' he said, 'am I to understand that there are *two* anonymous letter-writers in this one small village?'

'There *were* two,' said Mrs Bradley gently. 'There seems very little doubt that one of them was the late Mrs Dalby Whittier, the Fullaloves' housekeeper.'

She watched the young man closely as she made this statement. Emming went crimson and his eyes blazed. He stood threateningly over the small, black-eyed woman.

'You can take that back!' he cried furiously. 'She would *never* have done such a thing!'

'Don't loom,' said Mrs Bradley composedly. 'Even if you did strike me it wouldn't help matters. It would not even give you satisfaction. I did not invent this information, you know. It can be proved. I'm afraid you must accept that as a fact.'

The young man sat down. He looked tired. The colour ebbed from his face and neck, and he shrugged his shoulders helplessly.

'Please go on,' he said. 'I'm sorry. She . . . she had a lot to put up with, you know.'

'I'm sorry, too,' said Mrs Bradley gently. 'Now I don't know whether you have ever examined the theory that her death may not have been an accident? The verdict of the inquest, you know . . .'

'I . . . you mean . . . you think she may have . . . ?'

'Not even that,' said Mrs Bradley, speaking very quietly. 'I think she may have let somebody know that she had stumbled on an ugly bit of truth. So you see why I want to find out about those anonymous letters. We *know* she wrote the one which went to my nephew. That has been proved. It also seems likely that she wrote one to Miss Hughes at the College. If she wrote two, she most likely wrote others of which we have never known because they exposed dark secrets, criminal ones, perhaps.'

'Yes, I see.' He walked to the window. Mrs Bradley half-turned in her chair and regarded his thin shoulders and narrow back appraisingly. He swung round. 'I can't help you,' he said. 'And I wouldn't, even if I could. She would never have told *me* anything about such a thing. I'm her son, as, of course, you know.'

'Yes, I do know. A mother would hardly confide to her son that she was the author of anonymous filth.'

She walked to the door. The young man swung round and sped her departing presence with an oath. Mrs Bradley turned on him.

'I should be careful how I used that word,' she said mildly. 'It has appeared in two of the typewritten letters. You don't possess a typewriter, I suppose?'

Emming followed her to the door and watched until she was lost to sight at a bend in the road.

She passed under the bridge which carried the drive from Jonathan's house to the College, and then struck up through the lane to Will North's place. But it was not Will she had come to see. Her business was with the brothers Wootton, who lived in the opposite house.

The brothers were both at home. She came to the point at once, realizing that with Gloucestershire countrymen nothing would be gained either by beating about the bush or attempting to approach the subject tactfully.

'Mr Wootton and Mr Harry Wootton?' she said.

'Ah, right first time, missus,' said Abel, the elder brother. 'What can us do for 'ee?'

'You can tell me the truth,' said Mrs Bradley, with a fiendish grin. 'How did you come to get yourselves mentioned in an anonymous letter to Miss Hughes?'

'Anonymous? That means somebody didn't put their name to it, eh?'

'Exactly.'

'That means no good were said of us, eh?'

'No good at all. Far from it. It accused Miss Hughes of allowing you to consort immorally with her students.'

The brothers looked at one another. Abel, the widower, opened a large, brown-toothed mouth in hearty Rabelaisian laughter. Harry, the woman-hater, muttered a dark, Welsh oath and spat into the open grate.

'Well, I never did!' crowed Abel. 'If that there ent a good un as ever I yeard! Come on, speak up, Arry! None of that there talk you picked up off old Tommy Evans! Speak English, man, and speak up!'

'Well,' said Harry, slowly, eyeing Mrs Bradley with suspicion and some resentment, 'being as it appears to have come out, here'er be, then!' He paused, and looked at his brother.

'Get on, lad,' said Abel, encouragingly. 'Get the load off'n thy conscience!' He roared again. Harry appeared to make up his mind.

'I don't want to get nobody in trouble,' he said, in his soft, thick burr, 'but young immen be a bit too lively nowadays. I was smoothing over the potato patch way back be'ind the College when one of the young immen her comes up to me and her says, "Us be keeping Hallowse'en," her says, "and it'd be a bit o' fun," her says, "if you and Abel was to come along to it. We'll have tur-mut lanterns and put sheets on us, and have bobbing for apples and . . . well, you know the sort of thing," her says. "Do come. The more the merrier!"

'Well, it weren't much in my line, but I talked it over with Abel here, and we decided it wouldn't do no 'arm, specially as Emma was going to join in and wanted us for company, like, so us went. Well, what should one of them there uzzies do but stick me in one of the rooms downstairs all by myself and plant me in front of a looking-glass. It were purty dark, and there was a deal o' giggling outside, and then one on 'em comes in and starts reciting some jargon or other, and then, dang it, her slips between me and the glass and 'afore I knows what her's up to, her gives I a smacking great kiss. I never saw her face, 'cos her back was to the glass and it were too dark, see? And a bloomin' girt vool I must a-looked! Made me so mad, it did, I give her a cuff on the – well – and a purty good squawk her let out.'

'I see,' said Mrs Bradley. 'Thank you very much, Mr Wootton. I am glad to have cleared the matter up. Girls, as you say, will do anything nowadays!'

Keeping a carefully grave countenance, she then put her next question, but neither brother could help her.

'Groanin' Spinney?' said Abel. He shook his head. 'Us have both been up over at the College since last Wednesday fortnight. Haven't been this way except to sleep till today. Will North could tell ee, mam, better than anybody else.'

Mrs Bradley knew this. She also proposed to speak to Ed Brown, the carter. She tackled Will North first. His information was exactly as she expected, except for one interesting addition.

The only people who had been in the woods during the past week were Deborah and Sally, looking for catkins, Tiny Fullalove (rather rough walking for him, Mrs Bradley thought, but still, he had accompanied Jonathan up there on the day the packet had been found), Obury at his badgers' sett, Mansell with a telescope and binoculars, and, the cuckoo in the nest, young Robert Emming.

'What was *he* doing?' Mrs Bradley enquired. Will did not know. He was muttering to himself and writing in a little book, and jumped a yard and a half when spoken to.

The carter, Ed Brown, could add nothing to this catalogue, but he also had seen Emming in the wood.

'Writing po'try to his best girl, I reckon,' said he, with his sly, shy grin. Neither man had seen any of the named persons drop anything, but Will could substantiate Mrs Bradley's view that the empty packet had not been in the wood very long before she found it.

Mrs Bradley was not very anxious to tackle young Emming again so soon after her previous visit. Nevertheless, one of the people in the wood had dropped the package, and Deborah and Sally, who had been into the wood for catkins, both denied all knowledge of it. Mrs Bradley believed them. She gave the matter careful consideration, and then asked first Obury and then Mansell about it. She told them her suspicion that it had been 'planted', and received in return a direct answer from each man. Neither used aspirin in any form whatsoever, and neither had seen the packet when he had been in the wood.

'And I've been around that badgers' sett enough,' added Obury.

She went to Tiny Fullalove. He said that he had seen the packet but had taken no notice of it. He was potting at the grey squirrels, he said. He and Will North had the devil of a job to keep down the little pests.

Mrs Bradley had heard about the grey squirrels from Will North, but she thought that Tiny's balance would not be sufficiently controlled yet to make shooting a very satisfying pastime.

She did not say this to Tiny, since she did not wish to appear to doubt him, but she decided that, after all, it would be as well to interview Emming in case he heard of her questioning the others.

He received her suspiciously, but agreed that he had been in the spinney.

'I'm writing a little book on fungi,' he said in a surly tone which showed unwillingness to give her any information. He denied having seen the packet, but added, in a disagreeable tone, that it was not his business to act as a blasted park-keeper. Mrs Bradley, interested to note how seriously her previous visit had upset him, returned to the manor house.

Here Jonathan had news.

'The police have got a move on at last!' he said. 'Bill Fullalove is going to be exhumed.'

Mrs Bradley rang up the Chief Constable.

'Have the insurance doctor present? Yes, if you like. This is all a lot of ballyhoo, you know. There is no reason whatever to suspect that Fullalove was poisoned!'

'There are some grounds for suspecting that a fraud has been worked on the insurance company, though,' said Mrs Bradley. 'I want the insurance doctor to be allowed to help carry out the autopsy, and I want to be there myself at the exhumation.'

'No place for a woman!'

'It is a place for a knowledgeable citizen,' said Mrs Bradley, serenely. 'If I never see anything worse than the slightly decomposed body of a healthy man, I shall account myself fortunate.'

The exhumation was carried out three nights later under the usual conditions of darkness and secrecy. The morbid ritual had been begun during the daylight hours, when about half the necessary quantity of earth had been removed. The rest of the soil and the coffin itself came up at between ten o'clock and midnight.

By the light of hurricane lamps the damp coffin was transported to the vicar's tool-shed, emptied that day for the purpose. A couple of trestles supported a stout board – actually the sexton's fowl-house door, the birds being lodged for the night in a derelict hen-house at the bottom of the doctor's garden. This hen-house had been coopered up for the occasion by Abel Wootton, and the hens transported in a cart lent by Farmer Daventry. The cart had been driven by Ed Brown, and was covered with some old tennis nets provided by the doctor's wife and daughter.

Apart from the gruesomeness inseparable from even the most scientific dealings with an exhumed body, there was but one dramatic incident.

The doctor who was there in the interests of the insurance company exclaimed with great assurance:

'Oh, yes! This is the chap I vetted! But he shouldn't have pegged out like that! How long was he out in the snow?'

Nobody could answer this question. The police, Mrs Bradley realized, were satisfied that the exhumation had been, in a sense, unnecessary, for, since there was now no question of fraud, and since it seemed unlikely that the autopsy would show any positive indication of foul play, from the Chief Constable's point of view he had been right all the time.

He said as much to Mrs Bradley as they walked back towards his car.

'Can I offer you a lift?' he added.

'No, thank you,' she replied. 'I am going to walk back.'

'It's after midnight, you know.'

'Yes. I am unlikely to see the fairies, but who knows but what I may encounter the parson's ghost?' She spoke clearly, and heard a shuffling sound from the shadows.

She shone her torch on the gate of the nearest field, opened the gate, closed it carefully behind her, and struck out across the stiff grass.

It was a moonless night, fine and rather cold. There was no path to follow, but, ahead of her, and looming against the sky, she could just make out the trees of Groaning Spinney. By crossing the field steeply uphill on a north-west slant, she knew that she would come to the ghostly gate. She took her time. That there was somebody ahead of her, she knew.

When she topped the rise she involuntarily stood still, for

there, hanging over the gate, was an eerie, dead-white face most curiously lighted as though by phosphorescence.

Mrs Bradley walked nearer. When she was within distance she stopped again, took a small revolver from her skirt pocket, aimed with some care, and was rewarded by the sound of a loud explosion and the disappearance of the face. Then she ran for the shelter of the trees.

There was a path through the wood, but she did not use it. She waited and listened. Nothing stirred.

'You'll be tired before I shall,' she thought, and, with her back against a stout trunk and her revolver re-loaded, she waited patiently for half an hour. Still nothing else stirred. She still waited. At last, after about another half hour, she was rewarded. From the opposite side of the gate came the gleam of a torch. Someone was homeward bound.

Satisfied that she knew who it was, she did not attempt to follow. She remained still for another hour. Nothing else happened. Then she heard shouts in the distance, this time behind her. She turned and saw the light of another torch. Her nephew, who had waited up for her, had grown anxious, and had telephoned the Chief Constable's house until the great man, arriving home, was able to tell him that Mrs Bradley had set off to walk home across the fields. Guessing that she was making for the ghost-gate, Jonathan had come out to find her.

They walked back together, and during the walk she gave an account of the exhumation, its results so far as these were known, and then mentioned the balloon painted with phosphorescence which some practical joker had placed on the haunted gate.

She was up very early next morning and went straight through the Spinney. There were the remains of the balloon, harmless enough to see. She did not touch them. She went back to breakfast, spent an hour in writing to friends and in answering some questions sent to her by the psychiatrist she had left in charge of her London clinic, and then went to Tiny Fullalove's bungalow.

The woman who cooked and cleaned for him came at eight in the morning, got his breakfast, tidied up, went home for an hour, and then returned to cook his lunch. She was coming back for this second visit when Mrs Bradley met her and walked with her to the bungalow.

'I doubt he'm out,' said the woman when Mrs Bradley told her that she had come to see Mr Fullalove. 'He isn't generally here when I come back. He walks round the estate, like, on his job.'

'I've come from Mr Bradley's house,' said Mrs Bradley.

'Well, ee don't want to go all back there profitless,' said the woman, producing the key of the door. 'Will ee come in, then, and wait, mam, or will ee leave me with a message, like, do ee think?'

Mrs Bradley elected to wait. She was assisted in arriving at this conclusion when she saw a typewriter on the side table. Although she knew the answer, she asked the woman whether it was a new one.

'Brand new,' the woman proudly replied. 'Mr Fullalove only brought it in from Cheltenham yesterday. 'Tisn't for him, though, I believe. He brought it in for one of his London friends, who's writing a book, so they tell on. But there! Mr Fullalove's that good, he'd do anything—'

'Indeed?' said Mrs Bradley. 'It looks a very nice one.' She stepped negligently up to it and raised the cover. Then she tore a leaf out of her notebook, inserted it in the machine, and, watched admiringly by the woman, who betrayed neither surprise nor resentment at this free handling of her employer's property, tapped out a hundred words with the rapidity of machine-gun fire.

Then she removed the piece of paper, scanned it, pushed it into her pocket, and waited composedly for Tiny to return. When he came in she remarked on the new machine and said that she had tested it.

'I hope you don't imagine that the anonymous letters were typed on it,' said Tiny, helping himself to a cigarette. 'Oh, sorry! Will you have one of these?'

'No, to both remarks,' said Mrs Bradley. 'I came to ask you a leading question.'

'Yes?' He looked warily at her.

'Who killed Mrs Dalby Whittier? Do you know?'

'I? Of course not! How should I? If I did I should go to the police. I believe she was set upon and robbed.'

'Robbery with violence?'

'Well, I know she was poisoned, but that would mean poor old Bill or me.'

'It *is* rather difficult about the poison,' Mrs Bradley agreed. 'Do you think she had found out something which somebody did not want known?'

'Now, look here,' said Tiny, seating himself astride a chair and resting his arms on the back. 'What *is* all this? Are you asking me whether there was anything fishy about poor old Bill's death, too?'

'Well, *was* there anything fishy about it, Mr Fullalove?'

Tiny drew at his cigarette, took it out of his mouth, looked at the lighted end, and then tossed the cigarette into the fireplace.

'Damned if I know,' he said. 'And you know that female who claims to have been his wife? Well, she came here yesterday to show me her marriage lines. I told her roundly, and not mincing my words, that they were a forgery. She kept calm and said that she could prove differently. I told her to go to hell with her proofs, but I'm pretty certain, somehow, she's telling the truth. One thing, I'm not in actual *need* of poor old Bill's bits and pieces, otherwise I'd be inclined to fight her. As it is, if the lawyers pass her off as Bill's lawful wedded, I suppose I've had it. Oh, well. That's life, all right. But I think Bill might have told me he was married!'

He lit another cigarette and puffed at it, frowning thoughtfully.

'If anything more should occur to you,' suggested Mrs Bradley, 'I wish you would tell me what it is.' Tiny nodded. Talking through the cigarette, he said:

'Sure. If there's anything to tell, I'll tell it fast enough. But I shall tell it to the police, you know. I don't like amateurs muddling about with crime.'

Mrs Bradley took this delicate hint as a sign that her host would be glad if she would terminate her visit. She rose as if to go.

'I hope nothing happens to Mrs Clarence Fullalove,' she said distinctly; and had the satisfaction of seeing Tiny's jaw drop, so that the cigarette fell to the floor. She cackled harshly. 'And one more thing,' she added. 'Are you the practical joker who tied a balloon on to the ghost-gate at the top of Groaning Spinney?'

'No, I'm not. Sounds a kid's trick.'

'I'm pretty sure whose trick it was, and it seems rather like the "ghost" that your friends Mr Mansell and Mr Obury saw on Christmas Eve, after your cousin had been to see my nephew.'

'A balloon?' said Tiny. 'I shouldn't think that would deceive Obury and Mansell. At least, it might deceive Obury – he believes in ghosts!—'

'Don't *you* believe in ghosts, Mr Fullalove?'

'Good heavens, no! Why should I?'

'I thought that perhaps long residence in India—'

'Look here,' said Tiny uneasily, 'what are you getting at?'

'At some tales Ed Brown has to tell.'

'Oh, Brown! He's half-baked!'

'Is he? I hadn't realized that. Oh, well! By the way, there seems no doubt that your cousin died of cold and exposure, just as was thought at first.'

'Then what did you mean by asking me—?'

'Nothing at all. Just one more question, and then I can go back to London: where, on the estate, were those children from the Church choir?'

'The little devils I clouted? You can find out for yourself. I don't see what business you have to come here and interrogate me.'

'I have no business whatever to do so, unless it may be to save you from the hangman.'

'Oh,' said Tiny flippantly, his small green eyes intelligent again and all the exasperation gone from his voice, 'don't you think the little woman of Bill's has done that?'

'If your cousin could be proved to have been a murderer's victim, yes. But there is also the case of Mrs Dalby Whittier to be considered.'

'Look here, sit down again,' said Tiny. When Mrs Bradley had complied with this request, he continued, watching her warily, 'have you got something up your sleeve about that? I had nothing to do with it, you know. She left here on Christmas Eve afternoon. I don't know which way she decided to take to get to the bus stop, but the place where she was found wouldn't be on any possible route, as you probably know. Somebody poisoned her. Because she lived here you think that I must be the guilty person. Is that it?'

'If the police are not to think so, what other explanation can be given?' Mrs Bradley enquired.

'There's only one,' agreed Tiny. 'Bill did it, and then he committed suicide either through fear or remorse.' He laughed. 'You can forget that one. Old Bill never did either of those things.'

'No,' said Mrs Bradley, 'I don't believe he did. Then won't you co-operate with me to find the real murderer?'

'Not if it means sticking my own neck into the noose! Dash it all, I don't want old Bill's memory to be mud, but he's dead, when all's said and done, and it wouldn't help him for me to get myself hanged.'

This reasonable point of view won Mrs Bradley's approval. 'When do you expect to recall your dogs and cats from their foster-homes?' she enquired. Tiny's face twisted. She thought he was going to cry.

'He's hard enough to commit a dozen murders,' said her nephew. 'The question is one of motive. *Why* should he have poisoned the woman? That's the question. And, equally, why should he have let that cottage of his to this supposed wife of Bill's? Dash it all, if she can prove her case, she's Tiny's worst enemy! Why should he go out of his way to help her to stay in the district?'

'What would you say is the simplest mathematical proposition?' Mrs Bradley enquired.

'Eh? Oh, two and two make four, I suppose. Why?'

'There *is* an answer,' said Mrs Bradley mildly.

CHAPTER 14

The Beginning of the End

'Alle we shule deye, thath us like ylle.'
Anonymous, c.1300

Mrs Bradley carried out her promise to leave the Cotswolds in order to visit her London clinic, but her return was to be sooner than Tiny Fullalove supposed.

'Not that anything more is likely to come out about the deaths,' said Jonathan, gloomily. 'It seems to me that the police are entirely lost. I don't know whether they'll call in Scotland Yard. I should almost think they would, as Mrs Dalby Whittier was really a London woman. But apart from the murder, which I suppose *will* be solved sooner or later, I still wish we could lay this anonymous letter-writer by the heels.'

'I still think it must be somebody in the village,' said Deborah, 'but I do wish I knew what you two were talking about the other day. I've racked my brains over and over, and I still can't imagine—'

'That's because you're prejudiced,' said Jonathan. 'Mind you, with regard to this last letter to Aunt Adela, well, Obury or Mansell would be certain to mention that they had met her. That widens the thing out a good deal, because they've heaps of acquaintances, I expect, because of their jobs. They must belong to societies.'

'Yes, that might account for the *last* anonymous letter,' agreed

Deborah, 'but it doesn't account for the others. We know that the first letter came from Mrs Dalby Whittier, and the others *may* have come from Tiny Fullalove, but, if they did – and I still can't see Tiny as an anonymous scribe – would he be likely to use the word? I shouldn't have thought that even the Authorized Version of the Psalms was in his memory, let alone the older form. What do you say, Aunt Adela?'

'I am on the point of departure,' Mrs Bradley replied. 'You had better work it out for yourself.'

'But I haven't a clue,' complained Deborah.

'Oh, yes, you have. It was you who put your finger on the spot. It had nothing to do with the vicar, so you ought to be able to—'

'But I don't want to!' said Deborah, turning very pale. 'It can't be what I think?'

'Oh, yes, it is,' said Mrs Bradley, nodding solemnly. 'Don't be afraid of the truth.'

'I wish you would tell me what you're both talking about,' said Jonathan, glancing from one to the other. 'Aren't we still referring to Robert Emming?'

'Yes, of course we are,' said Mrs Bradley.

After one startled stare, Jonathan laughed heartily. Deborah joined in. Mrs Bradley cackled.

'Well, if *that's* the best you can do,' said her nephew, 'you can keep your word-associations for your text-books! In any case, if you and Deb and I could work that one out, couldn't the anonymous letter-writer?'

'Now that *is* a thought!' agreed his aunt. Deborah looked dubious.

'It's rather – subtle,' she said.

Mrs Bradley did not debate the point, for it seemed to her self-evident. She returned to London next day and found herself involved in her own affairs for almost a week. But on the Friday evening it seemed advisable to give her hard-worked young secretary a break.

'Laura,' she said, 'take the weekend off and report for duty on Tuesday immediately after lunch.'

'Hot dog!' said Laura joyously. 'That means I need not catch a train back until after breakfast. Are you sure you can spare me?'

Mrs Bradley reassured her, and, having seen her off on the six o'clock train, she returned to her Kensington house and continued to cope with certain arrears of work which her holiday in the Cotswolds had made inescapable.

On the Saturday morning she spent four busy hours at her clinic, but on the Saturday afternoon she received by special messenger an invitation to join a friend of hers at the Ideal Home Exhibition. Mrs Bradley telephoned the friend and learned, not altogether to her surprise, that no such invitation had been issued.

She was greatly intrigued and not at all alarmed to discover that she was to have been the victim of a plot. She believed a genuine mistake to have been out of the question; the invitation had been brought by the special messenger with her friend's compliments, and the friend was named. However, she decided that a few elementary precautions would scarcely be out of place.

She had sent the messenger back with a written acceptance, and then went in her own car to the village of Wandles Parva, where she had her country house. It was all rather fun. She inspected her treasures, had tea in the housekeeper's room, dined at the village inn off rabbit pie and stewed rhubarb, and took the London road at just after eight.

The night was overcast and promised rain. The car burst a tyre just outside Guildford, and after the slight delay whilst George changed the wheel, she and her man went into the Lion for a drink and a snack.

'Have we been followed, George?' Mrs Bradley enquired as they sat at a small table. George had been provided with a pint, and his employer (out of deference to the rhubarb, of whose unsweetened effects she was dubious), had chosen a loathsome but efficacious mixture of port and brandy. The chauffeur set down his tankard.

'I am inclined to think so, madam. I could take the stretch into Esher a bit faster if you should wish it.'

'Do so, George. We might as well try their mettle. Swallow, George, and let us go out to the car under the cover afforded by this large and animated party which I see is preparing to leave.'

But there was no question of their being followed for long. George, a sedate and careful driver as a rule, had the itch common to all chauffeurs – he wanted to find out just how fast the car could go. It was almost new. He had run in the engine carefully and with love. The car was spoiling for a test. He passed other vehicles as though they were standing still, and, apart from his passage through towns, did not slow up until he reached Esher hill. From there, steady and unspectacular progress brought the car into Kingston, from thence to Richmond, and so home.

Mrs Bradley went to bed at just before midnight. She lay awake for half an hour and then passed into her usual refreshing but hair-trigger slumber. She was awakened by a sound so slight that less keen ears, or a sleeper less accustomed to wake easily, would not have detected it.

The sound came from the narrow, iron-railed verandah which decorated the first floor of the tall, old house. Mrs Bradley stretched out a claw-like hand and pressed the starting-knob of the radio-gramophone which she had installed as a burglar alarm some months previously.

There was a slight whirring sound from the apparatus, and then the most uncarthly sound of seven dogs barking at once. She had never had occasion to use this record before, but there was no doubt of its efficacy now. There was a crash, then came cries and shouts from her rudely awakened servants, and the sound of feet on the staircase. Her French cook, Henri, forewarned, came bounding in, flourishing his carving knife. There followed a Gallic screaming from his wife. This was Mrs Bradley's French maid, who, previously rehearsed, was issuing commands and injunctions to the ghostly and intangible dogs.

Mrs Bradley switched off the radiogram and switched on the light. The bedroom curtain stirred a little more freely than usual. She suggested to Henri that he should descend to the area to find out whether anyone was hurt. She herself dressed quickly and went into the tiny front garden to reassure the neighbourhood.

Henri, threatening a fallen man with the carving knife, was blowing vigorously at the same time on a police whistle. To his subsequent disgust, his employer, having accepted a statement from the injured man, poured a glass of gin over the fellow's waistcoat and explained him to the police as being drunk and having fallen down her area steps. She added that he was a guest and that he was still on enclosed premises.

'He can't do much more harm at present,' she said, in response to Henri's lamentations that the man was not to be charged. 'I have another enemy who already has more than an idea, I fancy, that I am on his track. But you are a brave man, Henri, and I value your services beyond rubies.'

Henri still wagged his head reprovingly at her, and then he shrugged and laughed.

'The dogs on the record, they are magnificent, madame. The man might have broken his neck.'

'I am rather sorry he did not. It would have saved trouble in the end,' Mrs Bradley responded. She returned to Jonathan's manor house next day, taking her small revolver with her. The injured man had been carrying a Commando knife, and although he declared, probably truthfully, that he always carried it, and that it was a souvenir of the war, she had thought it best to deprive him of it.

'I shall not keep it,' she had told him. 'That might seem dishonest. But if you want it you will have to get it.' And she had given a flick of her supple wrist and lofted the handy little weapon on to her roof. 'And only just in time,' she had added severely, 'for here come the police, and a nice thing for you if they found *that* on you and I charged you with breaking and entering! The next time you become my guest, Mr Fullalove, I shall be obliged if you will leave your weapons at home!'

'I'd forgotten the damned thing!' growled Tiny. 'And the police will have to call an ambulance. I've busted my knee again!'

Mrs Bradley took no special precautions on the journey down to Jonathan's house, except the special precaution of going by car instead of by train. She drove by way of Maidenhead, Henley and Oxford, and told George not to hurry. The flat Middlesex fields faded into the sky. The landscape between Hounslow and Maidenhead was green-grey, blue-grey and brown with the promise of spring. There were, on both sides and in front, the ineffable width of the sky and right to the dim horizon the bright March ploughing.

Maidenhead was a bridge across a river, a congested High Street, and the witchcraft of Maidenhead Thicket, all scrub and hawthorn bushes and muddy, secret little paths. Henley was old houses and a straight stretch of water, followed by a Roman fair-mile of slightly uphill road.

Broad roadside boundaries of weeds and nettle, deep, straight-sided ditches, grass which would later grow as high as hay, woods through which the early spring sunlight was chequered and dazzled the eyes, accompanied the car to the bridge at Dorchester and past the long length of Dorchester Abbey. Soon the car passed the strange flat buildings of Littlemore, and so through Iffley and over Magdalen Bridge to the Mitre.

Mrs Bradley would have preferred to spend the evening in Oxford, and to have visited the theatre, (which was giving *Great Catherine* and *Androcles and the Lion* on the same bill), but she was anxious to reach Jonathan's house at a reasonable hour so she compromised by visiting friends in North Oxford and staying to tea. She set out for Cheltenham at six.

There was daylight left. George, realizing that his instructions of the morning were now to be disregarded, accelerated as soon as

Oxford was left behind. He had taken the Woodstock Road, and the landscape became ghostly. By the time they reached Chipping Norton it was dark. It had been the chauffeur's own fancy to take the Woodstock Road instead of the shorter and more usual route westward through Eynsham, Witney and Burford, and Mrs Bradley often wondered afterwards what had prompted his decision, for at just beyond Chipping Norton the car ran out of petrol.

'I can't think what's happened, madam,' said George, greatly distressed. 'I filled up in Oxford while you were lunching at the Mitre. I thought we had enough already to take us through, but to make quite sure I saw the tank filled at the Long Wall Street garage. I can't make it out at all. I'm very sorry, madam.'

'Are we leaking?' Mrs Bradley enquired.

'No, madam. There seems nothing wrong. All the same, we've run dry. My best plan would be to walk back into Chipping Norton and bring back a man and some cans of juice. I've got coupons for more than we shall want. We've less than another forty miles to do all told. I can get the garage chap to help look for a leak if he helps me to carry the petrol. I'll fix it, madam, don't you worry.'

'I should not dream of worrying, George. I have implicit faith in you. Such implicit faith that – never mind. Do as you suggest.'

As soon as her man had gone, she took out her little revolver, inspected it, settled herself comfortably and awaited her chauffeur's return. She was not seriously anticipating danger, but she could not help wondering what would have happened if the car had taken the Burford road and had stopped before it reached Northleach.

She blamed herself for the theft of the petrol – for that was what it had been; she was clear about that. George had brought the car round to the house of her friends at just after four, and she, knowing that she was staying until six, had sent out to tell him to go and get some tea and not to hurry over it, but to leave the car where it was.

It must have been during his absence that the petrol had been siphoned out of the tank. The street was a very quiet one. It would have been easy enough for anybody with sufficient nerve to have done the deed whilst the party inside the house were in the drawing room, which overlooked the back garden. Between four o'clock and five the chances were that not a soul had been about.

It might have been the work of an ordinary petrol thief, but she could not help chuckling at the thought of a baffled enemy waiting to waylay her somewhere along the stretch of lonely highway beyond the Cirencester crossroads, and she was still conjuring up a picture of the scene when George, who had his own methods of persuading garage hands into action, came back with two young men in overalls and four gallons of petrol in cans.

Mrs Bradley did her part by rewarding them handsomely for their trouble. There was general agreement that the tank did not leak, and George, who had been informed by Henri of a cat-burglar whom his employer had deliberately shielded, took no chances, but drove Mrs Bradley into Stanway, and almost to Beckford before turning south through Bishops Cleeve for Cheltenham.

'And now for Mr Emming,' said Mrs Bradley, 'for it is our duty to protect the general public.'

Once out of Cheltenham George hurried. But nothing untoward happened. Mrs Bradley and her man were hungry, but as soon as they reached the manor house, where Jonathan and Deborah were awaiting them, Mrs Bradley merely popped her head out of the car, greeted them, intimated that she would soon be back, and George drove on up the village street and stopped at Emming's lodgings.

The carpenter and his wife were in bed. Mrs Bradley knew this from the absence of lights. She did not leave her car. She sat and waited. Emming turned up on a motorcycle two hours later.

George closed in on one side and Mrs Bradley on the other as he dismounted.

'Well, and how did you find Oxford looking, cully?' George enquired, in the over-familiar accents of insobriety. Emming, who, in the darkness, had not noticed Mrs Bradley, drew away from George and said nervously:

'You go to bed, old boy! Just you go off to bed.'

'You were in Oxford,' said George thickly. 'You siphoned my petrol.' Emming shoved him off.

'You be damned for a liar!' he said. 'Of course I haven't been in Oxford. Get out of here and go home!'

'So that's two of you,' said Jonathan soberly, when he had heard the story of Tiny's exploit on the balcony. 'You twice, and——'

'Two of us? Not Ed Brown?'

'What made you think of Ed? No, it was the gamekeeper, Will North, who nearly caught it. Lucky for him he's an observant, cautious sort of bloke, otherwise he might have had his head blown off.'

The essentials of the story, which Jonathan related with great liveliness, were that, on the second morning after Mrs Bradley's departure for London, Will North had been out on his rounds when he saw a shotgun leaned up against the haunted gate at the top of Groaning Spinney. Wondering who could have left it there, since neither Jonathan nor Tiny was likely to have done so, Will went up to the gun and had a look at it. He did not touch it at first because he thought he knew every gun on the estate and possessed six or seven of his own. He could not recognize the gun, so he went up to the fence, ducked through it to come out on the side against which the gun was leaning, and was just in time to hold up Ed Brown who was coming that way with a wagon. Ed had been about to get down to open the gate.

It was Will's sharp eyes which had spotted the thread tied to the trigger. He realized that the gun was at full cock. Then occurred a curious incident. Will had gone forward to warn Ed, and the carter had walked towards him to see the thread. At the same instant a bird which had accompanied Ed across three fields also saw the thread, and, apparently deciding that it would help in making its nest, it had pecked at the string. The gun went off, fortunately into the air, so that it did no harm to anybody, and the bird flew on to Ed's shoulder and chattered complainingly of the noise.

Ed was for picking up the gun, but Will restrained him. He himself remained on guard over the gun, and sent Ed for Jonathan.

Mrs Bradley listened with the most intense interest to this story.

'Then, as I see it, Ed *was* the most likely person to have been killed or injured,' she said. 'I wonder whether it was known that he had to come that way?'

'A good many people *could* have known it, but to my mind it leads back to Tiny Fullalove,' said Jonathan. 'And if it *is* Tiny, you're not too safe here, are you? After all, he *told* you he'd hurt his knee again, but we haven't any proof of it, you know.'

'If you don't mind having me, I should like to stay here again for a bit,' said Mrs Bradley. She looked extremely cheerful. 'It is not an easy matter to break into this house, and in the open I am prepared to take my chance. As to Mr Fullalove, I can soon find out from my good young friend Detective-Inspector Gavin of Scotland Yard whether he is in hospital, and, if he is, where.'

'Could he give any explanation as to what he was doing on your verandah?'

'Not a satisfactory one. He said he had mistaken the house.'

'But you think—?'

'I really don't know what I think, child. One hates to think that one might be the corpse in the library!'

CHAPTER 15

The Gun

'Then sing, ye Birds, sing, sing a joyous song!
And let the young Lambs bound
As to the Tabor's sound!'

William Wordsworth

Politicians whose lives are threatened go about with a police guard but are expected to act as though assassinations are figments of the imagination. Mrs Bradley behaved in this way, but she was not a politician and she had no police guard. Her nephew, therefore, insisted upon accompanying her wherever she went. This chivalrous conduct worried Mrs Bradley because she knew how horribly scared Deborah must be all the time that Jonathan was out of the house.

She tried to persuade him not to come, but he was determined to escort her. What was more, he always carried a gun.

'The anemones are beginning to come out,' said Mrs Bradley on the third morning of her stay. 'I shall go out today and gather them.'

'Oh, no, not today!' said Jonathan. 'To begin with, they fade as soon as you pick them, and then I'm on the bench from ten o'clock onwards.' Mrs Bradley grinned triumphantly.

'I know,' she said. 'Just for once, I want to go out by myself.'

Jonathan and (for his sake) Deborah protested, but Mrs Bradley had an object in mind beyond wood anemones, so at just after nine she set off, accompanied by Will North as far as the village. At the lane by the inn she left Will, and turned up by the same way as the party had taken on a previous occasion when Mansell had been their guide.

Her objective was the lonely bungalow, and her business was with the woman in the blue dress. How far she was justified in obtruding herself into this woman's affairs she neither knew nor cared, but she was still intrigued by the theory that the woman was Tiny Fullalove's wife and not Bill Fullalove's widow.

The uphill walk seemed shorter than it had done on the previous occasion, and soon she was within sight of the long barrow. She had plenty of time on her hands and had told Deborah not to wait lunch, so she walked on up the hill to find out whether Mansell had been able to begin work.

She could make him out from some distance away. He was certainly digging and he had two companions. One she recognized at once as Miles Obury. The other, when she came nearer to him, proved to be the young choirmaster, Emming. Of village helpers there was no sign at first, and then she noticed Ed Brown. He was on his knees pegging out a measuring string, and Mansell's body at first had screened him from view.

All four men were so much absorbed in what they were doing that they did not notice her until she spoke.

'Good morning,' she said. 'Can I be of any assistance? You all look extremely busy.'

'Yes, we are,' said Mansell, leaning on his shovel. 'That's far enough, Ed. It's only for a first trial. If you *can* spare a minute, Mrs Bradley, I wonder if you would mind climbing to the lower end of the barrow and planting this stick as soon as I ask you to stop?'

'It would give me great pleasure,' Mrs Bradley replied. 'You wish to obtain an orientation, no doubt.'

Mansell neither contradicted nor confirmed this view. He said:
'It is just to test a theory. Now, Miles, you climb to the upper

end of the barrow, and plant *this* stick. Then we shall have the angle we want, I hope.'

'Do I stop when you call out to Mrs Bradley?' enquired Obury, taking the stout white stake which Mansell handed to him.

'No. You are to plant your stick when you hear my whistle. I don't know whether I shall sound that first, or call out to Mrs Bradley. All right. Off you go. Please don't hurry, Mrs Bradley. We are not at all pressed for time. I don't expect to attempt more than the beginning of my trench this morning.'

Mrs Bradley began her upward climb. She had further to go than Obury, but her walk was not as steep as his. She took her time, as Mansell had suggested, and was not at all surprised to hear his whistle before she had reached her objective. She looked to her right and saw Obury beginning to knock his stake into the turf with the small mallet with which he had been provided.

Then, faint but clear, came the order to her to stop. She stopped obediently and knocked her stake firmly into the ground. Mansell had a theodolite. She saw him motioning first to Ed Brown and then to Emming. The two of them took up positions directly in line with the two points set up respectively by herself and Obury.

Mansell cupped his hands and called to them to return to the dig. They did this leisurely, and, by the time Mrs Bradley was back, two measuring lines at an angle of about sixty degrees, with a centre line bisecting them, had been pegged out by Ed and Emming under Mansell's skilful directions.

The men then began to dig three trenches and Mrs Bradley noticed that Emming worked faster although not as skilfully as Ed. Mansell took no part in the actual digging and Mrs Bradley, perceiving that there was nothing useful that she could do, walked onwards up the hill.

As soon as she gained the further side of the barrow, she made a detour and crawled through a spiny gap between the hawthorns. Then she made a fairly long cast across a hilly field and so up from the east to the top of the barrow.

'Unseemly curiosity of an elderly psychiatrist,' she said to herself as she spread out her waterproof, lay on it and peered cautiously over the top of the ancient mound. The four men were still working. This time Mansell had taken up a shovel and was as busy as the others. When the men spoke she could hear quite clearly what they said.

As she watched, Emming stopped work, wiped his face and then began to clean his tool with a stone which he had picked up. At this, Mansell consulted his wristwatch, and suggested that it was time to knock off for lunch. Emming went towards the village and the two friends struck off in the same direction, although soon Mrs Bradley could see that their path diverged from his. Ed Brown sat down on a pile of sacks which the excavators apparently had brought with them, and took out his countryman's bundle of food and a can of tea.

Suddenly, from the woods to the right came Will North, as usual carrying his gun and with his gamekeeper's bag slung over his shoulder, but without his dog Worry. He called out a greeting to Ed and came over to have a chat. The three men had quite disappeared. None of them had given so much as a glance towards where Mrs Bradley was lying, and she, to preserve secrecy, had prudently withdrawn so that the slope of the barrow hid her.

Will and Ed talked for ten minutes by Mrs Bradley's watch. She had crept forward again. Then Will went off on his own errand, whatever that was, and Ed sat down again.

To the left there was a flurry of birds; then, (at the same instant, it seemed to Mrs Bradley), there were the sounds of two rifle shots, and Ed tumbled into the trench that he had been digging. Will North came running, and so did Mrs Bradley. Both knelt by the trench. Ed turned over very slowly and favoured Will with a wink.

'If you wouldn't mind acting like so be you thought I was done for, Will,' he murmured, 'you'd be doin' me a favour like them there old birds over yonder.'

'You aren't hurt, then?' enquired Will.

'Not a hair singed, but that ain't somebody's fault,' muttered Ed. 'I knowed summat was up. Felt it all day, like. Felt it ever since that there old gun went off by Parson's Gate.'

Mrs Bradley got up and gazed as though with compassion and grief into the trench. Save to a bird or from an aeroplane, Ed, she knew, was invisible except from very close range. She spoke to Will North.

'Be off, Will, as though you'd gone for help. If you see anybody don't speak to him unless you can trust him absolutely. Come back, if you can, with the Woottons. They're staunch enough and can keep their tongues still. By the way, where's Worry?'

'That's what I'd like to know,' Will replied. 'Not like him to go off on his own this long. Sent him out for his walk, same as I always do, but he hasn't come back. I was looking for him when I saw Ed first.'

He strode away. Mrs Bradley sat down on her waterproof and waited. Will was gone almost an hour. He came back with the two gardeners and with George, Mrs Bradley's chauffeur, who had been giving the brothers a hand with a motor mowing machine which had gone wrong. The three men had a hurdle with them, a bit of local colour which Mrs Bradley welcomed.

Solemnly the grinning Ed was raised from the trench and laid on the hurdle. Mrs Bradley spread her waterproof over him and the four men bore his light weight off towards Will North's cottage.

Mrs Bradley had seen where the bullet had snicked up the earth on the edge of the barrow. She picked up Ed's fork and excavated carefully, sprinkling earth by handfuls into the trench as though she might be covering up bloodstains. There was little hope, she felt, of finding the pellet. It would have gone too deeply into the soil.

She was still engaged in her deception when the three men who had gone off to lunch returned.

'Hullo! Ed Brown gone home?' asked Emming. Mrs Bradley pointed to the trench which was now almost half-full of soil.

'You'll have to leave your digging for today, I'm afraid,' she said gravely. 'The police, you know. Ed Brown was shot at, just after half-past twelve.'

The comma indicated in her voice prevented the statement from being a lie, but this fine shade of meaning was lost upon her hearers.

'Ed Brown?'

'Shot?'

'Who did it? – Some damned carelessness somewhere!'

Mrs Bradley replied to the last speaker, who happened to be Obury.

'There is no proof of who did it. As to carelessness, it seems to me that criminal negligence is the mildest description to apply to the occurrence.'

'Negligence? – Well, yes. There seems no reason to be shooting over this hill. I suppose some idiot saw a rabbit and took a pot shot. Sort of person who ought not to be allowed to handle a gun.'

'I thought I saw Will North,' said Emming.

'Well, I want to get back,' said Mrs Bradley; but back where she did not say. 'As for Will North, I fancy he can be trusted with a gun!' Mansell looked in a gloomy way at his dig, and then began to gather his impedimenta together. Obury and Emming helped him. The last Mrs Bradley saw of them was three rather dejected-looking figures making for the village by the route they had followed to go off to lunch.

She turned her back on them, and was soon at the lonely cottage. There was no sign of anybody about the place. The little garden was springing to life, but it was overgrown and untidy with plants that should have been cut down or dug up during the previous autumn. The windows were closed; the door – for Mrs Bradley tried it very cautiously – was locked.

Nevertheless she knocked. She even went so far as to peer in through the curtained panes. It certainly seemed as though the occupant was out, but to make certain she knocked a second and then a third time, but still there was no response.

Mrs Bradley was about to give up when she saw the woman she wanted coming down the hill from the direction of the village.

'Good day,' said the woman. 'I am sorry, but I'm not a churchgoer.'

'And I,' responded Mrs Bradley, 'am not a district visitor. I am wondering whether I can interest you—'

'And I don't want to buy anything,' said the woman. 'Just because I've come into a bit of money—'

'Oh, you *have* come in for it, then? There has been a great deal of talk, naturally, but none of us really *knew*.'

'People should mind their own business and let me mind mine. But villages are all alike!'

'Are you thinking of settling in the village, I wonder?'

'I don't know yet. There's a lot of things to see to.'

'There must be. Oh, well, I suppose I might have saved myself a journey. I wasn't going to try to sell you anything, you know. I just wondered whether I could interest you—'

'Well, in what?'

'In the death of Mr Clarence Fullalove,' said Mrs Bradley, pronouncing this name with great distinctness. The woman eyed her for a moment. Then she said:

'You'd better come in and sit down. I was just going to make a cup of tea.'

'Thank you, I never drink tea quite so soon before lunch, but I would very much like to come in.'

The cottage was almost unfurnished. There was nothing in the room except a small deal table and a couple of chairs. The floor had one rug and was otherwise bare. There were curtains at the window but they were faded and shrunk.

'It's not much of a place,' said the woman, 'but it will do until I get my rights, which I *shall* do, believe you *me*!'

She was a spiteful-looking creature, Mrs Bradley thought. Men had been egged on and nagged on to commit murder by such women. Referring to the question of the 'rights' she asked:

'Are they likely to be contested?'

'They'd better not be! That fine brother-in-law of mine would like to see me slip up, but he won't have the pleasure, thank you! However, I wouldn't put much past him! I've had the place broken into twice already since I've been here. I've got proofs, you know, of who I am, besides my marriage lines, and you might as well be a witness just in case of accidents. If I show you, will you stand by me if anything gets stolen? You seem respectable, even if you can't keep your nose out of other people's business.'

'I am here on my own business,' said Mrs Bradley mildly. 'To-day a man was deliberately shot at, not so far from here. I want to know whether you saw anybody carrying a gun.'

'Shot at? What goes on in this place, for goodness' sake? My poor old hubby found dead in the snow, a poor old girl poisoned, and now a shooting match! Thank God I've never had to live in the country! I like a bit of peace and quiet, not these sort of wild goings-on!'

She laughed nervously. Then she pulled open the table drawer, jerking angrily at it when it stuck half-way. Her hands were trembling.

'See here,' she said. 'Here's my lines and here's my proofs. What have you got to say to that?'

'Nothing,' Mrs Bradley replied, picking up the marriage certificate, 'except how interested I am.'

The husband had been Mr Clarence Fullalove, she noticed. The date was 1922. She handed back the documents.

'Strange you married so young,' she said.

'As for anybody with a gun,' said the woman, 'I met a tall, black-haired fellow who passed the time of day, and was potting at every bird and rabbit he saw.'

'Oh, yes?' said Mrs Bradley. 'That scarcely sounds an accurate description to me.' She raised her voice. 'Worry! Worry!' she called. A yelp, not very far distant, answered her.

The woman ran over and shut the window, and then turned to face Mrs Bradley. But Mrs Bradley put her aside and wrenched open the kitchen door. She called the dog's name again. There was no doubt about the answer.

'Where is the key? I am going to let him out,' said Mrs Bradley composedly. The woman swore at her.

CHAPTER 16

The History of Worry

'Follow on pitie, flee trouble and debate.'
William Dunbar

'But whatever made you think of *her*?' asked Jonathan, when the ecstatic Worry had been restored to Will North.

'I felt that Worry had either been injured or decoyed. I realized that the woman wanted to keep me at her bungalow. There seemed no reason why she should. I guessed she had seen me with Will. I met him out on the hill. I knew she must have heard the shot which was meant for Ed Brown. She did not mention it. The shots from that gun which was tied to the gate at the top of Groaning Spinney were meant either for Ed or for Will. It seems likely, from what was attempted today, that Ed was the intended victim, but, now I know that his dog was stolen, I believe that Will may equally be among the hunted. Worry hates that gate. In other words, the dog did not see a ghost that day: he smelt somebody who didn't or doesn't like him.'

Jonathan began to laugh.

'If you don't know what made you suspect that she had the dog, why don't you say so straight out?' he demanded. 'Now, look – and don't hedge over this! – what about this shooting business today? Whatever the truth about the shotgun that was tied to the gate, was today's bullet really meant for Ed?'

'Well, Ed seemed to think it was. If so, it's a good thing he is second cousin to the birds! He thinks they saved his life for him today. By the way, one of Will's guns is missing. It will be discovered that the shot was fired from it, I think. Worry might have been decoyed so that the gun could be stolen.'

'But Worry might not have been at the cottage. Will usually takes him out with him.'

'Yes, that is true. You know, there is one small point that rather bothers me in this case. We heard that Ed Brown did not like what he saw of Tiny Fullalove in India. He did not like his treatment of Army mules. Yet when I first saw Tiny he had the company of those two affectionate cats and of those two obviously adoring dogs. I wonder what Worry thinks of him? And we still haven't traced those animals, by the way.'

'Oh, well, a man may be fond enough of his own animals and not kind to other people's, don't you think?' said Jonathan, playing to the opening gambit as usual.

'It could be so, but I should think it is unusual. A dog-lover usually gets on with all dogs. A cat-addict likes everybody's cats.'

'Mules might come in a different category, though, from domestic pets. They can be the most obstinate brutes. I think maybe I will talk to Ed upon the subject. Not that he's an easy chap to get anything out of. I might be able to find out, too, what ideas he has about that shot. If it really was intended for him it's time the police made an arrest. I suppose you suspect Tiny Fullalove?'

'He is the one person I do *not* suspect. I took the trouble to ring up the police, and my friend Inspector Gavin was able to supply me with the name of the hospital to which he was taken following his fall from my Kensington balcony. He is still there and unable to walk. It was very clever of him to fall so clumsily.'

'Yes, I see. That gives us something to think about. You know, if young Emming had been murdered instead of his mother, we might have known by this time where we were.'

'You mean she kept him? Supplied him with money? Yes, there isn't much doubt about that.'

'I imagine not. And she may have become very tired of it. But there seems no earthly reason why *he* should have murdered *her*. Besides, he's got nothing against Ed Brown, so far as we know.'

'If Ed Brown is in possession of some important information,' said Mrs Bradley, 'Mr Emming might well have something against him! And then, as I say, there's Will North, who noticed the piled-up snow on that badger-watchers' platform. As for Tiny, I'm afraid we can't prove that he came to my house with the intention of handing me my quietus. He may have come merely to have a quiet chat, or had mistaken the house, as he said.'

Jonathan looked unconvinced.

'Well, I don't know,' he said. 'Anyway, let's tackle Ed and see what he's got to tell us.'

Will North was not at home when Mrs Bradley arrived, so, to keep up the fiction that the house was supposed to be empty, Mrs Bradley left it and Ed was commanded by Jonathan to nip across to the cottage belonging to the Wootton brothers. These were both at home and had been let into the secret because they lived far too near Will to be kept in ignorance of the fact that he had a permanent guest.

'Now, then, Ed,' said Mrs Bradley, when she had joined him, 'I'm going to ask you some questions. You need not answer them, but if you choose to answer you must be exact.'

'Questions?' said Ed. 'I've had questions enough from Mr Tiny! "I beant a liar," I says, "without good cause." I never told him nawthen. But, oh, mam, I know ee mean it for the best, but I be fair sick of being cooped up here like a broody old hen.'

'I'm sure you are,' Mrs Bradley agreed. 'And I don't think that what I have to ask you will have any bearing on what Mr Tiny wanted you to tell him. Here goes, then: First, how did the dog Worry get to Mrs (well, we'll call her for the moment) Bill Fullalove?'

'He followed Mr Tiny,' replied Ed, who seemed relieved at the form of the question. 'Any dog – and that dog in partic'lar – would follow Mr Tiny anywheres.'

'But mules wouldn't?'

'Mules, mam?'

'I understood that Mr Tiny did not get on with mules.'

Ed scowled.

'That's right enough. But dogs he did.'

'And Worry followed Mr Tiny to Mrs Bill's. I see. All right, Ed. I think that's all.'

'Thought ee was goin' to ask some questions,' said Ed, looking puzzled.

'I have asked them, Ed. All except one, that is. Can you guess that one, I wonder?'

Ed shook his head. A blackbird which had come to perch on the doorstep found the door open, recognized Ed, sang a satisfied, short aria, and flew on to the carter's head.

'So there you are, you old you, you,' said Ed. Mrs Bradley nodded slowly, and went quietly out of the house.

'Tell Ed to pop back as soon as he can,' she said to Abel Wootton, who accompanied her to the door.

Fortunately Ed was a bachelor, so that there was no Mrs Brown to be soothed, informed, and persuaded to keep her mouth shut, and not to let it be known that Ed was still in hiding in Will North's cottage. To keep up the deception that he was dead, Doctor Fielding had called at Ed's own empty cottage, and a rumour that the police doctor had also seen the corpse was allowed to circulate in the village. A blanketed figure (made up of a couple of bolsters) had been carried solemnly from Will North's cottage to Ed's home, and the village policeman had mounted guard to shoo away inquisitive youngsters.

The deception, as everybody concerned completely realized, could not be kept up for long; there was the question of an inquest, for example; but Mrs Bradley hoped to delay rumour until she was ready with her proofs. These she proposed to test and then to impart in serial form, as it were. She tried them first on the Chief Constable, who was a good deal more shrewd than his conversation sometimes indicated. She went over to see him.

'I don't see what you've got to go on, you know,' said the Chief Constable, who was not too sure that he ought to lend himself to Mrs Bradley's theories. Mrs Bradley slowly shook her head.

'Let us recapitulate,' she said. The Chief Constable settled himself in his own most comfortable armchair, filled his pipe, and settled himself to listen.

'Fire away,' he said.

'Well, first, there is the question of Worry,' said Mrs Bradley.

'Question of what?'

'You mean Who. Worry, the gamekeeper's dog. The story of Worry is brief but significant.'

'Let's have it, then.'

'Very well. I came here first two days before Christmas Eve; in other words, on December the twenty-second. On the following day I went for a walk with Deborah and Jonathan and we saw the ghost-gate at the top of Groaning Spinney. We went on to the Fullaloves' bungalow where I met Tiny. I took an instant dislike to him. I learned later that he was disliked by several other people. My own dislike you may dismiss as mere prejudice, but these others all had some grounds for their distaste.'

'Who are they? – And what were their reasons?'

'My nephew Jonathan did not dislike him *at that time,* so I will mention him first. He grew to dislike him when he learned that Tiny had annoyed Deborah.'

'Yes. Bit of a heel,' said the Chief Constable. 'Forget when I first learned things about him. Wants kicking, but I always thought that.'

'Possibly. His own cousin may have disliked him. I mention Bill next because there is no certain information except that he is said to have given Tiny a black eye. Tiny is not the kind of man to get over a thing like that very easily.'

'You don't suggest he murdered Bill on the strength of it?'

'No. But, all the same, somebody in the village (or somebody who has visited the village recently) wants us to believe that Bill died in the snow as the result of an overdose of aspirin – not an overdose large enough to kill him or large enough to leave distinct traces in the body, but large enough to make him very sleepy. The person who wants us to think that Bill's death was brought about in this way took the trouble to "plant" an empty packet of aspirin tablets where I should find it, and, I have little doubt, watched me pick it up and saw me throw it away.'

'You tampered with evidence?'

'It wasn't evidence, and it might have been misleading. One of the two persons who saw that I was not to be misled had a good but crude try at breaking into my London house a short time ago, whether with the intention of murdering me, terrifying me or of having a confidential chat has not been established.'

'Tiny Fullalove!'

'Yes.'

'But why should he . . . ?'

'Exactly. Why should he give away the aspirin trick if it was the method he himself had used to get rid of his cousin? The inferences are either that he did not get rid of his cousin, but that he knew who did, or else that the aspirin method was not the method used, or else that Bill was not murdered at all but really did die accidentally or did commit suicide. In the last case, Tiny wanted to incriminate some innocent person.'

'Well, what about the dog?'

'I'm coming to the dog. On our way home from the Fullaloves' bungalow we saw him. He was terrified of the gate at the top end of Groaning Spinney. Now I am not a subscriber to the belief that dogs can see ghosts. They may be able to do so, but until there is more evidence that they can, I prefer a rational explanation of some of their reactions. Well, Worry would not pass the gate until his owner came up. In Will North's company the dog showed no more fear. Whatever was frightening about the gate lost its power in Will North's presence. The obvious deduction is not that the dog saw the ghost, but that it had had some unpleasant experience which it connected with the gate when it was by itself. What that experience was we shall probably never know. Will North apparently had no knowledge of it, for he merely remarked that the dog was not usually silly, and passed on his way.'

'You mean Tiny (we'll say) may have kicked or thrashed the dog?'

'We'll not say Tiny, for a moment, if you don't mind. It is much more likely to have been somebody else, but that someone I cannot (honestly) name. At least, not yet, because I haven't named my proofs against him yet.'

'How do you mean?'

'I tell you that I cannot explain yet, but this is what followed. After the gamekeeper and his dog had passed, I happened to look back. A man was leaning over the gate. I deduced at the time that it was Bill Fullalove, whom I had not then met.'

'Leaning over the gate where he was afterwards found dead? Rather a queer coincidence, what?'

'I suppose it might have been so regarded, but, from facts which have come to light since, I am not at all certain that the man *was* Bill. However, he was too far off for me to be certain. Whoever it was, I am pretty certain that it was not Tiny Fullalove. For one thing, we had just left him at the bungalow; for another, well, Tiny is a dog-lover, and, as I have just argued with my nephew, a man who loves his own dogs and is loved by them, is not the most likely person to ill-treat somebody else's dog. Besides, Tiny, as the agent to the estate, would surely have a great sense of the value of a well-trained dog such as Worry, and would be one of the last persons to spoil his spirit by savaging him. Anyhow, that's mere speculation, so far. The next part of the story, as it concerns Worry, is this: somebody coaxed him away and hid him for a time. I advanced the suggestion that it was so that the man who took a pop at Ed Brown could steal one of Will North's guns, but this argument was very properly refuted by my nephew, who pointed out that the gamekeeper's cottage was often enough left empty, with neither the man nor the dog in charge of it.'

'What, then, do you suppose, was the reason for stealing the dog?'

'To entice Will North either away from his own cottage, or into that occupied by this woman.'

'How much easier it would have been,' said the Chief Constable thoughtfully, (apparently ignoring both these theories), 'if Mrs Dalby Whittier had murdered Emming! There we'd have had a clear case. I mean, she's bound to have been keeping him, don't you think? He had no visible means of support except the very small honorarium which he receives as choirmaster. He must have been living on someone, and Mrs Whittier was by far the most likely person, as she was his mother.'

'So my nephew has suggested,' said Mrs Bradley. 'But I'm glad you've mentioned Emming. He was the person I refused to mention just now. I believe him to be a murderer. There is only one difficulty. Why should Emming have killed his mother if she was his only means of support? That's what we have to work out. I *think* I know the answer, and I believe that very soon I can prove it.'

'So you're certain that Emming's our man? I'm not really very much surprised. But what's all this to do with Worry? You found him, I gather, in the cottage now occupied by Bill Fullalove's widow.'

'In spite of the fact that she showed me a certificate of marriage—' began Mrs Bradley.

'She did! Have you seen the trustees?'

'No, I haven't. Tiny Fullalove is bringing a case in his own interest to show that the certificate is a forgery.'

'And is it?'

'I've no idea. I should scarcely think so.'

'Well, then . . .'

'But I don't think the woman is a widow.'

'If she isn't, then the certificate *must* be a forgery.'

'Not necessarily. It could be somebody else's certificate, that is all.'

'But how the devil could she get hold of such a thing?'

'Well, she might even have inherited it, you know.' The Chief Constable shook his head.

'Don't be aggravating,' he said. 'You think that this woman inherited somebody else's – in other words, the real Mrs Fullalove's – marriage lines? I say that that's preposterous!'

'Not under certain circumstances. I myself have a copy of the marriage certificate of my parents.'

'Yes, but you're not suggesting a relationship between the real Mrs Fullalove and this woman, are you?'

'Not a relationship exactly, no.'

'Well, if this woman *isn't* the real Mrs Fullalove she's going to have a pretty thin time when the trustees and their solicitors, and Tiny Fullalove and his, dig up their witnesses.'

'Yes, of course – if the witnesses are still alive.'

'You don't mean . . . Mrs Dalby Whittier and Bill Fullalove?'

'I don't think they were the witnesses.'

'What do you mean, then?'

'I think they were the married couple. Now that we know a little more, everything, in my opinion, points to it.'

'Then what about young Emming? Is he Bill Fullalove's son? I don't believe it!'

'No, he is either his stepson or Tiny's son. Of that I am also convinced. His story, as he told it some weeks ago, is partly true.'

'You can't stop there, woman. I begin to see what you're getting at, but for goodness' sake tell me more!'

'All in good time,' said Mrs Bradley. 'Then there is this question of Will North. To the murderers Will North is dangerous. He saw the unaccountable heap of snow on the badger-watching platform.'

'Why the devil didn't he investigate?'

'He was on his way to the bungalow and to help with—'

'Oh, of course, yes. But, still—'

'Therefore Worry was decoyed so that Will would follow. Will did follow, and would have found his dog, and would probably have been murdered in that cottage, but for the mistake that one of the murderers made.'

'Emming?'

'Emming. He affected to pop at Ed Brown, but I fancy Will North was the target.'

'I'm off to talk to Ed Brown,' said the Chief Constable decidedly. 'You'd better come along, and bring Jonathan.'

'Mr Emming?' said Ed, looking at his questioner with sly amusement. 'Oh, him and me, us get on pretty well together mostly. Fond of birds, he is, and wanting to know their names and where to look for the nests.'

'Is he to be trusted with nests?'

'Oh, yes. He's all right, like. Don't steal no eggs nor nothing. Oh, ah. He's all right.'

'Are you a member of his choir?'

'I be, too and all. Tenor, I be.'

'You really know him very well indeed, then.'

'Well, no, I wouldn't say that. He'm too much of a gentleman, like, for me to say as how I know him.'

'A gentleman? What makes you say that?'

'Well, I reckon he be. Wouldn't you call Mr Tiny a gentleman, mam?'

'You mean that Mr Emming is Mr Tiny's son?'

'Stands to reason, I reckon. Not much doubt Mrs Dalby Whittier was Mr Tiny's wife. If her weren't, her were Mr Bill's wife. I couldn't make no mistake she were wife to one on 'em, and Mr Emming confess to being her son.'

'Yes, but it might be very important to know which of the Fullaloves was Mrs Whittier's man, you know, Ed.'

'Well, if I 'ad to guess, I'd say Mr Bill. Stands to reason Mr Bill wouldn't have taken out no insurance, else. But I reckon, too, as this new young 'ooman, er's Mr Tiny's.'

'Why?' asked Mrs Bradley, deeply interested in this view.

'It's like this,' explained Ed. 'Living by myself I 'ave time to turn things over in my 'ead, like. And what I ben thinkin' is this: Mr Bill never should have died like that. There was summat wrong about it. I reckon as 'ow the two of 'em was going to 'ave the one insurance between 'em, so, payin' only the one premium, either on 'em could benefit, no matter which one died.'

'But the Christian names?' said Mrs Bradley, startled to hear her own theories proceeding from Ed. Ed shook his head pityingly.

'When I was out in India,' he said, 'there was a bit of a case, see? Mr Tiny, 'e was 'ad up for cruelty to an 'Indoo. That's why he come 'ome. It was a real bad case and I 'ad to give my evidence. That's when I found out 'is name's William. Well, Mr Bill bein' called Bill, which 'is name may or may not 'ave been, it made it very orkard in front of the law. So I reckon Mr Bill got 'imself insured, and Mr Tiny was to 'ave the money if anything 'appened to 'im. Whereas, if, as it seemed most likely, it were Mr Tiny as died first, well, nothing amiss about the name – it's still down as William Fullalove. That's why I reckon *this* wife is Mr Tiny's, and the policy were Mr Bill's.'

'I agree with you entirely about the policy, Ed, but I still don't see how you make out that the claimant is Mr Tiny's wife and not Mr Bill's wife.'

'Stands to reason. Nothing 'aven't 'appened to she,' said Ed, with sombre realism. Mrs Bradley nodded.

'Who shot at you, Ed?' she demanded. 'And why were you expecting that someone would?'

'That were Mr Emming,' said Ed. 'Mr Emming helped Mr Tiny move Mrs Dalby Whittier from Groaning Spinney to the place where she were found.'

'How on earth can you know that?'

'I watched the birds. I knowed there were something going on.'

'But not *murder*!'

'Not till I went and 'ad a look.'

'What did you see, then? And where?'

'Nothen but footprints.'

'My nephew, Mr Bradley, saw them, too.'

'Then he knows as much as I do.'

'Did you follow them?'

'Didn't need to. I see old Simon Crow a-flutterin' hisself down along by Farmer Daventry's field. *He* knowed a dead un, I reckon, and I knowed '*im*. There wasn't nothen else to it.'

'Which day was this, Ed?'

'Let me see, now . . . I reckon 'twud a-been Christmas Eve, all right.'

'It couldn't have been! The footsteps you saw were in the snow. It didn't snow until Christmas night.'

'Unreliable witness,' grumbled the Chief Constable, leading the way to his car. 'Home, Bates. Nothing more to be got out of him, I suppose?' he added, as the big car slid over the bridge.

'Nothing at all,' said Mrs Bradley, cheerfully. 'But what he says confirms our own suspicions. Of course, the point about the footprints was rather interesting. They were first seen on Boxing Day. Miss Hughes, Mr Mansell and Mr Obury all saw them.'

'They were seen after that, though, weren't they?'

'Well, perhaps not the same ones. My nephew saw long footprints on the twenty-eighth or twenty-ninth.'

'In Groaning Spinney?'

'Yes. He then found Mr Bill Fullalove's dead body. Presumably that also had been moved.'

'But *rigor mortis*? And the position of the body as it leaned across that gate! Surely he must have died where he was found?'

'There are plenty of gates around here,' said Mrs Bradley. 'I should say that they moved him from one to the other, that's all.'

'Good Lord! That would upset the time scheme of the death completely!'

'Yes, I know, but it is a theory I have held for some time.

'The devil you have! Why, that means that Tiny—!'

'Yes, I know.'

'Well, what do you make of Ed Brown?'

'Lots of things, but nothing very helpful. What do you?'

'Dashed if I know. He's a natural, but he's as sly and as cunning as only a natural can be.'

'Do you think he knows more than he has said?'

'Yes, I do. But how do we get it out of him?'

'I cannot say. Perhaps we shan't need to do so.'

'All that stuff about birds,' said the Chief Constable thoughtfully. 'Never known such a chap for birds – and other wild things, too. And he does know a fair amount about this affair. Do you think a little bird told him?'

'Nothing could be more likely. But it is extremely doubtful whether the same or any other little bird will tell *us*!'

'Will *you* tell *me* something? – What about young Emming?'

'Oh, Emming typed the anonymous letters, that's certain. And Emming knew that his mother wrote the earlier ones. He must have been the person who posted the one that came to Jonathan about Deborah.'

'Couldn't that have been Tiny Fullalove?'

'Well, yes, it might have been. Did you search Emming's lodgings, though, for a typewriter? – And with that I must be going.'

'No, you don't. You're coming indoors again. I want to hear more about all this.'

CHAPTER 17

Point-to-Point

'Behold him (priests) and though he stink of sweat
Disdain him not.'

George Gascoigne

'Do go on,' said the Chief Constable, when they were settled in his study in front of the fire. He looked lovingly at his pipe. 'And don't hurry. If I stir from this room I shall be expected to dispense tea to the Women's Union. I don't know how it is, but the parsons seem to have shed quite a few of their social duties since the war. Wiping Emming off the slate for the moment we are left with . . .'

'Shadrach, Meshach and Abednego,' said Mrs Bradley. 'In other words, with Mr Obury, Mr Mansell and the ghost of Parson Pile.'

'Say on. This promises well.'

'It fulfils its promise. Figure to yourself last Christmas Eve.'

'Filled a bran-tub for my nephew's kids. Nearly set the house on fire trying out the candles on the Christmas tree. Gave a tramp half-a-crown instead of setting the dogs on him. Was rung up about a burglary at Cirencester.'

'Nothing of which affects my narrative. At the manor house we entertained two guests. They were not, properly speaking, my nephew's guests, but were the friends of the Fullaloves. We put them up because the bungalow is small. Before midnight they went out for a walk . . .'

'In heaven's name, why? The night was as black as pitch!'

'One went to see badgers, the other to debunk ghosts.'

'And . . . ?'

'I don't think there were any badgers, but there definitely was a ghost.'

'Another of these balloon things?'

'Oh, you heard about that, did you? Well, I wasn't there, but that may have been what it was.'

'But what was the aim and object?'

'It is impossible to say with any certainty.'

'But they put the thing up again, later. That beastly balloon thing, I mean.'

'To detract from the significance of the first occasion, probably, and to make the gate a special object of interest, knowing that on this second occasion it had no criminal connections. You see, I fancy that more than the official guests were present at the disinterment of Mr Clarence Fullalove.'

'Yes, but what about this ghost business on Christmas Eve?'

'A rehearsal, I fancy, for moving the body of Bill Fullalove.'

'Bill was still alive at that time.'

'Yes. He had been got out of the way by Tiny. As a matter of fact, and as you probably already know, Bill Fullalove came to the manor house whilst his friends were out, and had a very short talk and a very short drink with my nephew Jonathan.'

'Faking an alibi, I should say, for the time of Mrs Dalby Whittier's death.'

'She must have died soon after lunch, you know. The belladonna would have acted fairly quickly. You won't give up the search for those two dogs and the cats belonging to Tiny, will you?'

'No, no. To find their bodies and show that they died of belladonna poisoning would be tantamount to proving that they were poisoned at the bungalow and by the curry. Even *I* can see that, and it would leave Tiny Fullalove with a good deal of explaining to do.'

'I quite agree: may I go on?'

'Do, do. You have a most constructive mind.'

'Young Emming visited us on Christmas Day. Miss Hughes, from the College, came, too. Emming had a grievance against Tiny Fullalove. He accused Tiny of unkindness towards some of his choirboys who had trespassed on Jonathan's land in order to gather holly.'

'Little brutes! Pulling the place to pieces, as likely as not!'

'I know. That's the interesting thing. As Miss Hughes, a kindly and merciful person, pointed out, boys can be pests and usually are. But boys who can be and have been pests, rarely, if ever, go to complain to their choirmaster of the way in which they have been treated. Our ability to "take it" is, as a nation, at once our glory, and our shame.'

'Leave politics out of it, dash it! You mean these kids split to Emming and he took it up with Tiny Fullalove?'

'We don't know whether he did or not. The inference is not that the boys complained, but that the incident had been pre-arranged, and that Emming himself was a party to the arrangement. He had to show that he and Tiny were at war and not in collusion – a mistake.'

'When did this business take place?'

'That did not transpire, but it is easy enough to find out. By the way, it was not Tiny's habit to clout the boys. That also is interesting.'

The Chief Constable went to the telephone.

'Bring Bob Wootton up here,' he said, 'and as soon as ever you can. I don't care where he is, or what he's doing. You know where he lives, and I want him quick. Why do you think it was such a mistake for Tiny and Emming to appear to fall out?' he added, when he had put the receiver down.

'It connected them,' Mrs Bradley explained. 'They should have remained poles apart.' She elaborated this thesis whilst they awaited the arrival of Bob Wootton.

Bob was small, dark, wary and shy.

'Well, Bob,' said Mrs Bradley, 'this gentleman is a policeman, so just you mind what you say. What he wants is the truth, the whole truth and nothing but the truth, and as I know exactly what your answers ought to be you take great care that I am satisfied.'

'Yes, miss,' said Bob, with a squirm.

'Well, sonny,' said the Chief Constable kindly, 'it's this way. How many of you boys picked holly on Christmas Eve?'

'I dunno,' said Bob, with a glance at Mrs Bradley's bright black eye.

'Good man. Never give others away. But you were one of them, weren't you?'

'Yes, sir.'

'Where did you go for the holly?'

'Over Marlin Wood.'

'Think again, Bob.'

'Well, p'raps we might have gorn a bit further. It got dark.'

'In other words, you weren't in Marlin Wood.'

'No, sir.'

'Where, Bob?'

'Please, sir, we didn't know we done wrong.'

'All right. I'd just like to know where you were.'

'That copse be'ind Claygate.'

'There's no holly there. Come on, don't be a coward. Where were you?'

'Please, sir, half over Groaning Spinney, and Mr Fullalove caught us, and he give us one to get on wi'. Please, sir, we didn't know there'd be any trouble. Mr Fullalove never interfered with us boys last year. He knowed we went there for 'olly. Mr Emming got leave for us to go.'

'I expect he thought the new owners might not like you so near the house. Now, Bob, answer me this: did you see or hear anything in Groaning Spinney – and I'm not prompting you, mind! – which might lead you to think that Mr Fullalove didn't want you there?'

'No, sir, nawthen, sir. And there wasn't even many berries on the 'olly.'

'It doesn't help us,' the Chief Constable said to Mrs Bradley when the boy had gone. 'The whole thing seems to hinge on Groaning Spinney. One more reference to it doesn't make any difference.'

'Be that as it may,' said Mrs Bradley, 'I still say that there is the question of Tiny Fullalove's bad temper. If he didn't clout the boys *last* Christmas, why tackle them *this* Christmas? No, it is as I have said. He had to be shown to be a brute so that Emming could quarrel with him openly. It was a bad mistake, but it was the way they had worked things out. There was another reason, too. He had given permission – you heard what that young boy said – for the choir to pick holly in the Spinney. He did not go back on his word. That might have looked suspicious. Murderers are for ever allowing for the slip which *doesn't* occur! No, he lay in wait for the lads and chased them away from the body. I should certainly think that's what happened. I wonder what time it was when the boys met him?'

'Before dark, anyway. They wouldn't gather holly after dark if they thought it was all right to get it. But if they *did* think it was all right, I can't see why the youngster stalled so badly about the place they were in when Fullalove caught them.'

'Oh, just that he connects the Spinney now with the punishment, and has an after-effect of guilt connected with it. He's probably often been in mischief and gets into trouble with his aunt.'

'Yes, I see. So Tiny Fullalove and young Emming are our men. I can't understand about Emming.'

'Bad heredity, probably from both parents. There was no real need for him to have continued to send out those abominable letters, yet he did so.'

'But he seemed such a harmless young fellow.'

'Nobody is harmless who nourishes a twenty-eight-year-old grudge against society.'

'His illegitimacy, you mean.'

'I think so.'

'But what can I do? We've still no proof.'

'You can have him charged for sending the letters.'

'Yes, I could do that, if you're certain. But what about the type-writer? We can't do anything until that's traced to him, you know.'

'You should go and look in Mr Mansell's dig.'

'Eh?'

'That's where I think you will find it.'

'Yes, but . . . Of course, he did help Mansell up there. He was there with Ed Brown. I suppose . . .'

'You suppose correctly. It was he who dug the longest and deepest trench. I noticed that particularly. The far end will now be filled in and the turf replaced. The typewriter will be underneath that turf.'

'Let's find the typewriter, then.'

'And in Emming's presence. Right.'

What emotions were in Emming's breast when the Inspector, in plain clothes, and a police-sergeant, in uniform, presented themselves at his lodgings and requested him to accompany them on a walk, Mrs Bradley could only guess. She was not privileged – having no official standing – to be a member of the party, but weight was added by the inclusion of Mansell (whose dig it was) and Jonathan, representing Miss Hughes, for the dig was on College territory.

Jonathan retailed the facts as soon as he returned to the manor house. At the first mention of the typewriter Emming had turned insolent. He declined to give information of anything he had buried in the dig, and challenged the police to find the machine, and, if they found it, to relate it in any way to him.

Upon this, the sergeant and Mansell, watched by Jonathan and the Inspector, had begun the work of re-digging the filled-in end of the trench. The typewriter was soon discovered, but Emming denied all knowledge of it. This, in the event of its discovery, had been anticipated, and the next move of the police had been to charge him with the dissemination of the objectionable letters. He denied the charge.

'All the same, we know where we are, sir,' said the Inspector, reporting to the Chief Constable later and in Mrs Bradley's presence. 'He typed the letters all right. We've tackled his landlady. She said at first that she'd never heard the sound of typing, and didn't know what a typewriter would look like, but she remembered hearing the noise when the sergeant tapped on one in Emming's room, although she's positive she'd only heard it once before. He must have typed all the letters but one when she was out. He denied ever having had a typewriter, but she's prepared to swear to the sound and to the date.'

'The date?' said Mrs Bradley, when she heard this. 'What about the date?'

'December twenty-ninth, mam. She works for Mr Baird, as you know, and found him preparing to leave for Edinburgh for Hogmanay. He'd forgotten to mention it and he gave her her money, and told her to wash up and go. It was one of her regular mornings, of course, so that Emming was not expecting her to come back so soon, and he was using the typewriter when she arrived. He stopped as soon as she came in, but she recognized the sound when we reproduced it for her.'

'She doesn't sound to me at all a reliable witness. For one thing, had she never noticed the typewriter in his room?' demanded the Chief Constable.

'Apparently not. He kept the room clean himself and had his meals downstairs in her kitchen. She seems a woman without much curiosity, sir, and Emming paid the rent regularly and was nice to her children. We never had any occasion to search her cottage, of course, so we didn't find the typewriter when we were looking for it before.'

'What is his explanation for burying it?'

'He doesn't give one. Denies that it's his machine and suggests, of course, that whoever knew it was there is the person who put it there. We've got the job now of tracing it to him. It's a fairly new one, and it's a portable. It will probably be up to the Yard to take up the trail in London, but we're going to try Gloucester, Cheltenham and Tewkesbury first. It's only a matter of routine to find out where he bought it, but, of course, it may take some time. Still, I think it's all nice and in the bag, sir. Pity is, it doesn't help us over Mrs Dalby Whittier's death.'

CHAPTER 18

The Hunt is Up

'For sure in courts are worlds of costly cares
That cumber reason in his course of rest.'
Nicholas Breton

'So it's all over bar the shouting,' said Miss Hughes.

'Do you think you've a very strong case?'

'No, I don't,' Mrs Bradley replied.

'It seems almost a pity – don't you think? – that you did not give Mr Tiny Fullalove in charge when he entered your Kensington house.'

'It was much more fun to turn on the record and frighten him almost to death,' said Mrs Bradley, with a ferocity which her hearer had not expected. 'The plots which he and young Robert Emming concocted against Bill Fullalove and Mrs Dalby Whittier were vicious in the extreme, and I am not inclined to show mercy to either of them.'

'Just exactly what was the plot, then? I can trace some of it from what you have told me, but not all.'

'Briefly, it was this: the insurance policy was to be taken out so that it could benefit either cousin if the other one were to die. There was not much likelihood that the insurance people would insist upon seeing the body of Mr William Fullalove when he was reported dead. Bill Fullalove was willing enough to subscribe to the fraud. What he had not the brains (or perhaps the imaginative villainy) to realize was that Tiny was capable of turning the fraud to his own advantage, even to the point of murder.'

'But you still cannot prove that Bill *was* murdered?'

'No.'

'Still less, *how* he came by his death?'

'No, but I have no fewer than eight clues up my sleeve.'

'Good heavens! Can you tell me? – or shouldn't I ask?'

'I will tell you. Two dog-chains, two dog-leads, one oak, one pine and two beeches.'

'Who planted the empty aspirin packet? – I can't attempt to solve your cryptogram.'

'It seems to have been Emming, and that is where more villainy comes in. Emming was not only determined upon his mother's death and upon the death of Bill Fullalove, but he is now also bent upon incriminating his fellow-conspirator.'

'When did you first tumble to the notion that Tiny and Robert Emming were in league?'

'Well, I soon noticed a physical resemblance which set me wondering. At Christmas time I remarked that Emming reminded me of someone, and I was not content until I had worked out who that was. It did not take very long, in spite of the fact that Emming looks effeminate.'

'I still don't see why that should have indicated to you that they were in league.'

'It did not, at first, but I soon realized how much each stood to gain if Bill and his legal wife, Mrs Whittier (so-called) were out of the way. Bill's was the first-planned death, although it came second in point of time. It was very well planned. It was to appear accidental. All the conspirators needed was cold weather. Tiny made the plan, I fancy, but he had to have an accomplice to help him carry it out. He found out, I think, (mind, this is mostly a theoretical reconstruction), that Emming was blackmailing Mrs Whittier and so proceeded to blackmail *him* into helping to murder Bill.'

'I begin to see the point of your chains and trees now. How utterly horrible!'

'Indeed it was. Well, the terrible plan being made, the conspirators got rather a shock. Bill and Tiny quarrelled. Bill not only gave Tiny a black eye, but told him that the insurance policy was of no use to him, as he (Bill) had a wife. That sealed Mrs Whittier's doom. To do Emming justice, I think the only hand he had in her death was to help transport her body from the bungalow to where it was found.'

'Yes, I see. Now what about the fraud? – that intrigues me very much.'

'Well, as I see it, it hinges on Mrs So-Called Bill Fullalove. She is, of course, wife to Robert Emming, and as part of the plot she was given Mrs Dalby Whittier's marriage certificate after the woman's death. This gives her the necessary claim to the insurance money. Armed with it, she can come in as an unknown but unimpeachable claimant to the Fullalove five thousand pounds. This she is to share with her husband, Emming, and also with Tiny Fullalove.

'That arrangement, of course, in reality suited nobody. Five thousand pounds is not such a very large sum that it can be shared with much advantage among three people; therefore it became necessary for Tiny and Emming to make chess-like moves in order to . . .'

'Double-cross one another?'

'Exactly; and therein lies our advantage. I do not believe for one moment that Tiny Fullalove intended to murder me when he made that strange attempt to enter my Kensington house. I think he came to tell me that he was in possession of information that would incriminate Emming. After all, if Tiny could eliminate the Emmings he would (as Bill's next of kin) be entitled to the whole of the inheritance.'

'You say "eliminate the Emmings". Surely it would be sufficient for his purpose if he could eliminate *Mrs* Emming?'

'It would, but he dare not do it.'

'Oh, I see. You mean that he would be suspected immediately if anything happened to the only other (apparent) claimant to the money?'

'Exactly that – particularly as he already knows that I suspect him. His only chance now, as I see it, is to get rid of Emming, who alone knows the full intricacies of the web they have spun together, and then to frighten Mrs Emming into giving up her claim.'

'Would that be difficult?'

'No, I don't think it would. She does not seem to be a woman of much education or character. I think that a combination of daring her to prove that she was married as long ago as 1922 . . .'

'Really?'

'Oh, yes. I saw that at once on the certificate of marriage she showed me. I realized then that she was what I had suspected her to be – a mere imposter. In fact, when I saw that she claimed to have been married at approximately the age of eight—!'

'You interest me very much. Please do go on. And tell me. Since *you* saw the point of the date, would not the lawyers see it, too?'

'Of course. That is what Tiny Fullalove depends on, I should think. As for Robert Emming, who cannot openly visit the cottage, I doubt whether he has so far set eyes on the certificate. Of course, the woman may lie about her age. If she claims to be fifty, and no birth certificate is called for, all may be well. But I could wish that we had another witness besides yourself to what I am saying. Would you mind very much if we had a member of your staff in?'

'Not at all. In fact, Diana Bagthorpe has been listening behind the door of my inner sanctum all the time. It would put matters on a regular footing and promote mutual restoration of "face" were I to bring her in.'

The small, rotund, india-rubber Physical Training lecturer, upon this, was immediately installed in the extra armchair, and she delighted Mrs Bradley by recapitulating succinctly and without error the conversation which had already been held in her hearing.

'And I suppose you've never thought that Ed Brown, Farmer Daventry's carter, might have had something to do with it, have you?' she enquired.

'I have turned the thought over in my mind more than once,' Mrs Bradley replied, 'and I am inclined to give Ed a clean slate. It is true that he could have been the messenger who took the note to Anstey's house at the time of Bill Fullalove's death and Tiny's injured kneecap, but, then, you see, so could Robert Emming. And I do think that the plotters would have realized that the fewer people there were in the plot, the more chance it had of success. I must say that I was rather glad when we were able to trace the possession of the typewriter to Emming – or, rather, that the police are now in a position to trace that typewriter to where it was bought.'

'Talking of Ed Brown,' said Miss Bagthorpe, 'I assume that he is still in the land of the living as no inquest upon him has been held.'

'You are quite right, and we shall not be able to hide the truth much longer.'

'If it can be shown that Emming purchased that typewriter, he will have to explain why he sent the letters, will he not?'

'Yes. Why did he? I have realized that it was a case of "like mother, like son", but I don't think that is the full explanation,' said Miss Hughes.

'No, of course it is not. I think Emming argued in this way: if the anonymous letters suddenly ceased, people might begin to wonder what had happened to the writer, and, naturally, the longer Mrs Dalby Whittier's death could be kept secret the better. Bill Fullalove's death the plotters did not intend to hush up. That was to save Tiny Fullalove from being suspected. As soon as it was known that Bill was missing, Tiny would be questioned. The manner of Bill's death is still not proved . . .'

'What do you yourself think?'

'I think his drink was doped and that then he was set upon in Groaning Spinney by Emming and Tiny, a sack put over his head to muffle sounds, and himself secured to four trees. The trees show signs, but Bill Fullalove's thick winter gloves and clothing protected his skin from marks which would otherwise have been made by the dog-chains and leads. He was an easy victim, I would say, because he was taken entirely by surprise and would have been drowsy. The body, except for the head, was then covered in snow, and when he was almost dead he was hoisted up over a gate so that the body could receive the attitude desired. Then he was carried to the ghost-gate and his body inclined over that. Emming then made himself scarce, and the too-clever Tiny faked an injury.'

'How utterly horrible and wicked!'

'You may well say so.'

'Why do you think Bill came to visit your nephew on Christmas Eve?'

'I think he suspected something when the cats and dogs disappeared. I think he had decided, perhaps, that Tiny's story about the cats and dogs was rather thin. However, he did not communicate anything to Jonathan, and while he was out the murderers, I imagine – but this is the purest guesswork – staged a rehearsal of his own death. That would account for the "ghost" on Christmas Eve.'

'Why didn't he confide in your nephew, do you suppose?'

'I don't know. Perhaps the fact that Mansell and Obury were expected back and might interrupt the confidences decided him – or perhaps he expected them to be present, and was nonplussed.'

'I can't see that it made any ultimate difference whether he told Mr Bradley or not.'

'No, I agree. My nephew would hardly have deduced Mrs Dalby Whittier's death.'

'And what are you going to do now?'

'I am going to wait. The typewriter, as I say, will be traced to Robert Emming and then he will be exposed, but, unfortunately, not for murder.'

'What will happen to this Mrs Robert Emming at the cottage?'

'Nothing, until Tiny Fullalove is released from hospital. After that, I would not go bail for her chances, or for Emming's, either, if she remains where she is. The trouble is that, until she is the victim of at least one murderous attempt, it is going to be very difficult to make out a cast-iron case against Tiny Fullalove except upon Emming's evidence, and *that* will be highly suspect. Tiny is a very clever man. Almost nothing of all this can be traced directly to him at present. Even Ed Brown's evidence can only incriminate Emming, it seems to me.'

'What about you yourself? Are not you in danger from these men?'

'I think not, now. They will realize that by this time all I know or guess I shall have told. I don't think that either of them would now take the risk of trying to get me out of the way, and I am glad to say that Will North is now similarly circumstanced. He has told all he knows. But I am worried about Ed Brown. He knows far too much for his own health. I have attempted to persuade him to take refuge at my London clinic for a time, but he won't consider that at all. He says that he is well able to take care of himself, but Emming must be getting desperate, and is entirely without scruple, and Ed has not yet told all he knows. At least, that is still my belief. I wish I could get out of him what he is hiding.'

'Yes. But *did* Emming kill his mother? That is a thing I find incredible.'

'Well, although the poison was administered at the bungalow, Emming must be an accessory both before and after the fact, and would be found guilty, I have no doubt, equally with Tiny Fullalove, by any responsible jury. I wish we could find those dogs!'

'So we wait and see. I don't much like the sound of that, you know. Are you really going to do nothing more?'

'My nephew tells me that I am going out hunting,' Mrs Bradley replied.

'I believe the local hunt can show quite good sport. The pack is small – and the whole thing not a bit like the Cotswold proper, I believe – but if you don't object to chasing wild creatures I think you may enjoy yourself quite heartily.'

'I have no very strong feeling either for or against the fox,' Mrs Bradley explained. 'But I dislike to hunt otters and deer.'

'Deer I can well understand, but why otters?' Miss Hughes enquired. 'They are surely as destructive of fish as foxes are of poultry.'

'Yes, I know, but I don't care for fish,' said Mrs Bradley. Her hearers refused to accept this unreasonable answer, and a long and animated discussion on hunting, shooting and fishing went on until Mrs Bradley had to go home.

Sally had come to meet her with the car.

'It isn't far, I know,' she said, 'for you to walk, but it's getting dark, and Jon and Deb are anxious. Besides, I'm going back home tomorrow morning, so I might as well see as much of you as I can. Jon says he brought you here, and he would have come for you, too, but he's had to go over to Greenstreet. Dinner will be a bit late. He'll be back about half-past seven.'

'That reminds me,' said Mrs Bradley to Miss Hughes, 'although I really don't know why it should, of a very minor but still fascinating mystery in connection with this case. After the typed anonymous letters began to come in, my nephew feloniously purloined from the Fullaloves' bungalow this engaging piece of typescript.'

She produced the typed quotation which the executors had found in the natural history book.

'Why,' said Miss Bagthorpe, 'isn't that what Robert Emming typed out on Miss Bathwell's little machine when he came one day for our advice on an oratorio that he proposed to write for the church choir to sing?'

'Oh, of course, there is a typewriter in the College,' said Mrs Bradley.

'I told the police so, and invited them to make tests. Actually there are two typewriters here. My secretary, Miss Bathwell, has one and I have one of my own. The police, although they seemed not very eager to remain in College for long – they found a plethora of students embarrassing – tested both machines and assured themselves that neither had been used for the anonymous letters. And that reminds me. On the same occasion as he did the typing, Mr Emming borrowed a book from the College library which I believe he has not yet returned.'

'What book?' Mrs Bradley enquired.

'*Nature's Traffic Lights.*'

'I beg your pardon?'

'I know, but the book *is* called that. It describes and illustrates various poisonous berries and fungi. It is really a book for young children, but the students, especially those from urban areas, find it very useful in identifying such plants as the deadly nightshade, for example.

'Belladonna!' exclaimed Miss Bagthorpe dramatically.'Wasn't that the poison . . . ?'

'Which killed Mrs Dalby Whittier? Yes, it was. And you lent the book to Emming, and it was found at the Fullaloves' bungalow. I don't know that we can use it in evidence, but it certainly offers some interesting corroborative detail. It certainly does not seem a book which one grown man would ordinarily lend another. A great light dawns on me, by the way. Emming is a Londoner. Tiny Fullalove has spent much of his life in India. Ed Brown is known to be knowledgeable about wild birds and may equally be so about wild plants. What if Ed's guilty recollection is of being asked to identify the berries of the deadly nightshade? The question could have been asked casually and among such a host of others . . . and the name of the poison itself, belladonna, is probably entirely unknown to Ed, so I may be wrong. On the other hand, it is amazing what country people *do* know.'

'I believe you have got something there,' said Sally to her aunt on the homeward drive. 'You had better jog Ed Brown's memory.'

'It will have to be done circumspectly, then,' Mrs Bradley

replied. 'I cannot, at this stage, put a leading question. I must give the matter some thought.'

Sally went off next day, and Mrs Bradley, having pushed a note under Will North's door, went by car to Pinxworth and then walked. George put the car up at the public house, and, unknown to his employer until she stopped to admire the view (and, turning, saw him), trudged stolidly behind her with one of Will North's sporting guns sloped professionally over his forearm. Unknown to his employer, he had kept this gun in the car since the visit to Oxford.

Mrs Bradley's walk, although apparently aimless, was, in reality, guided by careful planning. She was extremely worried about Ed Brown. All her attempts to get him into a zone of safety had failed. Ed was already chafing so bitterly against his captivity that she had more than a suspicion that he escaped when Will North went out, and roamed the woods between Will's lodge and the manor house. It could only be a matter of time, therefore, before the fact that he was alive and well was all over the village.

Having seen her chauffeur trudging faithfully in her wake, she stopped for him to catch up with her.

'I am making for Rolling,' she said, 'and I shall be quite safe, George. However, if you would care for a walk of fifteen miles . . .'

George glanced down at his leggings.

'Are you sure you'll be safe, madam?'

'Yes, George. My enemies are in London, conferring together. The police are faithfully trailing them. I am on my way to a *rendezvous* with Ed Brown. We are proceeding by devious and divers roads so that no one in the village will suspect what is in the wind.'

'You have persuaded Brown to seek his own safety, madam?'

'I don't know. I doubt it. But he has something to tell me which I must hear from his own tongue and before witnesses. The fact is, George, I have discovered that Ed Brown's life is not safe until it is generally known that he identified for Robert Emming and Tiny Fullalove the plant called deadly nightshade. We cannot meet openly, so I am relying upon Ed's woodcraft to bring him across country. We shall have part of our talk in the Chief Constable's stable yard.'

'Yes, you would scarcely entice Brown into a house, madam.'

'So I thought. We shall meet at the Greening crossroads and stroll gently stablewards. During our stroll I shall obtain from Ed the information I seek.'

'Police witness will be required, madam, I take it?'

'Yes. Ed Brown will not see them, but they will be there.'

'I thought the bungalow had already been searched for belladonna, madam.'

'It has, but it has not been searched for a preparation concocted by a gifted amateur from the fruit of the deadly nightshade.'

'How do *you* think the poison was administered, madam?'

'I *did* think of several possible ways: in mince pies, in rum, in blackcurrant jam, in coffee essence, in giblet soup. No doubt one could think of more—'

'I wonder they didn't use bamboo splinters or powdered glass, madam, Mr Tiny Fullalove having lived in India.'

'Tiny, I think, would not have been a party to that, because, had the method been discovered, he, and he alone, would have been the suspected person. Nevertheless, his Indian experiences *did* come into it. The poison was administered in curry. Now, George, I shall want the car to meet me at the top of the Hangman at half-past ten tonight. I do not propose to walk home.'

CHAPTER 19

Goblin Market

'O that I could my bed of earth but view
And smile, and look as cheerfully as you!'
Henry King

The air on the upland road was fresh to the point of being chilly.
Parted from George, who had vainly pressed the gun on her for
her protection, Mrs Bradley stepped out briskly and covered the
rising ground at a most surprising pace.

She had made careful study of the map and she made no mistake about the route. The sky was blue and the slight clouds were
high; here a stream ran, and there a bird flew suddenly out of a
coppice. The woods on the steeps looked like bluish smoke, or
climbed like a company of Green Howards.

Here and there in the valleys a chimney smoked or a small
train puffed white steam against brown escarpments. Here was a
terraced town with steps leading up from street to street, and here
was a huddled village, the houses clustering together as though
the snow were still falling and they were taking shelter from the
drift.

It was grand country, although the going was not at all easy;
and it was a grand day, although Mrs Bradley decided that the
clearness of the weather promised rain. She rested on an old
mounting block at the end of the first five miles, and beneath a
long-perished gibbet at the end of the first ten. There was no

longer any sign of the hangman's power, but as she sat there she could fancy a ghostly creaking which took her mind back to her first walk through Groaning Spinney.

The sound, however, was nothing more than the creaking of a nearby gate which was set in a stone wall almost overgrown by bracken the colour of umber. Mrs Bradley sat, in a reserved and lady-like manner, upon a flat stone which lay beside the gate, and walked alongside the wall because the path she was supposed to be following had been overgrown in the previous summer. A pocket compass gave her sufficient direction, and the slope, as the map had shown, was now downhill.

She came up with Ed Brown at the crossroads after five hours' steady walking and her two ten-minute rests.

'You must be tired, mam, I reckon,' said Ed, with his wary woodland smile. Mrs Bradley shook her head.

'I brought you out as far as this,' she said, 'so that you could show me where the white lilies blow on the banks of Arcady.'

'What, this time of year?' said Ed. 'I could show ee, come May or maybe June, where ee can get some wild lilies of the valley, like.'

'I didn't know they grew wild.'

'Well, no more p'raps they do, in a manner of speaking, but we get 'em in the Squire's Wood, back 'ome. Myself, I reckon, they excaped like, from somebody's garden, like all nature will if 'er can, but they be thick as the winter berries along Squire's Ride for them as knows where to look. But Arcady . . . no, I never heard tell of that place in these 'ere parts, as I knows on.'

> ' "Yet there, where never muse or god did haunt,
> Still may some nameless power of Nature stray,
> Pleased with the reedy stream's continual chant
> And purple pomp of these broad fields in May," '

said Mrs Bradley with great approval of this theory. Ed looked at her oddly.

'You didn't ought to call up sperrits from the vasty deep,' he protested.

'But I don't,' said Mrs Bradley. 'Only the deadly nightshade from its flowering bed. Titania herself was a little like the deadly nightshade, don't you think, Ed?'

'You was talking of lilies,' said Ed, uncertainly.

'Lilies or daffodillies,' said Mrs Bradley. 'It is all the same thing.'

'That, by a power, it is not, mam. Why, as I was telling Mr Tiny Fullalove . . . would a-ben last summer, that would a-ben . . . the deadly nightshade, that's one of the plants as children should learn for to know. But lilies, well, some of *them* be poison, too, I *have* eerd tell . . . and the deadly nightshade – well, we 'ad a young thing, not more nor six year old . . . I never 'eard the right name, mam, till then. Her died of it, her did.'

'So that's where they got the information,' said the Chief Constable. 'I've got the report from the London hospital here. Tiny Fullalove will leave tomorrow morning. Now, if only we could find the carcases of those dogs that Mrs Anstey fed with the curry, he could be charged formally with the murder of Mrs Dalby Whittier and this woman up at the cottage would have to go to court to be a witness. We've got enough for that, now that you've seen her marriage lines and noticed the date. But how to get at Emming, except over the anonymous letters, I don't yet see, unless Tiny Fullalove squeals. And we haven't got our full evidence yet about the typewriter. Scotland Yard are on the trail of it, but they may have to make hundreds of calls before they find the shop where he bought it. Trouble is, it's an American make, and a pre-war model. But the letters were typed on it. There isn't any doubt about that, and it wasn't bought around here.'

'I suppose you are looking for the belladonna at the bungalow again?'

'Yes, but it's hopeless, I fancy.'

'Try the bumby-hole,' suggested Mrs Bradley.

'The . . . ?'

'Well, I imagine that, in these enlightened times, the bungalow possesses a dustbin, but . . .'

'Yes. We've raked over the local sewage works long ago, but no luck. And if you mean the heap of refuse behind Tiny Fullalove's woodshed, and the woodshed roof, and all the guttering round the bungalow, and the bottom of the well, and the bottom of the rainwater butt, and inside the cistern and . . .'

Mrs Bradley cackled, and said that she was sorry she had spoken.

'I should think so, too,' said the Chief Constable. 'Have another try.'

'Has every pot and bottle been sent for analysis?'

'Every single one. They got rid of the belladonna at once. There isn't a trace of it left.'

'Hardly surprising. I should scarcely think you'd have any luck with that, but one never knows; and although we can now prove that Ed Brown had identified the deadly nightshade for them, we cannot prove from that that their knowledge was guilty knowledge. I think we must employ the technique of the shoot.'

'Eh? What shoot?'

'The use of beaters to start up the game.'

The Chief Constable looked uneasy.

'I'm not at all sure that I understand you,' he said. 'We have to go carefully, you know. Once Scotland Yard trace the typewriter (which they are absolutely bound to do in the end) we can charge Emming with uttering the typed letters, but there's nothing strong enough yet for a murder charge, as I say, unless Tiny Fullalove squeals, and somehow I don't believe he's the squealing kind.'

'I was thinking of Mrs Emming.'

'We've tried her, you know. She isn't easy.'

'She would be a good deal easier if she knew that her own life was in danger.'

'But it isn't in danger.'

'Not as long as it is perfectly certain that she isn't going to give any evidence away. But what if Tiny Fullalove thought she would?'

'Oh, I see. You mean . . . ?'

'I mean that the bleating of the lamb would tend to excite the tiger, particularly *this* tiger. And, as I think I said before, five thousand pounds isn't so very much when it's shared among three people.'

'You think the woman will claim two-thirds of the money?'

'Why should she not? She is in a position to point out to Tiny Fullalove that she may be the means of saving his neck. If Tiny had been the obvious claimant (which, as things stand, he most certainly is not) his position might have been awkward . . . Can't you hear her saying it? She's not a courageous type, but money is an amazing stimulant.'

'But we should still have to prove that Bill Fullalove was murdered, and that is just exactly what we *can't* prove, and, in my opinion, never *shall* be able to prove. We can't trace his movements after lunch on December 29th. We know he went out after lunch because Anstey said so, but, after that, we know nothing.'

'Except that the dogs and cats have disappeared. And, of course, Tiny must have misled Anstey into thinking that Bill had gone to Gloucester.'

'Yes, I know . . . or it may have been a genuine mistake on Anstey's part. People do get ideas into their heads. By the way, do *you* think it was a genuine mistake?'

'No. But what I think isn't evidence.'

'It probably will be,' said the Chief Constable, who, beneath a curmudgeonly manner, cherished an affection for Mrs Bradley's gifts and was rather put out of countenance at what seemed to be her negative results in this particular case. 'Smack it about, my dear, and let's get action. The papers are beginning to be shrill.'

'If that that bears all things bears thee,' quoted Mrs Bradley in solemn and sonorous Greek, 'bear thou and be borne.'

'That's all very well. But fair words butter no parsnips.'

'Do you like parsnips?'

'Not particularly.'

'Would you agree that it does not matter to you, therefore, whether parsnips are buttered or not?'

'Oh, but look here—!'

'We want Mrs Robert Emming's evidence.'

'We shan't get it. She's as guilty as the two men are, and she'll be as hard as a hammer over the money. You said so yourself.'

'Heads fly off hammers.'

'To the devil with your metaphors and quotations. I can't pull the woman in and give her third degree methods!'

'No. And I would not agree with your doing so, even if you could. But a friendly call . . .'

'Friendly?'

'Certainly, and we'll hope, for her own sake, that she has enough common-sense to beware of the Greeks when they come bearing gifts.'

The Chief Constable shook his head and returned rather sadly to earlier matters.

'What did you expect that we could do, even after Ed Brown confessed to having identified the deadly nightshade for Emming and Tiny, about Mrs Dalby Whittier's death?'

'All sorts of things. For one of them, I thought that you might possibly resurrect Ed.'

'Resurrect him?'

'Yes. I think that if Mr Emming saw Ed's ghost at the top of Groaning Spinney his reactions would be interesting.'

'I can't risk Ed Brown's life.'

'Of course not. It was just an idea.'

The Chief Constable regarded her with the deep suspicion he retained for her foxier suggestions.

'Hm!' he said non-committally. Mrs Bradley cackled and gave him a poke in the ribs.

'It would be something constructive, at any rate,' she remarked, 'and might save you a good deal of trouble.'

'You'll have to fix it, then. I wash my hands of it.'

'Oh, quite. I will let you know the results if I attempt it.'

'I accept no responsibility, mind.'

'No, no. I hear there is a meet at County's Green tomorrow. My nephew has offered to mount me. Shall I go?'

'Good heavens, yes! We're not like the Cotswold, of course. Just the local farmers, and ourselves, and so on, with plenty of push-bike adherents, as a matter of fact. But you ought to get quite good fun.'

'You are not going to the meet?'

'How can I, with all this on my hands? Anything may break loose at any minute.'

As though to prove the truth of these words, the telephone bell rang, and a calm voice at the other end of the wire announced that the typewriter submitted to Scotland Yard for examination had been purchased in Islington on the twenty-eighth of December. There was no clue to the purchaser, however, who had paid outright for the machine and had taken it away with him.

'No address, you see. But definitely a man,' said the Chief Constable. 'Now to find out whether Emming went to London on that date.'

'You will find that he did,' said Mrs Bradley. 'Moreover, when you *do* find out that he was in London on that date, it will not help you very much. He wouldn't have gone for the typewriter himself. He would have sent a special messenger.'

'Well, we must trace the messenger and get him to describe Emming,' said the Chief Constable. 'But it still comes back to the same thing. We can prove, if we stick at it long enough, that Emming typed those letters, but I'm hanged if I see how to pin murder on him.'

'The woman is the key,' said Mrs Bradley. 'We must find some way of getting her to talk.'

'That must be a legitimate way, then.'

'I agree, and I already have an idea.'

'If you mean your ghost-gate theory . . .'

'Partly, I do.'

'Look here, you're not to land me in the soup!'

'You have no fear, and *I* will have no scruples.'

'Lady Macbeth in person!'

'No. I have no ambitions.'

'Not even to be in at the death?'

Mrs Bradley cocked a bright black eye at him.

'I shall know about that tomorrow,' she replied.

CHAPTER 20

A View to a Death

'Nor hedges, ditches, limits, narrow bounds;
I dreamed not aught of those,
But in surveying all men's grounds
I found repose.'

Thomas Traherne

'It will be the last run of the season,' said Jonathan, swallowing scalding tea. 'I'm glad you're coming.'

Mrs Bradley, correctly attired in habit and top hat, grinned mirthlessly.

'I don't suppose I shall see much of it,' she observed. 'I'm too old for these capers.'

'Oh, rot!' said her nephew. 'The old man used to say that you rode straighter than he did. Besides, you'll like our country, and we're a most democratic hunt, you know.'

The horses were already in the yard. Jonathan put his aunt neatly into the saddle, mounted his bay mare and led the way at a walk out of the muddy yard and into the wood.

They were in good time, and left the horses to choose the pace up the long woodland ride, now quickened into life by the appearance of the first wild daffodils. At the edge of the wood the gorse was in honey-scented flower, and the sinuous treachery of blackberry sprays was as quick as the green of the hawthorn. The leaf-mould underfoot was as soft as a feather bed and about as resistant, and the horses took matters easily, walking delicately on through the woods until they came to the open country.

Here Jonathan jerked the bay mare into a trot until they reached the road. There the horses sobered again, and walked in single file on the grassy boundary.

The meet was at a place called County's Green, and the small local hunt was gathered in front of a white-painted Georgian house with a semi-circular lawn now in process of hoof-printed destruction.

Jonathan introduced his aunt to the people he thought she ought to know, and it was not long before the riders moved off.

The country around County's Green was less wooded and not so steeply hilly as some of the Cotswolds, but it was good, broad, undulating land, and, except for the inevitable stone walls, free from unprepossessing obstacles.

'No wire round here,' said Jonathan, as the hunt moved off across a billowing field, 'and the country's wide open. We ought to get a good run. There are plenty of foxes. As long as the hounds can be kept to one only, we should have a glorious time. Hullo! Look at *him*! Cheeky rascal!'

A brown hare was occupying the middle of the field. Suddenly he became aware of hounds and dashed away, staring anxiously behind him and almost running into a gate. The Huntsman reminded the hounds that their business was with foxes, and suddenly the hunt was inspired by the thrilling music of a find.

Mrs Bradley was a light-weight and was on a rather high horse. It was a gentlemanly creature, but it wanted to be up with the foremost. It got into its stride, its elderly rider nothing loth, and, grinning with pleasure, Mrs Bradley went past her nephew with a thunder of hoofs and a devil's dance of thick-flying clods, as the ten-couple pack fled on.

Jonathan shook loose the bay mare and soon caught up with his aunt. At a stone-faced bank he lost her again, for the mare pecked, whereas Mrs Bradley's nobleman, deciding that the bank was negligible, soared over it with a terrific lift of his haunches but as neatly as a ribboned jumper at a horse show.

The sun rose higher, the clods continued to fly, everyone was warm, and the first fever-heat of enthusiasm settled to a tattoo of hoof-beats.

'The unspeakable in pursuit of the uneatable,' yelled Jonathan, catching up with his aunt again as the hounds streamed into a sandy road and checked for an instant at the turn.

'Rubbish,' responded Mrs Bradley. 'The tushery in pursuit of the brushery is far more applicable.' She waved her whip towards a rather precious young man who was obviously clinging on for dear life and who was doing so badly that the motion of his tall, heavy horse resembled that of a Bactrian camel.

'Lor!' said Jonathan, awe-stricken. 'Do you think he learned to ride like that in a circus?'

His aunt by-passed this uncharitable remark, and the course soon changed. The hedge at the roadside was broad and could not be leapt from the difficult, low-lying track. The hounds found a gap, but the riders, except for the Huntsman (who discovered a thin place and pulled his horse through and over) were forced to jog-trot behind a milk-van until they came to a gate.

'Lost touch,' said Jonathan, for there was now no sign of the hounds. 'This way. Come on. I know it here. We'll soon pick up again.'

The way led along a path worn during the summer by picnic-parties, goats and marauding boys. In the foreground there was a wood. Skirting this, and guided by the sound of the horn, Jonathan and his aunt soon found themselves on a downhill slope and heading towards a wicket-gate into the woods. In front of them was the circus equestrian.

'Damn!' said Jonathan. He pulled up. 'Sorry. I'll get off and open it.'

The camel-rider, however, had no such scruples. He made a dash at the gate, had the salutary experience of a rightly refusing horse, and landed on the top of his head.

'Job for you,' said Jonathan to his aunt. Mrs Bradley abandoned her horse, opened the gate and knelt beside the stricken and unconscious egoist. Gently she felt for the injury. This was not very severe. The man had been wearing a top hat with his pink, and this had acted as a crash helmet. In a second or two he sat up, shaky but in possession of his faculties.

'Sorry,' he said. 'Silly trick.'

'You might have spiked your mare,' said Jonathan severely; but his aunt thought better of the young exquisite than she had supposed she would. She and her nephew helped him up.

'You had better trot off home,' said Mrs Bradley kindly. 'You've had a bad shaking. Which way do you think we should go?' she asked her nephew when the young man had gone, for, beyond the wicket gate, the woodland rides diverged.

'Let's follow this one,' said Jonathan, leading the way. 'If the fox has gone towards Gracebarrow we'll probably catch up with the others. The woods there are full of foxes. In fact, there's a legend, which is certainly borne out by my experience, that when a fox heads for Gracebarrow you may as well give up and go home. It's very bad going, for one thing, all scrub and uncleared woodland and overhanging branches and bogs and tussocky grass. Still, I think we'll press on and investigate.'

The narrow path they were following would only allow them to ride in single file. It mounted steadily and surely, and wove in and out among the trees and then through a carpet of bluebell plants.

'Glorious colour next month,' said Jonathan, pointing. After about half a mile the character of the woodland began to change. The ride became as wide as a road, the bushes had been cut back, and there was a border of wild anemones and a carpet of dog violets.

Jonathan reined in his mare and his aunt drew level with him. Raising his whip he pointed onwards and upwards, for the slope was still uphill, although now it was very gradual.

'Let's gallop,' he said. 'We've got a mile and a half of this, and it's simply grand.'

After the sauntering pace at which they had been walked, the horses were ready for a change. The ride became almost level, and the going was better than good. For half a mile the riders thudded along on ground which was soft and easy and yet firm enough to resist the pressure of hoofs.

Jonathan reined in again. The trees had thinned. The riders were on the sky line. Below them, field upon field, was undulating arable and pasture, two or three winding roads, wooded hills and the sun on the beeches.

'Lovely!' said Mrs Bradley. 'What is more, I can see the hounds.'

In the dale between a ploughed field and a dark little copse of firs, the white and tan hounds were speeding across the pasture.

'Come on!' said Jonathan. 'I know a short cut to get down there.'

Jonathan's short cut did not play them false and was not a severe test for the horses, but by the time he and Mrs Bradley had caught up with the rest of the followers, the hounds were at fault and the run was temporarily checked.

'Can't understand this,' said Jonathan to his aunt. 'It's a very sudden check considering how well the hounds were going, and we're nowhere near Gracebarrow yet.'

'Gone to ground,' said a stout farmer on a sweating chestnut. 'Known 'em do that at this very place before. I reckon us can give up and trot along home. Lost him properly this time, us have.'

But this dark view went unheeded, for in another moment there was a wild cry from a boy on a bicycle.

'Hi! Mister! Mister! He come out in Parson's Medder! Go you that way!'

A cart-track led past a farm and there was a scurry of straying fowls. There were no casualties, and, once through the farmyard, the riders came to a shoulder of land that mounted to a sparse little copse. Avoiding this, the pack scrambled under a broken fence and were up and over the shoulder and lost to sight. The

Huntsman and the Master put their horses at the fence. Someone dismounted and opened a gate. One or two followed the Master and there was a spill.

Mrs Bradley, whose medical training and social instincts took pride of place over her interest in chasing the fox, dismounted to attend to the damage.

'It's all right,' said the sufferer, wincing under Mrs Bradley's sternly exploratory hands. 'Nothing broken. Thought my collar-bone had gone, but it hasn't – this time. Lucky the falling is soft. I was a fool to attempt the fence on a hireling and on an uphill slant like that. You shouldn't have stopped. Look, please don't trouble any further. I'm staying at a pub over there, about a couple of miles away. I shall be quite all right.'

Mrs Bradley, having assured herself that the fall, although heavy, had indeed broken no bones, told her nephew to ride on. Then leisurely she looped the reins over her arm, watched her patient and her nephew depart, and led her horse up the hill in the direction which had been taken by the hunt.

At the top of the rise, she could see some woods, more blue than green except for a larch tree here and there, and some haw-thorns just breaking into leaf, and between herself and the trees was a grim-looking wall of Cotswold stone, the kind of obstacle which, although it was common enough, had, so far, been avoided by the fox. She led her horse to a stone stile, remounted and then walked him alongside the wall in search of a gate.

She soon found one. It was guarded by a young countryman who opened it for her at once, obligingly pointed out the route the fox had taken, and, wheeling an ancient bicycle from where he had propped it up, passed through the gate behind her, shut it carefully, and then mounted his machine and accompanied her, wobbling uncomfortably on the coarse grass. Together she and her bone-rattling escort rode across the next field and towards the woods.

'Ah, they've got to hunt him again, the cunning old fellow!' exclaimed the young man, as he and Mrs Bradley caught a glimpse of a pink coat in among the trees. 'This way, mam. There's an easy way in for them as knows. You'll be up on the old rascal as soon as any of 'em. Come you along o' me. Your 'orse won't take no notice of my bike.'

There was no doubt hounds were at fault. Mrs Bradley's escort dismounted, leaned his bicycle against a piece of chestnut fencing, swung away on foot to the right and introduced her into the wood by way of a bridle path guarded by a gate.

'He's dished us, I think,' said Jonathan, as his aunt and her escort came up. 'Headed back for his own country, I shouldn't wonder, or else gone to ground in here. Never mind. It's a lovely day. Shall we be ambling home, or will you wait to see whether we pick him up again?'

'I've had enough, if you have,' said his aunt, re-settling her hat, which a branch had knocked slightly askew. 'What's the matter with that couple of hounds?'

Apparently the Master had the same desire for information. The couple had their muzzles inside a badger's sett and were baying as though they were demented.

The Huntsman called them off, and, the pack suddenly finding again, the hunt streamed off through the woods.

'On a different scent, I'll lay,' said Jonathan, ducking his head to avoid a whip-like branch. He glanced round to find that his aunt had dismounted and, with her cyclist guide, was poking with a dead branch at the badger's sett.

'Blood,' she said, holding out the branch as her nephew came up.

'Rabbit,' said Jonathan. 'A stoat has killed one and dragged it in there, I expect. Come along, or we shall miss the fun.'

'I thought you had made up your mind to go home,' retorted Mrs Bradley. 'But just as you like. Ah, there we go again!'

They bent low on their horses' necks to avoid the whip-like twigs and were soon again on a broad ride through the woods. Mrs Bradley's crop dangled from her wrist, and in her hand she held the blood-stained branch which she had poked into the badgers' den. Jonathan, accustomed to apparent idiosyncrasies which would afterwards, he knew, prove to be useful behaviour, made no comment. His horse began to canter, and soon he and his aunt were scudding up-wind behind a pack in full cry, a yodelling Huntsman and an enthusiastic field.

The woods ended with a wooden gate easily negotiable. The take-off, a little spongy, was good enough, and Jonathan loosed his mare at it and was up and over. Mrs Bradley gathered her tall hunter, and up he flew, made a perfect landing, and galloped steadily onwards, on a slightly downhill track.

They were in open country once more and the fox was in view. There were screeches, hounds yelling, and all the climax of the chase, but there were oaths, too, for with the fox was a man on horseback, and he had the fox on a long lead.

'Good God! It's that scoundrel Ed Brown!' said Jonathan, breaking into wild laughter. 'It's his tame fox he's got there! We always suspected he had one or two, although he'd never own to it. What on earth is his game? And where the devil did he get a horse like – Damn it all! It's my Moonlighter!'

Observing that the game, whatever it was, was up, Ed leaned from the saddle like a cowboy, and released the fox. It immediately disappeared, and Ed himself dismounted, while the Huntsman and the Master, calling upon all disembodied spirits, rode up to him to know the how and why.

Ed seemed confused. His sly eyes caught Mrs Bradley's alert and interested ones, and, apparently discerning sympathy in her yellow countenance, he addressed himself to her.

'Please, mam, you be the best judge of what I bin doin'. You do know who's arter me and for why.'

'Yes,' said Mrs Bradley, whom the Master was eyeing askance while the Huntsman was persuading hounds to come away from the mouth of the artificially constructed 'earth' where Ed's tame vixen had gone to ground. 'I think, Ed, that we must forgive you. Where is Robert Emming now?'

'I dunno, mam,' said Ed. 'He daren't touch me while the hunt was going on, in case 'e should shoot an 'ound – or maybe the fox.' He smiled shyly at the fermenting Master and then at Jonathan, who, pointing to the horse, asked wrathfully:

'Who gave you leave to borrow Moonlighter, confound you?'

'I don't understand your tale,' said the Master, before Ed could reply. 'What's all this about shooting hounds and foxes?'

'Perhaps I had better explain,' said Mrs Bradley. 'Ed, the evidence of your crime is not very securely hidden. Look!' And she showed him the blood-stained stick. 'But I do not advise you to return that way at present.'

'He were after me, and I knowed it,' said Ed, almost sullenly. 'I rate meself higher than one old fox, I reckon.'

'So you *did* kill our fox, you villain!' said the Master.

'I had to lead him a dance,' protested Ed. 'He were arter me, I tell ee.'

'Nonsense, Ed,' said Mrs Bradley firmly. 'You've got a bee in your bonnet. Mr Emming and Mr Tiny Fullalove are still in London. What put such a notion into your silly noddle?'

'It was a dream I 'ad,' said Ed unwillingly. '(It's all right, Mr Bradley, sir. Me and your Moonlighter's old friends.) I don't 'old with takin' no notice of dreams. Dreams is in the Bible, and allus took notice of there, being interpreted.'

The Master caught Jonathan's eye, tapped his own forehead significantly, and the Hunt began to move off. Ed seemed not to notice their going. His expression became craftier than ever.

'You've got something on your conscience, Ed,' said Mrs Bradley. 'Something you haven't told me.'

'It come to me, like, when I told ee about the deadly nightshade,' agreed Ed. He fondled the horse, which was gently nibbling at his shoulder to attract his attention. '(All right, then, you old you, you.) Yes, mam, that's when it come to me. They poor old dogs, mam.'

'Good heavens, Ed! You saw them being buried!'

'I did, mam, too an' all. Mr Tiny and Mr Emming . . . and Mr Tiny cryin' all the time like an 'eart-broken gal . . . they buried them two poor dogs and them two little cats when Will North was over to Camphill on the Christmas shoot.'

'Will North?' asked Jonathan, puzzled. 'How does *he* come into it?'

'Of course!' said Mrs Bradley, looking affectionately at Ed. 'Will North's dog cemetery! How completely obvious!'

'But what an awful risk to take!' exclaimed Jonathan.

'Mr Emming, he were again it,' said Ed, 'but Mr Tiny, he says as 'ow 'is little dogs and cats be going to lie proper, like 'umans, you see, mam.'

'Yes, I do see. I do indeed,' said Mrs Bradley, gazing raptly into Ed's face. 'And I can see that you agreed, Ed. How did you come to be there?'

'Well, tell you the truth, mam, Will North, he don't go round there very often, but me, I go round and tidy up a bit and say a prayer for the poor old dogs and that, though I doesn't tell parson what I do. So when they come . . . Mr Tiny and Mr Emming . . . I just creep into the bushes, that be all.'

'Yes, I see. Nothing else, Ed?'

'Ah, there were one other thing,' confessed Ed. 'Mr Emming, he intend to kill Will North with that gun, not me.'

'I thought so at the time. As you fell into the trench, Will was directly behind you, and therefore in the line of fire. We must be thankful for Mr Emming's poor marksmanship.'

'Indeed, yes. It was only turning it all over in my mind afterwards, mam, I knowed what to think. I wouldn't 'ave done it, not for a bet nor nothing . . .'

'Exactly. I acquit you of complicity, Ed. I suppose the bet was that you could tell by the actions of the birds what was going on. Then, if Will got the shot in him, you'd have had to swear it was an accident.'

'That were it. Now I got my mind cleared . . .'

'But still not your conscience, Ed. You've been a nuisance. I want you to do something to atone for that.'

'I don't intend for to be mixed up in nawthen else no more.'

'You've got to do this, Ed.' She came close to the carter and muttered at him in witch-like tones. Ed started back. He looked horrified.

'Not me! Not me!' he protested.

'Oh, nonsense, Ed. And it *must* be tonight. We'll let Will know what we intend. Get up on Moonlighter again, and off we go!'

There was a telephone message at the manor. Deborah had taken it. It came from the Chief Constable. Emming and Tiny were expected to return that afternoon.

'I hoped so,' said Mrs Bradley. 'This is our last chance. First we must disinter the dogs and get a post-mortem for traces of the belladonna. Secondly, we must make certain of Mrs Emming's safety, particularly as she will be needed at the trial. Thirdly, we must carefully coach Ed Brown in the part he has to play tonight.'

'I can't see what those two went to London for. They could have conferred here,' said Jonathan.

'They've been making arrangements to leave the country and go to South America,' said Deborah. 'The police have knowledge of that.'

'Oh, I see; and they're coming back here to pack up, I suppose? Well, that suits us all very nicely.'

Disinterring the dogs was a grim task. Will North and the staunch Woottons performed it under Mrs Bradley's eye and under Ed's directions. Tiny's unfortunate pets were barely identifiable, but the vet from Cheltenham, called into consultation, swore to the horrid remains as being those of a setter and a bull-terrier, and the equally disagreeable relics of two cats proved that these had indubitably been Manx.

'And there won't be any doubt about the poison,' said Mrs Bradley, when Will had tidied up his cemetery and nothing remained to mark the empty graves except the freshly dug, loamy soil. 'And now for Mrs Emming.'

It was getting towards dusk when she and her nephew, accompanied by the Inspector and a policeman, reached the lonely cottage. The woman had lighted the lamp and drawn the blinds. Her head was silhouetted against the light. She started nervously when the Inspector tapped on the window.

'Go round to the front!' she called. 'I didn't expect you back yet. I thought you said the seven o'clock train, and back to your lodgings.'

'I don't think we're quite the visitors you thought,' said the Inspector, when she opened the door. 'I am a police officer and I've called to ask you a few questions.'

He pushed gently past her into the cottage. The others remained outside, but the door remained open and the conversation could be heard clearly. Mrs Bradley knew the Inspector to be an efficient, hardworking officer, but she had not suspected him of guile.

'I'm sorry to trouble you, Mrs Emming,' he said, 'but we've had an enquiry through from Scotland Yard about two gentlemen who seem in rather a hurry to get out of the country. As their objective seems to be South America, which is quite a long way from here . . .'

She did not question the title he had given her, and she did not allow him to finish.

'The dirty, double-crossing little . . . !' she screamed. 'He deserted me before and then found he'd got a use for me in his murdering monkey tricks! Get out of the country and do me down, would he! Not while I've got a tongue in my head to tell what I know, he damn well won't! Him and his rascal of a father! Come-by-night and fly-by-night, will he? I'll soon cure him of that, the . . . !'

Mrs Bradley touched her nephew's arm. They walked back towards the village under the thin light of the pale, remote and early evening stars.

'I think we can safely leave that to the Inspector and the constable,' she said. 'We have other fish to fry. Now, you understand your part, don't you?'

'Perfectly. I'm to get Tiny up to Groaning Spinney by ten tonight.'

'Exactly. And Will North will be with you. I myself will tackle Mr Emming.'

'My job will be easy. Tiny's still my agent, and Will and I have only to report signs of fire-raisers and poachers.'

'And Mr Emming will come with me whether willingly or not,' said Mrs Bradley, with relish. 'You to the bungalow, then, and I to the lodgings!'

'You'll look out for yourself, won't you?' said Jonathan, anxiously. 'He's a treacherous devil!'

'I am not proposing to be particularly above-board myself,' said Mrs Bradley. 'I hope Will North has placed the lantern in the right spot.'

Arrived at Emming's lodgings she asked when he was expected home.

'He's to be at Cheltenham at seven o'clock. I had a telegram.' His landlady showed it proudly. 'If he catches the bus all right at half-past seven I reckon he'll be in to his supper before nine.'

'Oh, well, will you please tell him that Mr Tiny Fullalove will meet him at the old place at ten o'clock tonight?'

'Mr Tiny? At the old place?'

'Yes.'

'Be that all as I'm to tell 'im?'

'Yes, please. You won't forget, will you?'

'Oh, no. I won't forget. But I thought Mr Tiny were from 'ome?'

'Is he? Anyway, that is the message for Mr Emming.'

She went straight from the village street to the College. It had taken some time to reach the village from Mrs Emming's lonely cottage, and the evening was wearing on.

'I want to borrow your typewriter for a few moments,' she said to a surprised but welcoming Miss Hughes. 'And if you've an odd crust that you can spare, I shall be glad of it.'

Fortified with sandwiches and coffee, Mrs Bradley took leave of Miss Hughes at half-past nine, and, having inspected and loaded her little revolver, set out to walk to Tiny Fullalove's bungalow. She went by way of the village, and got there in less than twenty minutes by walking fast. Arrived there, she found it, as she had expected, still tenanted, but at the end of five minutes Tiny came out and set off in the direction of the Spinney.

Mrs Bradley went up to the front door and pinned her typed slip just beneath the knocker. To her satisfaction the white paper could be seen quite easily against the dark paint. It bore the legend, in capitals:

GROANING SPINNEY

She retired to the shadows and waited. By half-past ten she decided to give up her vigil. It was evident that Emming was not coming. She supposed that after all he had gone to see his wife before he returned to his lodgings, and she wondered what kind of reception he would get after the Inspector's visit. She went quickly back to the village. 'I want you to come with me,' she said, when she had knocked at the policeman's door. 'And be quick. I think we may be too late already.'

Police-constable Mayhew had finished his supper and had, in point of fact, taken off his boots and his tunic preparatory to going to bed. He resumed them, told his wife, who was already upstairs, that he was going out on a job for the squire, and accompanied Mrs Bradley to the lonely cottage beyond the long barrow.

The cottage lamp was still alight and the front door was wide open. In the room immediately within were the bodies of Emming and his wife.

'She must have shot him as he opened the door,' said the constable, looking with bovine interest at the corpses. 'And then put the gun under 'er 'eart.' He examined the gun. It was the one belonging to Will North which had been stolen. The constable recognized it directly. 'You better go for Doctor Fielding, mam, while I stays 'ere and keeps guard.'

'I wonder she knew how to load it,' said Mrs Bradley.

'It's easy enough, once you're showed. I wonder what in 'eaven's name made 'er do it?'

Mrs Bradley could have enlightened him, but did not. She made all haste back through the starry night to the village, and, having notified Doctor Fielding and, from his house, rung up the Inspector, she set off for Groaning Spinney. Of pity for the murderers of Bill Fullalove and Mrs Whittier she felt not the slightest pang. She was anxious only to know the result of her ghost-gate experiment and to assure herself of her nephew's safety.

She met him at the edge of the wood.

'Who's that?' called his voice as she approached. 'Oh, it's you, Aunt Adela. I say, Tiny's conked out. Could you come and see to him? It's his heart, I expect. The ghost upset it. He gave a sort of moan as we came in sight of Ed hanging over the gate with the lantern light on his face, and fell flat. I'm afraid he's in a rather bad way.'

'Yes, he's saved the hangman a job,' said Mrs Bradley grimly, bending over the dead man whilst Will North held up the lantern. 'Can you two get him back to the bungalow between you?'

'I won't ask by what means you've taken the place of the Furies,' said the Chief Constable. 'I'll only say this: I'm most relieved that you did. Those two were as black murderers as ever came out of hell, and, of course, even with Mrs Emming's evidence, we might not have got a conviction.'

'I did not foresee the Emming deaths,' said Mrs Bradley. 'I thought that Emming might break down at the sight of Ed Brown's ghost. Tiny Fullalove's reactions do not surprise me. That fall from my balcony did his weak heart no good. It is better so. I confess I dislike the thought of hangings.'

'And I dislike the thought of reporters,' said Jonathan. 'We shall be swarming with them during the next few days as soon as they get to know of the Emming affair. Tiny's luck has held. It's Emming who will come in for all the mud.'

Mrs Bradley nodded slowly. Then she quoted solemnly in Greek:

'Fear not for him that departs from life; for after death there is no other accident.'

They were standing by Will North's cottage. In Farmer Daventry's field a lamb cried out for its mother. A blackcap flew out of the lilacs and pecked at the cardboard top on a bottle of milk. The lush land rose to a hawthorn hedge, the stable tower, and the trees. Behind the house, on the woodland bank, the wild strawberry ambled in faint flower.

VINTAGE MURDER MYSTERIES

dead good

*For all of you who find
a crime story irresistible.*

Discover the very best crime and thriller books on our
dedicated website – hand-picked by our editorial team
so you have tailored recommendations to help you
choose what to read next.

We'll introduce you to our favourite authors and the
brightest new talent. Read exclusive interviews and
specially commissioned features on everything from the
best classic crime to our top ten TV detectives, join live
webchats and speak to authors directly.

Plus our monthly book competition offers you the
chance to win the latest crime fiction, and there are
DVD box sets and digital devices to be won too.

Sign up for our newsletter at
www.deadgoodbooks.co.uk/signup

Join the conversation on:

KT 4/18

penguin.co.uk/vintage